POPULAR PUBLICATIONS — FACSIMILE EDITIONS

Terror Tales #8
(April 1935)

Starting in 1934, editor (and publisher) Harry Steeger unveiled *Terror Tales*: perhaps the flagship magazine in Popular Publications' so-called "Weird Menace" lineup of titles. Running for almost 50 issues, *Terror Tales* showcased some of the best suspense, mystery and terror stories to see print in the pulps. This facsimile of the April 1935 issue contains stories by Hugh B. Cave, Paul Ernst, Nat Schachner, H.M. Appel, Ray Cummings, G.T. Fleming-Roberts, and Arthur J. Burks.

Authors:

Hugh B. Cave, Paul Ernst, Nat Schachner, H.M. Appel,
Ray Cummings, G.T. Fleming-Roberts, Arthur J. Burks

Illustrators:

John Newton Howitt, Amos Sewell

1

Volume Two   April, 1935   Number Four

Cover Painting by John Howitt
Story Illustrations by Amos Sewell

Published every month by Popular Publications, Inc., 2256 Grove Street, Chicago, Illinois. Editorial and executive offices, 205 East Forty-second Street, New York City. Harry Steeger, President and Secretary, Harold S. Goldsmith, Vice President and Treasurer. Entry as second-class matter pending at the post office at Chicago, Ill., under the Act of March 3, 1879. Title registration pending at U. S. Patent Office. Copyright, 1935, by Popular Publications, Inc. Single copy price 15c. Yearly subscriptions in U. S. A. $1.50. For advertising rates address Sam J. Perry, 205 E. 42nd St., New York, N. Y. When submitting manuscripts kindly enclose stamped self-addressed envelope for their return if found unavailable. The publishers cannot accept responsibility for return of unsolicited manuscripts, although care will be exercised in handling them.

3

Classified Advertising

SATAN'S SEPULCHER

By Hugh B. Cave

(Author of "Enslaved to Satan," etc.)

There were stories of the devil's minions haunting the darker shadows of that bleak, deserted church—of corpses returned from the dead to set up a weird, unholy kingdom in the house of God! Were these red-robed fiends actually returned from hell? Or could they be man-inspired —more treacherous, more deadly and cruel because they were driven on by the evil lusts of living humans?

A Novel of
Evil Mystery

conspired to make a monstrous leering pile of the abandoned church building that thrust its black bell-tower into a winding-sheet of upper darkness.

Hilton shuddered, stared gloomily. The last time he had entered that gaunt pile, the building had been a place of worship. Now it loomed as dark, as forbidding as the crypt which lay deep down in its silent bowels. A "For Sale" sign hung beneath the drooling glass of a huge arched window.

Strange things had happened in the past six months. And the strangest, Bill Hilton reflected, was the summons which had caused him to drop work at the Hilton factory in Portland and come hustling back here to Northwood. That brief, frantic letter from Edith Darnell, begging him to rush back to his home city after he had been away for six long months!

And then—the look of terror, of something even worse, that had lurked deep in her eyes last night, when she had whispered fearfully of the things that were eating at her heart. When she had told him of her father and of this huge church, now abandoned, where the Reverend John Darnell had been minister.

"The bank owns it now, Bill," she had

R AIN splashed from a leaden sky, whispered against the gleaming folds of Bill Hilton's wrap-around trench coat and made puddles for his feet to slop through as he hiked along the tree-lined streets of Northwood's residential sector, toward the First Grace Church. Rain and late-afternoon gloom said, with tears gathering in those dark eyes. "There was some kind of mortgage and the bank took the church over, offered it for sale. For ages now it has been dark and empty and—and something else. Bill, something is happening to dad. And I—I'm afraid!"

She had sent for Bill Hilton because he alone, of all her friends, might be able to help. Before going to Portland to take over the Hilton factory at the time of his father's death, he had been studying at medical school—a keen student of psychiatry. He would know what to do!

Know what to do? After hearing the darkly sinister tale she had narrated, Bill Hilton had gone home—home to the big Hilton house which had lain unoccupied for the six months he had been away— and spent hours thinking of what she had told him. Now, gazing at Northwood's First Grace Church, he felt a slow sensation of uneasiness creeping through him. Reluctantly he climbed the broad stone steps and put a wet finger on the bell-button.

There would be a caretaker on the premises. A man named Eric Hefferen had been hired by the bank to come here and live with his wife and son. . . .

The great door creaked open. Dark eyes aimed a hostile glance at Bill's wet face. "Well, what d'yer want?" the man growled.

Bill stepped back involuntarily. This man's leathery face, his deformed, humpbacked body, were too much in keeping with the grim innuendoes beneath Edith Darnell's dark tale of terror. Bill Hilton shuddered. "You're—Eric Hefferen?"

"I'm Hefferen. What d'yer want?"

"I've come to look the place over. Here's a permit from the bank."

Hefferen reached out a stump-fingered hand and took the envelope, stared suspiciously at the enclosed slip of paper. The bank officials, openly defiant at first,

had been only too eager to issue a permit after learning that Bill Hilton represented the Hilton interests in Portland and was interested in the church from a commercial point of view.

Well, he had not lied about that. The Hilton Company did need additional facilities. If this gloomy old building could be transformed into a storehouse—

"All right," Hefferen grunted. "You can look around, provided you don't disturb nothin'."

Bill jammed his hands into the pockets of his trench coat and stepped forward. Behind him the door creaked shut and a key rasped in the lock. "If I ain't around when you want to come out," Hefferen grunted, "holler, or else come downstairs to my apartment. Me and my family live in what used to be the choir-room down in the basement."

If I ain't around! Like a ghoul in some dark temple of evil, the humpbacked caretaker dogged Bill's steps, trailed him upstairs and down, in and out of every silent chamber, everywhere—always around, always watching!

Dark, empty rooms echoed the hollow thud of Bill's feet. Grimy staircases led him into the bowels of the building where he prowled nervously through a monstrous cellar, explored gloomy recesses and sunken chambers that seemed waiting to suck him into their sinister depths. Once, pacing past a narrow, tunnel-shaped vault that was the crypt, he shivered, felt on his forehead a dampness that did not come from the sodden brim of his hat.

FOR an hour he continued his exploration. Darkness leered out at him, went with him; uncanny silence mocked the scrape of his plodding feet. And always, behind him, hung the contorted shape of Eric Hefferen, watching, gloating, sometimes obscenely chuckling over his apparent uneasiness.

"It ain't what you'd call a pleasant sort of place," the caretaker grinned. "Me and the wife and boy, we got used to it after a while, but even now it gives us the creeps sometimes when we hear footsteps and that sort o' thing late in the night. Every old buildin' like this has its queer noises."

Bill was glad when the ordeal was finished, when he could return at last to the main part of the church where the darkness was less sinister and where daylight, dim as it was, filtered through stained-glass windows. With the caretaker still trailing him, he walked slowly down the broad center aisle of the church, past rows of empty pews. And then, abruptly, he caught a sharp breath. . . .

The church had been empty before, utterly empty of everything except crawling shadows and dark spectres that were spawned in his own too vivid imagination. Now, in one of those shadowed pews, 'way up front near the chancel steps, sat an alien shape.

Bill took his hands from his pockets, stood staring. The newcomer was an aged, stoop-shouldered man sitting there in a dejected slouch, gazing dully, lifelessly, at the altar. Slowly, Bill moved forward.

He had to continue up the aisle, turn left and walk along the front of the church in order to reach his objective. Yet the old man did not turn his bowed head to look at him. He did not move; and behind Bill, old Eric Hefferen stared evilly and made mumbling sounds in his thick throat.

And then abruptly Bill knew the truth, remembered what Edith Darnell had told him last night. He had not exactly believed, at the time. The thought of any man, even one who was reported to be "queer", coming again and again to a place such as this, to pace like a doomed prisoner through the building's black catacombs—and that talk of hearing strange, weird music in the abandoned building,

of seeing spectral shapes and being warned to stay away on pain of death—

He had been inclined to doubt the girl's story. Yet here was proof that she had not lied! This stoop-shouldered, almost lifeless shape was John Darnell!

Slowly, Bill paced the last few strides, stood over the man and peered down. Good God, what was wrong with Darnell? What had come over him? How could he sit here, his head on his chest, his eyes wide open, his hands half-clenched on his knees, knowing surely that a friend stood over him and yet not even raising his head to acknowledge the friend's presence?

Bill reached out a trembling hand, touched Darnell's shoulder. "Mr. Darnell!" His voice was husky with a numbing dread that crawled through him. "Mr. Darnell, what's wrong?"

The man's head came up; his dull gaze focused. "Wrong? Nothing is wrong." The words were as lifeless as the pale lips that hardly moved while uttering them. A coarse stubble, grayish white, stood out on Darnell's gaunt face; his eyes were dull globules in pits of shadow, his body a pitifully thin, emaciated form wrapped in a worn overcoat. He had removed his hat and placed it on the pew beside him, and his hair was a gray mass that gnarled down the back of his thin neck. "Nothing is wrong," he intoned heavily. "Leave me alone."

Something was very wrong. Pity softened Bill's scowl and he leaned forward, gripped the older man's arms. "You shouldn't be here, Mr. Darnell. You're ill. Let me take you home and—" The words trailed off. Straightening with a jerk, Bill lurched about and stood staring at the swing-doors which led to the church vestibule.

THE doors had opened, groaned shut again. And a girl stood there, trim and slender in the wet raincoat that enveloped her. Her wide eyes gazed into Bill's frowning face. And then, quickly, the girl came forward, clung despairingly to Bill's arm and stared at her father.

"What—what has he been doing, Bill? Why must he keep coming here the way he does?"

Bill shrugged, forced his reply to sound casual. The paleness of Edith Darnell's face troubled him; that terror-stare in her eyes was all to indicative of unstrung nerves and an impending breakdown. "Nothing's wrong. Your father just came here to be alone where it's quiet. He knew you'd know where to find him."

She gazed at him queerly, stepped past him and said to her father: "It's almost supper-time, father, and I've made something you like. I—"

John Darnell stared at her, mechanically picked up his hat and pushed himself erect. Scowling, he glanced at Bill, at Eric Hefferen, as if aware of their presence for the first time. "I was about to go home, my dear," he said dully. "I am quite finished."

The girl took his arm and led him to the door. Just once she turned, peered questioningly at Bill. Her lips formed the words, "You'll come tonight?" and Bill nodded silently in answer. Then the swing-doors closed; Bill Hilton and Eric Hefferen were alone.

"He's a queer one, Darnell," Hefferen muttered. "Day after day he's been comin' here, prowlin' around. And sometimes I think them footsteps I hear late at night are his. He's got keys and can get in and out of here any time he wants to. If you ask me, I think he's goin' crazy."

As if corroborating that opinion, the voice of John Darnell came in a sudden amazing roar of violence from beyond the shut doors that led to the vestibule. The doors jarred open; Darnell's raging figure came hurtling through, his fists clenched, his eyes blazing with sudden mad passion. . . .

"They can't drive me out of it! It's my church! *Mine!* I won't be ordered to stay away!"

Like a madman he surged along the aisle, reached the chancel steps and swayed there, stood with his chest heaving, his face and throat drenched with sweat, his blood-rimmed eyes staring wildly at the marble figure of Christ above the altar. "Oh my God, why can't they leave me alone? Why—"

His voice broke, became a pitiful sobbing sound that gurgled to nothing. He would have pitched forward, sprawled in a sobbing heap on the white steps if Bill had not reached him in time and caught him. Gently, Bill held the stricken man erect.

"It's all right, Mr. Darnell," he mumbled words of comfort. "No one's ordering you out. No one says you can't come here."

"They do! I tell you they do! The devil himself—in my—my own church—"

Darnell's mad strength had died utterly, left him weak and trembling. He clung piteously to Bill's rugged frame, made vague moaning sounds when Edith came and led him away. The girl's face had become a white, drawn mask of terror, yet she shook her head negatively when Bill would have accompanied her to the door.

"I—I can manage," she breathed. "He'll come quietly now. You'll come over tonight?"

"Of course," Bill said.

He saw them go, heard the great front door open and groan shut. Then, scowling, he swung to face Eric Hefferen. "Darnell says he's been warned to stay away from here. What does that mean? Have you been—"

"Me?" The caretaker's eyes widened. "Lord, no! I never said nothin' to him.

He's just queer, that's all. Says he hears voices and devil-music and sees spectre-shapes and all that sort o' thing. He's crazy as a loon!"

Bill stared for a moment, then finally made for the door. Not until he reached the huge portal and heard the drumming of heavy rain against its thick panels did he realize that he was no longer wearing his trench coat. He shuddered, turned a half-circle and gazed into gloom toward the stairway that led down into the building's black cellar. Down there, in one of the many small chambers of the basement, he had stripped off the clammy coat and draped it over an empty packing-case.

Going down there after it would not be pleasant. Not after what had just happened. Even now Bill's nerves were vibrating queerly; he was beginning to understand how too many visits to this monstrous temple of gloom had twisted John Darnell's mind. But slowly he swung to Hefferen. "My coat's downstairs," he said. "Do you have a flashlight?"

Hefferen's ugly mouth curled into a grin. "Forgot it, did you? Now that's too bad." The hand that held forward the flashlight was like a monstrous spider with curled, hairy legs. "I'll be waitin' here for you," Hefferen leered.

CHAPTER TWO

Tomb of the Mad

BILL HILTON went downstairs alone, and going down those stairs was like descending into the dungeons of some huge medieval castle where darkness and silence increased with depth. A sensation of impending peril, brought on perhaps by that suggestion of evil triumph in the caretaker's face, stalked with him. Eyes wide, he stared into the ink-thick darkness as he prowled along the lower corridor.

He had left his coat in one of the small storerooms that led off the main cellar. Which room, he was not sure. The probing ray of the searchlight jumped ahead of him as he turned off the corridor and walked past the entrance to the crypt. Extending before him, he could see the shadowed cellar, a great low-roofed chamber floored with concrete, the boiler-room at the far end. Slowly, Bill paced forward.

And suddenly, out of the darkness, came a sound that pulled him back on his heels.

He stopped with a jerk, stood gaping. Instinctively his thumb slid from the flashlight button, plunging him into darkness. Dark dread welled up inside him, gagged him, corded the muscles of his tense face.

Again the sound muttered toward him through gloom. And this time it took form, became a low, throaty voice that possessed qualities not human. Droning through a darkness that crushed against Bill's rigid body, it uttered his own name, called him by it!

"Why did you come here, William Hilton?" were the gutturally intoned words. "Answer!"

Bill did not speak. His throat was tight.

"Then I will tell you!" the voice gave its own answer. "You came here to meddle in affairs of which you know nothing. You came to risk your life and your soul for the sake of satisfying a morbid curiosity! Take warning, fool! No longer may strangers come here to prowl about at will. This is the chosen abode of me and mine, who have come back from the Dark Beyond to live again in the shadow of life. Look—and be convinced!"

With a sudden convulsive jerk Bill stepped backward, smothered a cry of horror. As if conjured into being by the very intensity of his stare, a weirdly terrifying shape had suddenly taken form before him. Less than a score of paces distant, framed in the jet darkness of a narrow doorway, the spectral form stood motionless, studying him with grim interest.

Chill fingers touched Bill's spine. A wild thought stabbed his brain that this thing before him, this terrifyingly inhuman thing from some dark hell beyond man's knowledge, was merely a freak of his own imagination, made tangible by the power of black premonition. But he knew better. He had imagined no such spectre as this! This thing was real, was possessed of the powers of speech and movement.

Yet it was not human! The truth surged through him like a blast of storm-wind. One red-robed arm was extended toward him, and the hand, terminating in a pointing forefinger, was leprous white, white as the wax of candles which had once burned in the church above!

A scarlet robe covered that emaciated frame. Matted hair hung over the thing's obscene eyes; its face was a cadaverous gargoyle covered with a thin, mottled layer of vile flesh.

And Bill Hilton stared in horror as the lips writhed open to speak again. His eyes bulged at the spectral body before him, at the strange purple discoloration of one side of that frightful face, at the unearthly tenuous glow that emanated from the thing's dead flesh, enveloping it and rendering visible every dread detail.

"Go, William Hilton! Go and do not return! There will be no second warning!"

The spectral form stepped backward, seemed for an instant to sway on the threshold of the black chamber from which it had glided forth. Then suddenly Bill Hilton knew that the thing was only an illusion. The unearthly glow still remained, as illusions of light sometimes linger in gloom for long seconds after the lights themselves have been extinguished. The monster was gone, gone back into the well of silence from whence it had come!

With it went the numbing dread that had held Bill Hilton rigid.

A snarl came from his throat as he lurched forward. The searchlight in his fist sent a stabbing shaft of lurid light into the gloom, showed him the empty doorway which had spawned the monstrosity. Blindly he flung himself over the threshold, his free hand balled into a fist that hung ready for emergency.

Then he stopped, turned a slow circle and again became prey to unreasoning fear.

The room was empty—empty of everything except a few hulks of discarded furniture. There was no other door, no other outlet.

Fear clouded Bill's eyes; instinctively he fell back a step. The thing had come into this room. Of that he was positive. But the room was utterly empty of any sound or movement, of anything alive or anything that had been alive!

He put a trembling hand to his damp forehead, mumbled incoherent words. Then, fearfully, he began a systematic search.

TEN minutes later, when he climbed the steep stairs to the upper part of the church, his mind was warped around a black suspicion that he, himself, was going mad. Even the sight of old Eric Hefferen standing at the big door, staring with beady eyes, was a relief from the evil darkness of the cellars. Struggling into the trench coat which he had found downstairs, Bill strode toward the man and gripped Hefferen's arm. A question rumbled in his throat.

"Listen. Who else besides you and your family lives here?"

Hefferen stared stupidly. "Huh?"

Harshly, rapidly, Bill told the man what

had happened, described the spectral shape that had confronted him downstairs. He had to talk, to clear his brain of sinister suspicions that festered there. But if he thought to arouse a sullen defensive attitude in the caretaker, he was mistaken. Hefferen backed away from him, stared with wide, white-rimmed eyes that slowly filled with terror.

"What—did his face look like?" The question was a whisper, barely audible. "Was it—was it all scarred on one side?"

Bill's mouth curled savagely. Scarred on one side? So long as he lived he would never forget that scarred countenance of evil! His hand seized Hefferen's wrist in a vicious grip. "What do you know about it?"

"Then—then it was!" Hefferen's voice rose to a wail; wild-eyed he stared around him, suddenly afraid of the gloom to which he had apparently become inured. "Annie was right! Only last night she said she seen it! It's Matthew Craven come back!"

"Who's Annie?" Bill snapped.

"My—my wife. Then—that's the meanin' of the footsteps we been hearin' late at night! Old Matt Craven—"

Anger blazed in Bill's narrowed eyes. "Snap out of it, will you? Who's Matt Craven? Why should he come here to prowl around?"

Eric Hefferen's stunted body trembled as if seized by a sudden fever. His thick lips quivered, mumbled husky words. "Matt Craven used to—to be a member of the church." Cringing, he tried to release his arm from Bill's grip. "He—he got cancer on the brain more'n a year ago and went mad and—died." The voice whined to a thin, tremulous whisper. "He died, I'm tellin' you! I seen them put him in the vault! Now he's back. Matt Craven is back!"

Bill released his grip, stood staring.

Despite a desire to believe otherwise he knew that old Hefferen was not acting.

But he had had enough—enough of creeping dread and strange, inexplicable happenings and whispering, sinister darkness. The gloom of the huge church had taken toll of his nerves. Grimly he said: "All right, open the door. I'm leaving."

Hefferen fumbled nervously for keys, seemed reluctant to turn his back as he sidled to the door. No longer did Bill entertain even a suspicion that the man's terror was anything but real. And then, abruptly, in the act of sorting the proper key from its companions, Hefferen jerked his head up and stood stiff as wood.

Down through the darkness from the upper reaches of the building wailed a sound that sucked the color from the caretaker's taut face, and froze Bill Hilton in his tracks. Once, twice, three times a lurid peal of insane laughter jangled its cacophonous way from somewhere high above.

Then it died to an obscene chuckle that gurgled into emptiness, left a pregnant silence more nerve-numbing than the sound itself. And Eric Hefferen, flattened grotesquely against the door, made blubbering sounds of utter terror.

"It's Matt Craven! I'd know that laugh anywhere! He laughed like that for days on end before he died! It's Matt Craven come back from the grave!"

Bill Hilton strode to the swing-doors that led into the church proper, pushed them open and stood staring. The lurid laughter had come from somewhere high in darkness, perhaps from the topmost part of the balcony. But the sound was not repeated. And up there, nothing moved. The balcony was wrapped in a shroud of gloom.

For an instant grim determination dragged Bill forward and the doors creaked shut behind him. Then he halted, knew that he had neither the courage nor the desire to go prowling again through hell-born darkness in search of a leering ghoul who could vanish at will. Whatever the secret behind that spectral shape, this was no time to seek the answer!

Shuddering, Bill turned, retraced his steps. This time old Hefferen's trembling fingers were able to thrust the big key into its lock, and Bill shouldered the heavy door open.

The chill rain that slapped against him as he stepped over the threshold, was as refreshing and as welcome as brilliant sunlight. With a sensation of utter relief welling within him, Bill hiked down the gleaming sidewalk, leaving the terrified, humpbacked Hefferen behind him.

DOWN there in the catacombs of the church it had seemed like midnight, yet the streets of Northwood were still pale with dying daylight, and the hands of Bill Hilton's watch pointed to only twenty past six. Scowling, he recalled that he had promised to drop in on a meeting of the board of directors at the Northwood Cooperative Bank, and report his findings. Only under that condition had he been able to obtain a permit to look over the church.

Well, the directors would be disappointed with his findings. So fas as the church-building itself was concerned, there was a possibility that the Hilton Company might be interested. But other things would have to be cleared up first.

It was seven o'clock when he got to the bank, and he wondered, without caring much, if they had waited for him. The bank itself was closed, locked for the night, but the door opened to Bill's ring and Mr. Leonard Aborn, bank president, greeted him with a trace of irritation. "Well, sir, good evening!"

Three men sat with Bill Hilton in Aborn's office. Aborn himself, large, grey-haired, with a round moon of a face and a blustering manner; Henry Greenwood, thin, exceedingly tall, with dark roving eyes and a distasteful habit of putting subtle double meanings into his dry comments; and Ellery Hamblin, middle-aged, soft-spoken, vaguely sentimental.

"Well, sir," Aborn said, "how about it?"

Bill shrugged. "I'm not quite sure."

"Huh? Now look here, Hilton. Frankly, that church is a white elephant. We're anxious to get it off our hands even at a sacrifice. Come down to terms, man, and let's see if we can't talk business. You've looked the place over pretty thoroughly and—"

Bill leaned forward, took his time about lighting a cigarette. He did not, he decided, like any of the three men he was dealing with. Least of all he liked Aborn. "Who—and what," he said quietly, "is Eric Hefferen?"

"Huh? Hefferen?" Aborn answered testily. "He's what he says he is—a caretaker. We hired him because he was the only man we could find who would take the job."

Bill nodded thoughtfully. "And who is Matthew Craven?"

"Who?"

"Matthew Craven!"

Aborn sat stiff, failed to suppress a noticeable shudder that shook his big body. "I see you've been—learning things." He exhaled heavily. "A year ago, Craven was one of the directors of this bank. Then he came down with cancer of the brain. He went mad."

"And died?" Bill asked softly.

"Yes, he died. He was buried in the church cemetery. Demanded, just before he died, that he be interred in a vault whose door could be opened from the inside. His only living relative is a young chap named Al Truman, who's quite fond of old Darnell's daughter."

Bill's eyes narrowed; without meaning to, he clenched his hands. Staring, he blew twin jets of cigarette smoke from his nostrils. When he spoke at last it was to say stiffly: "I can't give you an answer on the church yet. Sorry, but too many things are involved."

"But you've looked it over, man! You surely know whether or not—"

Ellery Hamblin, speaking for the first time, interrupted in a voice that contrasted strangely with Aborn's gruff outburst. "Hilton is right. There are many angles. One angle in particular involves John Darnell. Suppose we do dispose of the church property. What is to become of Darnell?"

Aborn's large mouth curled. "Who cares?"

"But I do. John Darnell is a friend of mine, a very good friend." There was almost a whine in Hamblin's thin voice. "I tell you the man has changed terribly since his church was taken from him. If it is taken altogether, God knows what will become of him!"

"There's no place for sentiment in business, Hamblin."

"But I tell you—"

Bill Hilton pushed himself erect, reached for his rain-soaked hat. The glint in his eyes was not a pleasant one. He was thinking of many reasons why Leonard Aborn might be so very anxious to dispose of the First Grace Church. And he was thinking, too, of what Aborn had said about Edith Darnell and a young man named Al Truman, who was a distant relative of Matthew Craven.

"I'll give you an answer later," he said tersely. "Right now I can't." Deliberately he pulled the door open, walked through the banking room and let himself out.

IT WAS dark when he got home. Pitch dark, and the rain had not let up. The big house was a looming hulk in a wet world of gloom, and the great elm in the front yard—the elm which had been a giant even before Bill Hilton had seen the light of day in one of those upstairs rooms—was like some Gargantuan monster flinging its grotesque arms to a moaning sky.

Wearily, Bill climbed the broad steps and let himself in. He had promised to visit the Darnells tonight. Already it was late. His clothes were drenched and he was hungry.

A gust of wind slammed the door behind him and he turned lights on, walked stiffly down the hall to the bedroom. The house was dark, musty, had lain unoccupied since he had moved out of it months ago to go to Portland and take over the factory at the death of his father. In its upper reaches, where twin gables angled grotesquely from a multisloped roof, the pounding of the rain was a sullen half-human voice that droned through every part of the building's bigness.

But Bill's thoughts were of something else, something infinitely more sinister and significant.

What had Aborn said about Matthew Craven? Craven had been a member of the board of directors at the bank, had died of cancer about a year ago. Raving mad at the time of his death, he had demanded to be interred in a vault which could be opened from the inside.

A scowl made dark crescents of Bill's eyes. He thought grimly of the spectral shape in the church, of Eric Hefferen's utter terror when informed of the spectre's appearance. Thought, too, of the many warnings which John Darnell had reputedly received, threatening him with death unless he remained away from the church which had been his for more than twenty years.

Finally he thrust open the bedroom door, strode across the threshold and snapped on a light. Water puddled the floor as he yanked off his trench coat and threw it with his hat on a chair. Damp hair hung in his eyes and he paced to the bureau, reached for a pair of military brushes that lay there.

His outthrust hand went suddenly rigid, hung suspended in space. Breath soughed to his lips as he stood staring.

The bureau-top was uncovered. In the center of its dusty mahogany surface, a white curled shape leered up at him. Slender, human fingers were hooked around a rolled tube of paper!

Bill's lips trembled, mumbled almost inaudibly: "Good—God!" Seconds passed before he forced his numbed body forward, extend his hand to touch that thing —that other hand—which squatted there on the bureau.

At his touch the thing tumbled backward with a dull thud and lay like an overturned crab. Some sharp instrument had been used to sever that hand from the arm and body it belonged to. The stump was a smooth flat surface. The hand itself was pale, slender, the kind of hand that might casually have raised a scented cigarette to a pair of lovely, smiling lips. Young lips, and alluring. Lips like Edith's. . . .

Darkness beat at Bill's brain and he stared mutely at the pale fingers, at the delicately tinted nails that spoke of loveliness and refinement. Breathing heavily he bent closer, forced himself to slide the tube of paper loose from the clutching fingers that held it.

Slowly, with bated breath, he unrolled it. . . .

CHAPTER THREE

The Temple of Torment

IT WAS a half-sheet of typewriter bond and bore rows of crudely hand-lettered words. Dark red words, scrawled in blood that had not long ago been wet, sticky, hot with life. Wide-eyed, Bill Hilton studied the grim message, read it from beginning to end. Then he stiffly dropped the paper to the bureau, where the bloody warning continued to leer up at him.

> By the hand of the dead this warning comes. Heed it! Let no word of what has happened pass your lips on pain of terrible death! Leave Northwood before this night is over and do not return! *Do not return!*

Mad words! Mad words for hard-fisted Bill Hilton to be staring at and believing! Yet cold sweat stood out on his forehead; fear was a sodden, tangible weight in his throat. Very slowly he retreated from the bureau, backed across the room and lowered his trembling body onto the bed. But his gaze remained fixed on the curled sheet of paper and the severed human hand whose very presence was even more hideously significant than the words written in blood.

Moments passed and Bill Hilton did not move. Somewhere in the room with him a clock ticked hollowly. Rain hammered against shut windows, created muttering voices in the upper reaches of the big house. And the voices took form, grew to a shrill, vibrant shriek that jangled in Bill Hilton's mind, repeating over and over the bloody words of warning.

> Go! Leave Northwood before this night is over! Go—and do not return!

Then, fists clenched, he pushed himself erect, strode to the bureau and stood there, glaring down. Words snarled from his curled lips.

"It's a hoax. The whole damned thing is an idiotic scheme to keep me from buying the church. As if I wanted the blasted place!"

But the thought flashed to him, who would want to prevent him from taking the church over? He stood scowling, forced himself to think things out. There was John Darnell, for one. And perhaps scattered members of Darnell's flock who still hoped to win the church back again. And even Eric Hefferen, who had a good job and would not want to lose it. . . .

Plenty of people might have a violent desire to prevent him from consummating any deal that would turn the church into a factory warehouse. And this—this idiotic message written in blood—was a fantastic scheme to scare him from town before any such deal could be completed.

He backed away, sneering. But the sneer died as his gaze focused again on that other thing—on the hand which had held the note—and sweat beaded the base of his hair. After all there was nothing idiotic about a severed human hand. . . .

And because he could not bring himself to touch that hand again, he left it there, with the note beside it.

HALF an hour later, when he had changed into dry clothes and was ready to leave, the hand was still there, still curled in an attitude of supplication as if piteously begging him to—to help? Yes! that was it. He might be able to do something if he could keep the horror of these mysterious portents from taking over the sanity of his mind. There was nothing to all this, nothing that could not be solved by action and clear thinking.

With a feeling of utter relief, Bill locked the front door behind him and started for the home of John Darnell.

Rain spilled in huge drops from a jet sky, made a drenched dripping scarecrow of him long before he pushed open the gate of the Darnell home and strode up the walk. The house was a small brown cottage with trellised vines masking its low-roofed veranda. Vaguely, Bill hoped that Edith would be alone.

Edith . . . the name did queer things to him. For years before he had gone to Boston to attend college and medical school, he and she had been close friends. But John Darnell's wife had passed on; the responsibility of caring for an aging father had fallen on Edith's shoulders.

She had been brave about it, despite the annihilation of her dreams for the future. She had made a home, taken care of her father ever since, just the two of them here in this small cottage a few streets from the church. . . .

Slowly, Bill climbed the steps, rang the bell and stood waiting. It was hard not to be bitter against some things—not against Edith or her father, but against a cruel fate which had blackened his own hopes for the future. Without knowing it, he was scowling when the door opened. But the scowl vanished when he stared into the face of the girl whose summons had brought him back to Northwood.

He knew then, as she spoke to him in a low, guarded voice, that she was not alone. Other voices, men's voices, were audible from the parlor. And the girl said almost inaudibly: "Bill, I've got to talk to you alone. We've got to find some way."

He closed the door, followed her into the parlor and stood scowling as she introduced him. Her father was there, sitting lifelessly in a big lounge-chair with a newspaper fanned out across his thin knees. Ellery Hamblin, the mild-mannered, plaintive little bank director who had endeavored to be human during the cold-blooded conference at the bank, sat nervously stiff and made birdlike movements with his pudgy hands. And a dark-haired, dark-eyed young man, wearing a close-fitting oxford gray suit and a greenish madras shirt, stood wide-legged, glaring.

"I—I don't think you know Al Truman," the girl said slowly.

No sign of emotion crossed Bill's stiff

face as he acknowledged the introduction, but the cords of his neck tightened and the muscles of his big frame went suddenly taut. So this was Al Truman! This was the only living relative of Matthew Craven, who had gone mad, and died, and, according to Eric Hefferen, had "come back!" The youth stared—stared with black, glittering eyes that seemed to smoulder behind half-shut lids as he extended his hand.

Edith Darnell glanced from Truman to Bill, seemed uncomfortably aware of the sudden chill that had invaded the room. Awkwardly she said: "If you people will excuse us for a little while, Bill and I have something to talk over." Her hand found Bill's arm, clung there as if seeking protection. "Come on, Bill. They can get along without us for a minute." Her smile was forced, faltering. "It's ages since I've really seen you."

Silently Bill followed her over the threshold, suppressed an impulse to turn and glare back into the dark eyes that he knew were hostilely watching his every step. Dully he wondered what Edith and Al Truman meant to each other, how far the affair had progressed.

HE ASKED her about that, asked her bluntly, with typical Bill Hilton lack of tact, as soon as they were alone. She stared at him, seemed surprised. "Why, it's nothing, Bill. Don't be silly! You *know* it isn't anything!"

She leaned forward, seemed very small and helpless as she looked into his eyes. "Bill, what about father? Do you—do you think he is—"

"I don't know," Bill said stiffly. He wasn't thinking of her father now, but of Al Truman. "I haven't had time enough yet to find out anything."

"But you saw him this afternoon in the church. You saw how suddenly he went —went—"

"Mad?" Bill narrowed his eyes, chewed thoughtfully on his lower lip. "Don't be too ready to call a man mad, Edith. That's one of the first things they drilled into me at school."

She took a long look at him. Edith knew Bill well enough to realize that he was evading the issue. "You've been to the church," she said—and there was a note of pleading in her voice that made him realize how much she was depending on him. "You've been there and seen dad. You've heard what he says about being ordered away from the place, and about seeing horrible things there. Oh, Bill, what *is* the answer?"

"You want me to tell you?" he demanded grimly. "You want me to tell Truman and Hamblin and all the rest of them? Then by God I will, even if it makes me out to be a madman!" Savagely he strode back to the parlor.

And he told them—told them everything, spilling the words out in slow, deliberate monotone, through a scowl that kept his hearers silent. "And that's the whole thing," he concluded grimly. "You can believe it or doubt it. John Darnell is not the only one who's seen things in the church; he's not the only one who's been warned. If you won't believe him, you can believe me!"

John Darnell had thrust aside the paper and was staring with wide, eager eyes, as though realizing that he had finally found a friend. Ellery Hamblin, saying nothing, sat with his mouth slightly agape, his hands massaging each other nervously. But Al Truman stood up slowly, leaned against the table and stared with narrowed unblinking eyes into Bill Hilton's face. His lips were curled into a sarcastic sneer. Without shifting his boring gaze he said deliberately: "Hilton, you're a damned liar."

The words came slowly, without too

much emotion, without any rising inflection of voice. They trailed into silence and lived on in the tomb-like silence of the room. Edith Darnell stared wide-eyed from one man to the other. Then a dark red flesh crept up from Bill's collar and carmined his face. His hands clenched into fists. He took a step forward.

Only the realization that both he and Truman were guests of the same girl—that they owed it to her to carry their differences elsewhere—stopped him. But the dark-eyed young man took that sudden hesitation to mean something else. He said tersely: "Hilton, your case is open and shut. Everybody knows it. Your job is to buy the church. If you can spread a lot of terror-talk around, the price goes down and the competition vanishes. But it won't work. We're wise to you."

The beseeching look on Edith Darnell's white face held Bill back. His big body trembled; his eyes blazed with a desire to use both fists on the sneering, taunting mouth of his accuser. But he stayed where he was.

"Look here," Truman flung out. "I've said I think you're a liar, and that's what I do think—a dirty scheming liar, playing for your own interests at the expense of Edith and her father. All right, I'll prove it! You've talked about seeing weird things at the church and of being warned to stay away. All right, show me! It's not far from here. Take me there and show me!"

For a moment Bill fought for self-control. A fuming retort died on his lips and he thought of other things, thought suddenly that Truman's proposition might have something more than jealousy and rage behind it. Slowly he nodded.

The others gaped. Edith Darnell took sudden steps toward Bill and clung to his arm. "Bill, I'm afraid! That church, at this time of night—"

He kissed her, held her in his arms and took his time to do a good job of it. When he turned, the light in Truman's eyes had become a look of pure unadulterated hate, so intense that Bill felt its almost tangible impact. Silently he strode to the door and followed Truman from the house.

FROM the house to the church neither he nor Truman spoke a word. Side by side they trudged along the sidewalk, hands jammed in their pockets, heads lowered against the driving rain. At the church, old Eric Hefferen answered Truman's insistent ring and stood gaping, obviously amazed at the prospect of intruders at such an hour.

"I can't let no one in without a permit," he croaked.

Truman's hate found an outlet. Savagely he thrust the caretaker aside, pushed forward over the threshold. Ignoring Hefferen's voluble protests he swung to Bill and growled nasally: "All right, we're here. Produce your spectres!"

Temper boiled again in Bill's face; again he controlled it only with an effort. A searchlight dangled from Hefferen's belt. Bill's hand curled around it, unhooked it. "I'll need this," he said grimly.

Without even a sideways glance at Truman, he strode to the stairway and descended in grim silence. The mumblings of old Hefferen died to a weird whisper on the landing above. Grimly, Bill headed along the lower corridor into Stygian gloom.

Twice before he had come this way, once on a tour of inspection, once to retrieve his forgotten coat. Because of what had happened on that last occasion he went slowly now, made sure that the white beam of the searchlight preceded him, probing every sinister pit of shadow. And behind him the dull steady thud of Truman's trailing feet was a nerve-wracking monotony, somehow pregnant with threat.

Warily, Bill slid past the entrance to the crypt, prowled into the huge cellar. Deliberately he advanced, then stopped, stood wide-legged and aimed the flashlight's beam at the door through which that red-robed spectral shape had vanished.

Truman, moving to his side, turned a sneering face and said sarcastically: "Well, what do we do now? Sit down and wait?"

In silence Bill strode forward. The door was closed; the flashlight's glare fell on a dangling padlock. Eyes narrowed with suspicion—suspicion spawned by the jeering attitude of the man beside him—Bill jammed he searchlight in the crook of his arm, fished a pen-knife out of his pocket and went to work.

It was a heavy lock, not easily picked. Moments passed and the only sounds in the huge cellar where the low sough of two men breathing and the dull rasp of the knife-blade against unyielding metal. Sweat stood out on Bill's face, left a wet streak on the back of his hand when he wiped it away. Then suddenly he straightened, shoved the knife back into his pocket and shouldered the door open.

Gripped in his outthrust fist, the searchlight cast a weird halo of light over the room's emptiness. Beside him, Al Truman said nasally: "Well, what now?"

A scowl twisted Bill's mouth. Slowly he advanced, glared into the room's dark corners. Bitter words welled to his lips as the chamber proved to be empty.

But those words died unuttered. With a sudden gasp Bill jerked about, stared wide-eyed at the doorway. His fingers froze stiff around the searchlight's metal cylinder.

In the doorway, glaring at him hostilely, stood a withered, hunched shape that was a woman—a woman whose approach had been so silent, so furtive, that neither he nor Truman had heard the whispering scrape of her feet, if indeed she had made any sound at all! Arms outstretched, she stood on the threshold like some black hag of hell, her gnarled hands gripping the sides of the door-frame. Swaying on stiff legs, she thrust out a crooked arm, aimed a trembling forefinger at Bill's face.

"Listen, you. Both of you! We don't like people that comes here and meddles in what don't concern them! Me and my man are paid to watch out for nosey people like you!" Those narrowed eyes were malignant as the eyes of a snake; that wrinkled, aged face was almost not human! Savagely she advanced, shook a fist in Bill's face. "Get out! And don't be comin' back, or—"

The words clipped off with an abrupt suck of breath. The woman's trembling body stiffened, turned jerkily toward the doorway as another sound moaned into the room. The sound was low, vibrant, beginning in an almost human whisper and swelling into the deep, throaty voice of a distant organ. Here in the depths of the abandoned church the sound was weirdly terrifying.

BILL HILTON abruptly stepped backward, gaped at the empty doorway as if expecting the sound to take the form of some menacing grey mass and come slithering over the threshold.

In a low, macabre dirge, weirdly blood-chilling, the guttural voice of the organ continued. And into Bill Hilton's pounding brain came a vision that seared his soul, stilled the breath in his throat—a strange, unreasoning vision of some spectral red-robed shape bunched forward on a wooden bench in the distant gloom of the organ loft—of bony, sepulchral fingers gliding over rows of dirty-white keys, creating music born in the depths of a death-rotted mind. . . .

His mad thoughts were dispersed by the

mumbling voice of Eric Hefferen's uncouth wife as she paced jerkily to the door. "At it again," the old woman was muttering. "At it again, he is, even after I warned him I'd beat some sense into him. Damned idiot!"

Mumbling to herself, the crone scuffed from the room, became a hunched grotesque shape in the hugeness of the cellar as she marched across the vast floor. The searchlight in her outthrust hand cast a jerky pool of white ahead of her, and her bent body moved like a contorted black bat silhouetted against the glow. Without a backward glance she turned into the narrow passage that led to the stairs.

Al Truman's trembling hand gripped Bill's arm. "Listen. I'm going to follow her! There's something queer about this!"

Bill said nothing, stood staring as the dark-eyed youth slipped over the threshold and disappeared in gloom. That weird, macabre dirge, emanating from organpipes in the church above, still rolled like a living thing through the cellar's darkness. Slowly, Bill dragged a deep breath, gazed around him.

He was alone in the room where that red-robed shape had vanished. Deliberately he made a tour of the chamber, again determined to find an explanation of the monster's disappearance. Spectral or not, that shape had possessed a voice, had not vanished through any solid wall! There would be an answer somewhere. There had to be!

There was—but more than twenty minutes passed before Bill Hilton stumbled upon the solution. By that time the glare of the flashlight had grown dim; the huge cellar was again silent, empty of the macabre moan of the organ. Prowling for the fourth time around that room of mystery, testing every inch of its mocking walls, Bill found the answer.

At the far end of the room the wall was of matched boards, and one of those boards moved as if alive under the pressure of Bill's fingers. With a sudden gasp he lurched backward, stood half-crouched, gaping. Where the blank wall had been was now a narrow rectangle of empty darkness, big enough for a man to squeeze through!

The searchlight in his hand threw a sickly yellow glare over the opening as he toed forward. His eyes were narrow in a taut, stiff face. Carefully he studied the mechanism of the hidden door, discovered that it worked on a spring-release and could be opened only by pressure upon a single one of its camouflaging panels. . . .

The room he entered was huge enough to put amazement in his staring eyes. The flashlight's glow was inadequate, revealing only part of a low-roofed, stone-floored chamber that extended deep into darkness. Warily he advanced, knowing intuitively that he was uncovering a secret as black as the catacombs that nurtured it. Something here was evil. Something here was so evil, so vile and horrible, that it sucked the cords of his throat to the surface and swelled them into livid welts on his neck.

Then, abruptly, he jarred to a stop.

The light in his fist had swung sideways, thrown its sickly halo over the wall at his right. In Bill's veins, dormant worms of terror—terror handed down through fear-blackened centuries—came to life. The thing he stared at was a dark symbol of all things unholy!

It was a great black mass that rose darkly from the floor and filled a huge section of the wall—a monstrous black shape fashioned of iron, in the form of a great bat's-head looming from floor to low ceiling, its hollow eyes glaring down into Bill's own, its gaping mouth festooned with twin fangs of horror.

Bill stood staring, knew that his heart

was beating with dull heavy thuds against his inflated chest. In God's name, what kind of room had he stumbled into? This long, low-roofed chamber with its smooth stone floor, its sound-proof walls and door . . . this gigantic leering hulk of iron that so strangely suggested a huge furnace and yet was fashioned to resemble the head of a monstrous bat. . . !

He stared, shuddered. This was the chamber into which that red-robed spectral shape had vanished after warning Bill Hilton that death was the penalty for again invading the forbidden catacombs of the church! This chamber, with its weird, heathenish accoutrements, its great bat's-head furnace that loomed like an altar in some buried temple of torment, was the spectre's dwelling-place! And he, Bill Hilton, had found his way into it, discovered its dark secret. He—

What was that?

CHAPTER FOUR

Screams of the Tortured

THE sound was a low whimper, nearly inaudible. Bill's big body swayed on stiff legs, feet rooted to the floor. His nerveless fingers tilted the light, aimed its meager halo to the left of the great bat's-head furnace. The sound had seemed to come from there.

Slowly he advanced, looked up and shuddered as he passed beneath the outjutting iron fangs in the bat's cavernous maw. The sound had come from somewhere beyond the wall, near here. Somewhere in darkness—

It came again—came in an eerie moaning whisper that chilled the flesh of his suddenly rigid body. This time it made words that sobbed vaguely, brokenly through the room. "Oh, God—help! Help me—" Words, almost inaudible, almost smothered by the noise of his own hoarse breathing!

The flashlight's glow swept the wall, came to a stop. Bill Hilton sucked in his breath and leaned forward, staring. His outthrust hand, cold as an inanimate lump of wax, closed over a protruding knob. Then the moaning sound came again as he steeled himself, turned the knob and inched open the narrow door that frowned out at him.

And with one hand frozen on the doorframe and the flashlight's glow yellowing the enclosure before him, he stood swaying. His eyes bulged; his lips formed a single soundless word. *"God!"*

The enclosure was no bigger than a cell. Wooden walls reared from a filthy floor, merged darkly with the low ceiling. And on the floor lay a contorted shape that was alive.

Horror came at Bill Hilton in a heaving, viscous wave, engulfing him, seeping through every pore of his taut body. He stared down into a face that was young, that should have been attractive —a woman's face gaunt with suffering, gray as dirty candle-wax. And the body that went with it was stark naked, curled in an attitude of agony unendurable.

Pitiful eyes gazed up into Bill's own, silently beseeching his help. Below the eyes, a mouth that had once been soft, sweet, now hung agape. Iron shackles encircled the girl's wrists, her ankles, her throat. Iron chains curled like black serpents from the shackles to massive rings in the wall and floor.

Bill Hilton stood stiff, held rigid by the black horror that surged through him, numbing him. Seconds passed and he did no more than stare. Then a dark rage germinated deep inside him and sent him lurching forward. He fell to his knees, put gentle hands on the girl's emaciated shoulders.

"What—how—?" The words died on

his lips as he realized the futility, the cruelty, of asking questions. There would be time for that later. "I'll get you out," he said. "Don't worry. We'll get out of here, both of us. Just—don't worry."

The girl seemed to understand, tried to summon strength enough to make words. Her lips quivered, her pale breasts swelled with an agonizing intake of breath. Incoherently, moaning words came into being. "Don't leave me here. Those horrible creatures will come back—"

Bill's hands seized the heavy chain that curled from her ankles to the wall. He stared down into her face. "How long have you been here? When did they bring you?"

"Days ago—" The voice was a sob, broken by convulsive shudders, as if memory were a dark horrific thing even worse than physical torment. "I—I answered an ad for a position in—in Dennis—and —oh, God, I can't remember. The man offered me a drink and—" A violent convulsion shook the girl's body; her eyes bulged to abnormal bigness, showed white rims of terror. "Oh, my God, no! No! Don't throw me in there!" She began screaming. *"The flames—"*

Her voice was suddenly so shrill, so violent, that it smothered another sound —smothered the creak of the sound-proof door at the far end of the chamber where that monstrous bat's-head leered down in darkness. Bill Hilton did not hear, did not turn. Intent only on his hopeless task, he redoubled his efforts to drag those iron chains from the unyielding staples that held them.

And in the dark hell-chamber behind him, cowled shapes moved slowly, silently across the stone floor, toward the narrow enclosure where Bill Hilton crouched above the girl's nude body.

HE DID not know, did not turn to see. Not even a whisper of slow-moving feet murmured through the chamber to warn him. He heard only the low moaning sounds from the chained girl's lips, was concerned only with his bitter conflict with iron chains that refused to yield their prey.

Wide eyes stared into Bill's own as he labored—wide eyes dull and glazed and loaded with mute supplication. Sweat oozed out in gleaming beads on his forehead and splashed his corded arms. And suddenly the girl's eyes looked beyond him, saw the red-robed spectral shapes that loomed in the doorway.

A shriek jangled from the girl's lips, tore madly through the chamber's silence. Bill Hilton whirled erect.

For a split second he gazed with black horror into the foul face directly before him, into a cadaverous gargoyle scarred with a livid patch of grafted skin. The name of Matthew Craven screamed through his soul. He gaped, saw other cowled figures in the gloom beyond the threshhold. Blindly he hurled himself forward beneath clutching hands that reached out to seize him.

He fought then as a dying man fights Death itself, knowing it is his last combat, yet that somewhere in a dim hovering outerworld of the unknown there may be a watching God who will offer a chance for life if the chance be earned.

His fists ground home, crashed into Matthew Craven's cadaverous face and sent the spectre stumbling backward. Clear of the threshhold, Bill lunged sideways to the iron base of the great bat's-head furnace, crouched there and met the snarling rush of cowled fiends who surged forward to annihilate him.

How many there were he could not know. Darkness was an evil shroud blurring all within it. In hell-born gloom he fought for life, for the right to liberate the moaning, naked torture-victim who lay chained nearby in hell's dark antechamber.

Legs braced, Bill used arms and fists with mad abandon. He *had* to win! If that wave of snarling hell spilled over him, his own battered body would be dragged to the alcove and chained beside the one that now lay there. Chained and held for some vile ritual in which the great bat's-head played a central part. What would come then, he did not know. But the girl—the girl had shrieked of *flames. . . !*

His wild eyes sought to watch the writhing darkness on all sides of him. Blindly his fists beat back every furious attack of surging ghoul-shapes that leaped to pull him down. Then suddenly a red-garbed arm lashed up, back; and Bill Hilton saw a small glass bottle gripped in vile fingers.

The bottle whined toward him, missed its mark as he jerked his head sideways. With a dull thud it crashed against the iron furnace, and liquid spattered in Bill's snarling face, seared in his eyes. Agony clawed at him with great curled fingers that could not be wrenched loose.

Screaming, he staggered from the wall, clawed at the buring pools of torment where his eyes had been. Cowled shapes closed in on him, were repulsed by the murderous flailings of his arms. What —what in the name of God had happened? Into what bottomless hell of screaming darkness had he been hurled, to fight—and *fight*—and—?

HE BATTLED instinctively, knew vaguely that he had to, or death would reach out its sucking tentacles and drag him down. But reasons, motives, were a gyrating blur; the word *fight* was a meaningless red monument in his brain, blazing there in agony. Fight! *Fight!* For God's sake, don't retreat! Keep going to the door!

They let him through because they had to, because he was a screaming, shrieking beast gone amok, no longer even allied to anything human. His body was a whirling juggernaut, an uncontrollable composite of flailing fists, knees, gleaming teeth stained red with blood not his own!

Agony spurred him on as black torment, beginning in his sightless eyes and surging in a roaring stream through his body, through his brain, made of him a monstrous beast so savage and violent, so intent on one thing only—*escape!*—that even a superior weight of numbers could not pull him down.

He left a bloody trail behind him, repulsed attack after attack before the threshhold yawned before him. Agony went with him and all things else were a gigantic blur without meaning. He was not conscious of lurching over the sill, of racing wildly through the room beyond, of hurling shut the door which he and Al Truman had opened, ages ago, by using a pen-knife to pick the lock.

Mad with pain he lurched through darkness, found his way somehow through the maze of catacombs that lay between him and freedom. Nor did he remember, afterward, how he left the church, how he stumbled up a short flight of wooden steps, hurled himself against a shut door until the door jarred open and precipitated him into cold wet rain, into a darkness where no black walls hemmed him in.

He knew nothing of all that; knew only that a soul-retching agony drove him on, that he was blind to the things about him because his eyes were no longer instruments of sight but bottomless wells of pain, and the pain was a relentless lash driving him on, on, through the Valley of the Shadow of Death.

He had escaped, but he no longer remembered from what, nor did he remember that naked moaning shape which had not escaped with him but had remained there in chains, to become object of the fiends' rage. The past was a black void in which snarling demons fought to drag him down.

Twice, as he blundered along the rain-soaked sidewalks, he stopped, and suddenly became a writhing, lunging madman, lashing out at red-robed spectres which existed now only in his diseased imagination. And always he went on, on, wandering through rain and darkness, driven by unending agony that began in his eyes, where liquid from a breaking bottle had splashed against unprotected eyeballs.

FOR two hours he staggered blindly along the downtown streets of Northwood, always moving, always struggling to remember, to think. And then the agony subsided; memory returned. Fists clenched, eyes wide with sudden awakening, Bill Hilton stood swaying on a rain-wet curbstone, glaring back into a blurred past.

Somewhere—somewhere in that mad vortex a girl had been moaning for help. A young girl, naked, chained. . . .

Bill Hilton raised his trembling hands and stared at them. They were bloody, scarred from their futile efforts to tear iron chains from a mouldering wall. Scarred, too, from beating and clawing at frenzied ghoul-faces, red-cowled monstrosities of darkness.

What had happened? Merciful God, what had he done? What had become of that nude, torture-wracked girl who had begged him so pitifully to help her?

He began to realize, dully, that he had abandoned her to the robed fiends who had sought to annihilate him. She was still a prisoner, still back there in the hell-room deep down in the church's black catacombs. . . !

She was at the mercy of living-dead horribles who would torture her and revel in the agony-shrieks that ripped from her throat. That monstrous bat's-head. . . .

He ran, then, plunged through the rain, toward distant lights, street-lights, and a winking amber eye that was an all-night traffic beacon. His actions were a blurred haze that afterward meant nothing to him. He was a dishevelled, drenched madman, stumbling, retching, stopping at last to blubber insane words to a uniformed policeman who stood gaping at him in amazement. Mad words of a naked woman, of red-robed fiends and a torture-room where a monstrous iron bat's-head leered down in a darkness of the damned!

Yet he knew enough to insist, to keep on insisting, and batter down the policeman's disbelief. He knew enough to give his name—to refrain from blurting truths which would have branded him a frenzied madman.

One gaping policeman—then two—scowling, listening, growling curt questions. And then a police-car droned through murk and rain, sped through deserted streets, and ground to a stop before the black portals of the First Grace Church. Old Eric Hefferen answered the incessant clamor of the doorbell, standing like a deformed gnome in the gloom of the doorway, fantastically attired in dirty white nightgown and huge leather slippers, frowning, shaking his head. . . .

"He's mad," Hefferen muttered, retreating from the wild glare in Bill's eyes. "Stark, starin' mad and nothin' else!"

Bill's hand clawed out, gripped the arm of one policeman. "I tell you it's true! That room downstairs—the girl—— Don't stand here wasting time! I'll show you!"

The policeman did not believe. They exchanged significant glances; one of them shrugged. But they followed as old Hefferen led the way, mumbling irritably to himself, swinging a searchlight in one gnarled hand. Down, down . . . heavy feet thumping on the wooden staircase, parading through the Stygian gloom of the downstairs passage, past the rectangular entrance to the crypt, into and across the great cellar with its concrete floor, its looming pillars, its stone steps leading down to a boiler-room.

Old Hefferen's wife came then, hobbling from the "apartment" occupied by the caretaker and his family in a distant part of the cellar. She was scowling, blurting querilous questions, staring with beady dark eyes and making quick, birdlike movements with her bony hands.

Her son, whom Bill Hilton had heard of but never before seen, accompanied her. Tall, big-boned, with a heavy tread that sent hollow echoes ahead of him as he took one step to the woman's shuffling three. Dark-haired, dark-eyed, suspicious. . . .

BILL HILTON reached the end of the huge cellar and stared helplessly at the door where he and Truman had picked the padlock. The lock was again in place, dangling from its rusty bracket. "It's in here," Bill sobbed. "In here and through a sound-proof door in the far wall—"

Hefferen's crone of a wife barked shrilly: "Through what?"

"A door. A hidden door—"

"He's crazy! Crazy as a loon! This ain't nothin' but a storeroom!"

"Open it," one of the policemen grimly ordered.

Hefferen rattled keys, drew the door wide, scuffed over the threshhold with the searchlight gripped in his outthrust fist. Bill Hilton stumbled across the floor and groped against the wall, pawed for the hidden panel, pawed frantically with trembling sweat-drenched hands. The others stood watching, Hefferen sneering, his wife staring with beady glittering eyes, the two policemen openly skeptical.

And there was no panel. No panel!

Sobs welled in Bill's throat and sweat smeared his face, seared his swollen lips. Wildly, frantically he sought what he could not find, what had been there but was there no longer. In the end he turned, stood glaring, his hair a damp mop dangling in his eyes, his chest heaving with the agonized labor of breathing.

"There *was* a door. I went through it! There's a room—a torture-room. And a girl—"

"He's out of his head," Hefferen muttered. "This here ain't nothin' but a storeroom. As for secret doors and all that sort o' nonsense, there ain't any around here that I ever come acrost. This here is a church. Who ever heard of secret rooms in a church? Huh?"

"I tell you there's a room beyond this one!" Bill blurted. "I was in it!"

"You been in a good many places tonight, young feller," one of the policemen shrugged. "Barrooms mostly, from the looks of things. And in a couple of fights, too, I'd say. Come on. It's time you went home before you get into any more trouble."

Desperation blazed in Bill's eyes and he stood stiff-legged, fists clenched, returning the mocking stares of his accusers. Savagely he strode forward, gripped Hefferen's arm. "Listen. I came here tonight with a man named Truman. Damn you, deny that if you can!"

"I ain't denyin' it."

"Where's Truman now?"

"Him? He went home."

"He—went home?"

"Look here." Firm fingers closed over Bill's trembling shoulder. "That's enough of this nonsense. Come along, you!"

There was no alternative, no hope.

Dully, Bill turned, stared at the wall where that evil doorway had opened to let him into the torment-chamber where a naked, tortured girl had lain in chains. The wall leered back at him, mocked him, hiding its hellish secret. Strong hands dragged him away. Slowly, relentlessly, he was forced across the huge cellar, upstairs to the church vestibule, outside into rain and darkness.

And one of the two policemen said grimly: "You get on home now and don't cause any more trouble. If there's a next time, it won't go so easy with you."

CHAPTER FIVE

Warning of the Dead

THE beat of unceasing rain drove madness from his brain, left him weak, weary, numbed by the turmoil and agony of the past few hours. He walked slowly without knowing his destination or caring where he was going. The horrors of the past were a gigantic blur in which strange shapes took form, leered out at him, then misted away into nothingness.

A naked girl, chained . . . red-robed fiends . . . a sudden jarring thud as glass broke. Acid—was it acid?—lashing his face, gouging his eyes. . . .

The stuff had been something more viscious than acid. He knew that now. It had eaten into his brain, robbed him of the power to think clearly, made of his memory a vast gray fog ever changing. Even now he could not recall certain dark details.

Al Truman—what had become of him? Gone home, Hefferen had said. Home? But somehow, vaguely, Truman was mixed up in the mad sequence of horrors that had preceded his going home!

Bill stopped, made growling sounds in his throat as he stared around. Through the dark fog that enveloped his brain intruded a sudden vicious desire to confront the dark-eyed young man who had so cunningly led him into hell. Up the street a neon sign advertised an all-night drugstore. He blundered into it, used the phone-book to find Truman's address.

The house was in the residential part of town, and Bill Hilton was a ghastly, gaunt-faced visitor out of darkness. His blood-rimmed eyes sought the name *Truman* above the bell; his trembling finger fumbled for the bell-button and clung there. Twenty feet distant a street-light cast its lurid glare through the rain, and Bill's face stared back at him from the glass pane of the door.

It was the face of a ghost, haggard, grayish white with great dark pits of eye-sockets in which the eyes glowed like red coals. Fever and terror and exhaustion had fed on his strength, made of him a weak, staggering shell that no longer even resembled the big Bill Hilton of yesterday.

He stared at his grotesque reflection in the glass, and groaned. But his finger clung to the bell. . . .

It was Truman himself who answered the bell's jangling clamor, jerked open the door and stood there, glaring, attired in black satin pajamas, dressing-gown and slippers.

"What in the name of God do you want at this time of night?" His dark eyes flashed with anger as he spoke.

"To talk—with you," Bill Hilton stuttered.

"Talk to me about what?"

Bill's red blobs of eyes narrowed, returned the man's glare without blinking. His hands gripped the sides of the door-frame, holding his swaying body erect. A black wave of unconsciousness came at him and fought to engulf him. He battled clear of it. "Listen, Truman." The words came thickly in a hoarse whisper. "You've got some questions to answer. You're going to answer them now or—or else—"

The dark-eyed young man snorted impatiently, but did not step back to let Bill enter. He exhaled noisily, curled his lips in a sneer that was all too familiar. "All right, I did desert you," he admitted curtly. "When I left you downstairs in the church, I was suspicious of the old woman and I followed her upstairs. She went up to the organ loft and gave her son hell for playing the organ. It seems he has a yen for going up there at all hours and playing the damndest weird music.

"Anyhow, I stood around the vestibule talking to old Hefferen, waiting for you to show up. I figured you were messing around downstairs and you'd come up when you got through. Then I got tired of waiting and came home."

Bill glared, swayed forward. "That's your story, Truman. What I want to know is—"

"I've told you all I'm going to! Now get out!"

"Get out? Not a chance. Not until I—"

The words stuck in Bill's throat. He saw a clenched fist coming, stared straight at it as it swung savagely to his face and became a huge dark blur before his eyes.

He made a feeble effort to ward it off, but he had no chance. The fist made crunching contact with his outthrust jaw, struck twice again with trip-hammer precision. And agony surged again in a scarlet wave through Bill's brain; the doorway, the snarling face of Al Truman, the guttural sounds that spewed from Truman's curled lips, all blurred together into one vast vaporous mass that was stabbed through with shafts of numbing pain.

CONSCIOUSNESS flowed back into Bill Hilton's brain in a dark wave, bringing with it a return of the agonies which had begun with the breaking of a little glass bottle in the bat's-head torment-chamber beneath Northwood's First Grace Church. He lay motionless, his half-open eyes staring at a low ceiling above him. Moments passed and slowly, dully, he remembered what had happened—as though those things had happened not to him but to someone else. . . .

Sunlight streaked the ceiling and puddled the crumpled covers of the bed on which he lay. It was his own bed in his own home. Wearily he sat up, put a groping hand to the throbbing part of his face and winced as his stiff fingers sent torment stabbing through him.

He was still dressed; his clothes were crumpled, damp. Blood from his face had stained the bed-covers. How, then, had he gotten home? His memory began with the sudden attack of Al Truman. After that there was nothing.

And the sunlight in the room was warm, bright. Hours must have passed since Truman's attack, since Truman's bludgeoning fists had climaxed other hours of agony and illness. Someone had carried him here to his own home and left him. Perhaps Truman himself had done that after battering him down.

It was an effort to get off the bed, to grope across the room and stand staring at the clock on the bureau. The clock's hands were together at twenty past four—four-twenty in the afternoon! That other thing lay on the bureau, too, and Bill closed his eyes as a violent shudder jerked through him. That curled human hand with its grim message of warning. . . .

He patched himself up, then. Stood for ten minutes under a hot shower and then, dressed in clean dry clothes, prowled into the kitchen and made something to eat. The events of yesterday, of last night, were fused in a dull haze that would not clear. When he had finished eating he lit a cigarette, went to the living-room and slumped in a chair near the fireplace, sat there and tried vainly to concentrate.

He stared straight ahead of him. Nearly three minutes passed before he realized, with a sudden intake of breath and a convulsive stiffening of his slumped body, what he was staring at.

Slowly, with bloodshot eyes agape, he pushed himself out of the chair, took faltering steps forward and stood with both hands white and taut on the edge of the living-room table.

The thing that squatted there at the base of the lamp was the mate to the thing that lay curled on the bureau in the bedroom. A pale, red-stumped human hand—a woman's hand—holding between its second and third fingers a rolled tube of paper.

His hand went out slowly, not to touch the pale, flawless flesh of that other hand but to pull the tube of paper loose and unroll it.

Crimson words stared up at him from the paper's curled surface.

> By the hand of the dead, William Hilton, be warned! Twice ye have intruded into the abode of the dwellers in darkness. Twice ye have been permitted to escape. There will be no third time! Leave Northwood now, and do not return on pain of death!

THE words quivered as the paper shook to the trembling of Bill's fingers. His tongue curled over dry lips, moistening them. Then the sudden jangle of a doorbell startled him so violently that the paper leaped from his nerveless hand and fluttered like a thing alive to the table.

Slowly, with fists clenched and dark dread beating at his heart, he paced down the hall to the front door and opened it.

Mr. Ellery Hamblin, of the board of directors at the Northwood Cooperative Bank, stood solemnly gazing at him over the threshold. Behind Mr. Ellery Hamblin, and vaguely ill at ease, stood Mr. Henry Greenwood, his compatriot. At Bill's puzzled invitation the two men paraded into the study—where there were no blood-notes, no severed human hands to startle them—and sat down.

Ellery Hamblin nervously moved his pudgy hands and leaned forward, screwed his womanish face into a frown. "It—it's about what happened last evening at John Darnell's house," he said awkwardly. "You know—about young Truman's abominable conduct. We've been hearing things, Hilton, that we thought you should know about."

"Well?"

"Truman is—well, he's quite a somebody in this town. Money, you know, and influence. And we've had it on good authority that he intends to bring suit against you unless you leave the city."

"He—what?"

"Now, now, Hilton, don't fly off the handle!" Hamblin soothed. "I'm only saying what we've heard, but it comes from a dependable source. Six months ago when your father was living, the idea would have been ridiculous. But people have sort of forgotten you since Mark Hilton passed on and you went to Portland to take over the reins. It's really quite probable that Truman with his influence could make things mighty unpleasant. Personally, I—well, I think you'd do well to—er—take yourself away until he gets over it. Then come back. The bank deal can wait."

Henry Greenwood, who usually said things with smirks and *double entendres,* stared vaguely with large round eyes and said nothing. Bill Hilton stood up, his hands on his hips, and glared.

"So I'm to be run out of town," he said with slow sarcasm. "Is that it? By an ascetic-faced playboy named Al Truman!"

"Well, he has threatened to use his influence—"

White-hot rage boiled in Bill, forced savage words to his lips. But the words died unuttered as he thought suddenly of a number of disjointed things that vaguely, sluggishly began to slide together and form a composite whole.

He thought of Al Truman's deceased relative, Matthew Craven, who had gone mad with cancer pain and died, and been interred in a vault which could be opened from the inside. He thought of red-cowled spectral shapes which belonged not among the living but among the dead; of severed human hands—and a naked girl chained in a strangely non-existant room where a gigantic bat's head, symbol of death, leered down in evil darkness. Of John Darnell, whose queer actions during recent weeks had caused his daughter, Edith, to send a frantic plea to Bill Hilton for help.

And of Eric Hefferen, the humpback, and his withered, vicious crone of a wife, and their son, who wrung weird, terrifying music from the dark pipes of an organ. . . .

Somehow, now, there was a tie-up. There was meaning and reason, and a monstrous ever-swelling mist of horror that sucked those many disjointed things into its black vortex!

"I'll think it over," Bill Hilton said quietly. "Get out now, both of you. Later, I'll get in touch with you."

Ellery Hamblin frowned, put out a twitching hand. "You—you're going to leave town for a while?"

"I said I'll think it over."

The two men left, Hamblin still frowning, Greenwood seemingly bewildered. Quietly, Bill closed the door after them.

And just as quietly he went to the phone and called the Darnell home. Edith Darnell answered.

"Listen," Bill said without preliminaries. "Listen, Edith. I want you to be very careful what you do for the next several hours. Watch your father's every move. Don't let him go near the church and don't go there yourself, whatever you do! Do you understand? This may be the last you'll hear from me for some time, but don't worry. I think I see daylight."

Her answering voice was heavy with anxiety. "But, Bill! What's wrong? What—?"

"Don't worry," he said evenly. "Just be careful. Above all, don't say anything to Truman. You'll hear from me later."

HE HUNG up. Half an hour later when he left the house he carried a suitcase in each hand and, instead of taking a cab, walked downtown to the Northwood depot. He walked slowly, spoke to several people who knew him, made sure that he was seen and recognized by others.

A train for Portland was due at six-ten. He took it. Darkness blurred the town of Northwood as the train roared on its eighty mile journey.

But Bill Hilton did not travel the eighty miles; he left the train at Milton, a small town less than ten miles from Northwood. He checked the two suitcases at the Milton depot, climbed into a cab and said curtly to the driver: "Drive to Northwood, in a hurry!"

He left the cab on the outskirts of town, pushed his big hands deep into his pockets, and walked the rest of the way.

His destination was the First Grace Church.

Dark premonition told him as he made his way through night-shrouded streets of Northwood's residential sector that he was deliberately parading into peril. Two severed human hands clutching bloody notes of warning were conclusive proof of that, even if his mind and memory were not already black with the agonies of his last visit to Northwood's temple of torment.

He, Bill Hilton, was acting the part of a sentimental damned fool, for the sake of a woman who might even now be with a dark-eyed, ascetic-faced young man who perhaps had found the secret to her heart.

The hour was late. Darkness was solid, heavy; occasional street-lamps were pale beacons leading him on. Nearing his destination, he went more slowly as the realization of his peril increased with each forward step. Ahead, the dark hulk of the church loomed gaunt and huge, its great bell-tower rising against an evil sky.

He stared up. And suddenly, with a bone-jarring jerk, he pulled to a halt.

Up there—high up in the topmost part of the great tower, where in the past the huge bell of Grace Church had intoned its calls to the faithful—something had moved. The thing was white and small and frantic against a background of ribbed blackness, where man-high openings in the stone structure provided a grim appearance of prison-bars. The topmost room of the tower *was* a prison—not because the apertures between huge ribs of stone were too small to permit the escape of a human body, but because the tower itself rose straight and sheer into upper darkness, high above the sloping slate roof of the church itself.

And up there in that great shaft a woman was frantically gesticulating, screaming as she sought to attract Bill Hilton's attention!

The thin wail of her voice trailed down to him, stopped the breath in his throat as he caught the stark terror that accompanied the incoherent words. Stiff as stone he gaped up, until that white, frantic shape against its sinister background was indelibly etched in his soul.

He knew that voice, knew the lips that shrilled it forth! The girl up there, imprisoned in the tower's bell-room, was Edith Darnell!

CHAPTER SIX

Red Hell of Torture

THE events of the next few moments were never more than a dark murk in Bill Hilton's brain—a dark murk made up of running, stumbling, hammering frantically on the great front door of Northwood's Grace Church, of bellowing wildly for old Eric Hefferen to come and open the damned thing. Of staggering away from the great barrier at last and sobbing along the wall—of leaping, clutching with curled fingers, dragging his aching body over a stone window-ledge, smashing with frantic fists at one of the huge stained-glass windows. . . .

Hands and face were gouged, bloody from contact with jagged glass when he tumbled to the floor inside, stumbled erect and lurched into darkness impregnable. Blindly he raced down the carpeted church-aisle into vast gloom beneath the great overhanging frown of the balcony. Sobbing, he staggered upstairs, up flights of stairs that curled endlessly into blackness. Up—up—

There were doors that had to be wrenched open, others, locked, that had to be shouldered down, cursed, battered loose by physical assault. Only a black-souled fiend of hell could have conceived a bell-tower so high, so choked with black musty rooms and treacherous stairways.

Rooms—rooms on every level, some of them alive with crawling shadows as the stained-glass windows let in murky lesser darkness from outside. Some of them filled with great hulks of old furniture that rose to block Bill Hilton's path. And always a thick black snake of bell-rope reaching up, up through floors and ceilings, to the topmost chamber of all.

In the end, Bill Hilton's sobbing form reached the final door of all—the door of the bell-chamber far above the night-shrouded streets of Northwod — and hurtled against it.

A padlock clanked against the wood and he fought it with blind unreasoning fury. The door jarred open, flinging him lurching over the sill.

Flat against the wall, staring at him, stood the girl he loved, her trembling, cowering body only half covered by the torn satin of a white evening gown. A whimpering moan spilled from her lips as she swayed forward. She would have fallen, but Bill's outthrust arms caught her, held her. Dully she stared up into his face, mumbled again and again: "Oh, thank God! Thank God you found me!"

He stared around, shuddered. The chamber was small, hardly more than a cat-walk around the monstrous iron bell that hung black and silent in its midst. Against the far wall hung something that loomed white and still in death.

Bill's eyes bulged; horror crawled through him. That contorted, naked form, slumped in the embrace of cruel ropes which held it half erect, was the girl he had seen before—the girl he had discovered lying in chains in the room of the great bat's-head furnace downstairs. Dead, now. . . .

And Edith was sobbing, moaning words as she clung to him. "I—I shouldn't have come, Bill. Oh, God, I know it. But dad was missing from home and I knew he would come here and I had to find him!" Her white, terrified face stared up at him, pleading with him to understand. "Eric Hefferen let me in and—

then I don't know what happened. I was alone, calling dad's name, and—and something seized me, dragged me up here and tied me and left me here. I got loose and—"

The words tumbled wildly from her lips, went shrilling through the room's grim silence. "I got loose, but the door was locked on the outside! The only way out was to jump—from there." She pointed a trembling hand to the man-high openings in the great circular wall of stone. "I tried to attract someone's attention, and then I saw you on the sidewalk—"

"Easy now," Bill said grimly. "We're not out of this yet." His hand gripped hers, squeezed hard. Slowly he led her to the shattered door that angled grotesquely inward on one hinge. "We've got to go quietly. Follow me, now."

Fretfully he moved forward. . . .

Too late, his staring eyes pierced the treacherous gloom at the head of the stairway and saw the great black blur that hurtled toward him. Breath stuck in his throat; he jarred backward, flung up both arms in futile defense.

For a fraction of an instant he gaped point-blank into a leprous, cadaverous countenance that reeked of death. Then something blunt and black whined through space, crashed with sledge-hammer force against the side of his head.

CONSCIOUSNESS returned weirdly, crawling in a vague dull drone of macabre melody. It came and went, came again, tauting Bill Hilton's aching brain with its inconsistency. Moments passed while he lay in a dark stupor, aware of the physical torment within his raging skull—aware, too, and puzzled by, the undulating unearthly death-dirge that came at him in vibrant waves, engulfing him. Perhaps *this* was death. . . .

When he opened his eyes, the illusion

was increased. A deep lurid glare seared his eyeballs, ate its way into his brain and brought agony. The weird wailing world about him was a world of dull crimson, of dark red shapes moving in distorted space—a macabre world, strangely terrifying.

And with returning consciousness, with a sluggish realization of the *meaning* of those things, came a wave of soul-retching terror so proportionately worse than physical agony that the agony became as nothing.

Bill Hilton stared, abruptly realized where he was. The red-glowing room that extended before him was the chamber of torment in the bowels of the church. Glaring down at him through the room's bloody haze were the leering eyes of the gigantic iron bat's-head furnace. And he himself was a naked, fantastic offering—naked and battered and bloody, hanging in cruel bonds against a wall that exuded abnormal heat.

Knotted ropes stretched from iron rings in the wall to encircle his wrists and hold his arms at shoulder-torturing extension. A rope loop rawed his throat. The floor hung barely within reach of his dangling bare feet.

Great God, no wonder returning consciousness had brought agony. The torture of such a position could drive a man mad!

He groaned, stared through blurred eyes at the scarlet hell confronting him. Terror clawed at him as he realized that the room had changed since his previous visit. That weird, undulating death-dirge came from the throats of red-cowled ghouls who sat with their backs toward him, sat in rows of wooden benches facing the crimson maw of the furnace.

And that huge vat, fashioned in the shape of a bat's gaping mouth, was an inferno. Heat billowed from its scarlet depths. Red tongues of flame leaped in

a *Danse Macabre* far back in its yawning throat. And something else had been added since Bill Hilton had come here before; something of frightful, horrific significance.

Terror ran with his blood, reached the nerve-ends of his body and sent a prolonged shudder through him. This was a room of darkest hell, a torture-room fit for the vilest inquisition! The weird contrivance in front of the furnace-mouth was an endless broad belt, turning slowly, relentlessly, like the caterpillar of some huge tractor. Gleaming rows of spikes protruded from its upper surface. Handcuffs were riveted at intervals to its sides. . . .

Any human being flung onto that slowly moving hell-device and shackled there would be gouged by the thing's gleaming iron teeth, would be dragged writhing and screaming into the red maw of the furnace. And as the belt continued to revolve, the charred, cremated, torn body of the victim would reappear for sadistic eyes to feast upon.

Even now, red-cowled figures were advancing through the room's dull glare, dragging with them a struggling victim!

Instinctively, Bill Hilton fought the bonds that held him. Already the heat of the room had made a dripping, gleaming distortion of his naked body, sucked sweat from his agonized flesh. Convulsively he lowered his head, fought to get his teeth on the rope loop that encircled his throat. If he could do that. . . .

BEFORE him the assembled ghouls were swaying to the rhythm of their weird dirge—swaying like dark, bloated, formless gargoyles on the rows of wooden benches that faced the furnace. Out of darkness had come the cadaverous monster who was evidently their leader—the scarlet-robed fiend whose name was Matthew Craven.

Matthew Craven—a madman risen from the dead, with hell's own lust incarnate in his obscene face as he stood facing the spectral fiends of his congregation!

Bill Hilton's teeth gnawed savagely at sweat-smeared ropes. His eyes gaped wide. Into his seething brain surged a question that chilled the sweat of his straining body. Where was Edith? In the eternity that had passed since unconsciousness had crashed down on him, what had become of her?

Madness rolled over him in waves of mental agony, and he realized suddenly that the hideous death-dirge of the ghouls had ceased, that the room was alive with the terror-shrieks of the writhing victim who was being dragged toward the great furnace.

Arms folded, leprous face full in the scarlet glare from that roaring maw, Matthew Craven stood leering. And the victim—the naked, shrieking victim whose death-agonies were to supply these red-cowled fiends with sadistic delight—was Leonard Aborn, president of the Northwood Bank!

The man's cries curdled Bill's soul, put new strength in his gnawing teeth. Already the rope loop at his throat was chewed half through. The bonds that held his wrists were saturated with sweat—sweat produced by terror, and by the savage heat of the torment-chamber.

And the red-robed ghouls paid him no attention. They were content to lean forward, to stare avidly as the shrieking victim was hauled toward a horrible death.

Matthew Craven stepped back, reached a leprous hand to touch a lever that protruded from the furnace-side. The endless belt stopped. Cruel hands forced Aborn's naked body down over sharpened steel teeth. The screams that retched from his throat shrilled in red horror to the room's far corners. Steel shackles, ringed to the belt, closed over his wrists, his ankles.

Again Craven's hand touched the lever. Slowly, horribly, the great belt began its journey of death. And as the assembled ghouls watched in gloating silence, that naked writhing body moved toward the black bat's fuming throat. . . .

The lips of Matthew Craven were intoning words in a high-pitched wailing sing-song, but Bill Hilton heard them only through the marrow-melting dread that had him in its grip. Words—significant, hideous syllables of horror—chanted their lurid way through the room's madness!

"Again are we gathered here, O Brethren of the Night, O Worshippers of the Dark Soul of Hastur! Again, despite interference from ignorant ones who know not our purpose, we assemble by the undulating waters of Hali to pay homage to Bethmoora, the Ever Mighty. Grant us thy favor, O Prince of Darkness! Harken to our supplications, O Yuggoth! Receive our offerings and look upon us with favor, O Mighty Yian!

"Pain and torment we offer thee. Suffering and anguish we send thee in return for thy favor. In the name of the Great One of all Greats, whose name is forbidden the lips of even the faithful, grant that we be freed of the bonds of earthly limitations!

"These are our offerings, these wailing unbelievers who come to you in torment and in terror, knowing not their privilege. Three of them we offer— Take them into thy dark embrace and feed upon their sufferings in the vales of unbounded night where nameless ones walk in shadow. Carry them to thy temples of torment where they may shriek and writhe for thy pleasure throughout all eternity!

"These we offer thee now! And before the night is done, O Nyarlathotep, we offer thee the rituals of the Blackest Mass and kneel to the inverted cross of a false Christ in thy name. . . . Hear us, O Lord of Lords! . . ."

Horror words, rising in shrill crescendo above the soul-searing agony screams of a naked victim whose writhing body moved slowly into the avid maw of the bat's-head furnace! But Bill Hilton's enormous eyes watched a second victim —watched a white cringing figure that was dragged forward out of darkness.

Edith! The second victim was to be Edith Darnell!

TERROR seized him, made of him a frantic, struggling beast as he strained futilely against the bonds that held him. But the girl's captors paid no heed to the hoarse cry that retched from his throat. Relentlessly they drew her forward, while the resurrected corpse of Matthew Craven continued to intone words of dark evil.

"Hear us, O Hastur! . . ."

Leonard Aborn's shrieking body was gone, gone into the red hell that awaited it. Again Craven's leprous hand touched the lever, brought the great belt to a stop. Cruel hands seized the girl's arms and dragged her closer.

Bill's teeth finished their savage task, sawed through the sweat-soaked rope that bound his throat. And at the same instant, a door at the far end of the room jarred open—the same hidden door through which Bill Hilton had prowled once before! And a dishevelled, contorted shape burst over the threshold, hurtled like a flung scarecrow into the red hell of the torture chamber!

The intruder was John Darnell—like a shaggy beast gone amok. The aged minister surged forward, arms outflung, face convulsed into a screaming gargoyle.

He had a dozen yards to go before reaching the rows of wooden benches that supported the room's red-cowled occupants. But before he had covered half that distance, those cowled figures were erect and facing him. One old man against a score of sadistic fiends!

But Bill Hilton was free now, had known all along that he could free himself if only the rope around his throat could be severed. His sweat-drenched wrists tore themselves loose from the slithering grip of wet bonds. With an animal snarl Bill hurtled clear of the wall!

After that, the room was a nightmare-chamber of red-flamed, screaming action in which Bill Hilton was ever the vortex. His clenched fists drove surging red-robed shapes away from him, cleared a path as he roared toward the girl who stood silhouetted against the crimson blast of the furnace. And before he got to her he scooped a chair into the savage grip of his fists and swung it in murderous half-circles, crashing it against the vile faces that loomed in his way. . . .

He had no thought for John Darnell. Darnell had a gun in one frenzied hand and was using it to send screaming bullets into the room's red hell of horror. He could take care of himself!

But Bill Hilton was unarmed. Clawing fingers raked his naked body, gouged flesh in bloody strips from his heaving chest as he fought through the circle of fiends who sought to drag Edith Darnell back into shadows. The prolonged agony of the past half hour had robbed his big body of strength; yet he found new power in the black rage that surged through him.

Savagely he hurled aside the girl's captors, gripped her slender waist and swung her behind him. Then a monstrous raging figure lunged at him—Matthew Craven!— And one of Craven's leprous hands gripped a gun!

BILL HILTON made a split-second decision and flung himself forward. The gun roared as he made contact. Agony raked the corded muscles of his upflung arm, and the impact of the bullet swung him partly off his course.

But his groping hands seized their prey, jabbed with crushing force against that spectral throat and heaved Craven back. The gun arched through space, firing again as it left Craven's fingers.

Borne backward by the force of Bill's mad charge, Craven staggered three steps, stumbled with an insane shriek against the steel-toothed belt of the torture machine. The fiend's huge body crashed downward, lay impaled while pain made a writhing, squirming horror-shape of it. Robed arms flailed empty space on both sides of the belt—and then one of those horrible hands made contact with the lever that bulged from the side of the furnace. The belt shuddered into motion!

But Bill Hilton had gone mad, mad with pain and hate. His clenched fists still battered the impaled body, even as it moved away from him toward the scarlet inferno of the bat's maw.. His raking fingers clawed that spectral face, gouged savagely, tearing flesh, ripping madly. So pain-wracked was he, he did not realize until afterward that the face which the moving belt finally carried away from his frenzied fists—the face that became a livid, crimson countenance of terror as roaring flames leaped out to engulf it— was not the cadaverous face of a corpse. Not until later did he remember those mad moments and realize that his clawing fingers had torn loose a bloody, sweat-drenched mask, uncovering a twisted face that was neither weird nor spectral—but human. . . .

That face belonged to Ellery Hamblin, director of the Northwood Bank!

But Bill did not know, then. The bat's-head furnace had claimed its shrieking victim. Bill stumbled back, caught hold of Edith Darnell's hand and dragged her through the room's mad shambles toward the door—dragged her past the rigid, snarling shape of her own father who stood with a menacing revolver levelled at the room's crimson occupants.

Staggering, Bill reached the aperture, thrust the girl through it. Right behind them John Darnell backed through the red haze. The gun wavered in Darnell's fist; a groan welled from his throat and he swayed against the wall, near collapse. Bill flung him over the threshold, leaped after him and clawed at the door with both hands.

And then, not until then, Bill Hilton slumped to his knees and pitched to the floor, unconscious. . . .

LATER, he stared up at a bedroom ceiling in the home of John Darnell, and Darnell himself sat at the bedside. Mr. Henry Greenwood, of the board of directors at the bank, sat stiffly nearby.

"You should have said all this before," Darnell was saying through a scowl. "If we had known from the beginning that Hamblin had confiscated funds from the bank, we might have realized other things."

"But I tell you I didn't know!" Greenwood's voice was a plaintive wail. "Aborn probably knew—and was murdered because of it. But the rest of us didn't find it out until the police came to the bank this morning and we checked back over a period of months. Hamblin stole a vast amount of money. He schemed to replace it before we discovered the loss.

"According to one of the cult members who knew his secret, he first conceived the idea of organizing an ordinary thrill cult and persuading wealthy persons to join it, paying him handsomely for the privilege. It was a pet idea of his anyhow. He had leanings in that direction."

Greenwood wrung wet hands, blinked his watery eyes and stared feebly into the older man's stern face. "Then—Hamblin elaborated on that idea, took a few wealthy persons into his confidence, appeared to others as the resurrected madman, Matthew Craven. He played his part well, convinced some of his potential cash-customers that they could win eternal life through devil-worship, appealed to others through promises of mystic rites, orgies —to still others, through fear. . . ."

"These people actually believed him to be Matthew Craven?" Darnell asked.

"I—I don't know," the banker stumbled. "Probably many of them were aware of the hoax. But my God, man, you've seen the list of names! They're the type of persons who have too much money, who look for the ultra-sensational in entertainment. The type who are satiated with ordinary thrill stimuli and want something different. Hamblin knew what he was doing! He schemed, planned everything. He hired Eric Hefferen to be caretaker, paid the man and his family handsomely to keep their mouths shut. Everything was planned to the finest detail. Even the door to the horror-chamber could be utterly concealed by the lowering of an artificial wall-section. . . ."

"From the very beginning," John Darnell scowled, "I suspected some black deviltry. And when my daughter was missing last night, it was the hand of God that guided me to that room of hell. Otherwise she and Bill Hilton might have gone the way of those other victims— others, equally innocent, who were obtained through underworld connections and dragged to the church. I tell you, Greenwood—"

He stopped talking, turned abruptly in his chair as the door opened behind him and Edith Darnell entered. A vague smile touched John Darnell's thin lips; he glanced toward the bed, stood and motioned to Greenwood. Quietly he and Greenwood left the room.

The girl came and sat by Bill's side, stared down into his face. She saw that he was awake. Softly she said: "Bill— you asked me a long time ago about Al Truman. He sent a note this morning— for you."

Bill opened the envelope and read the words written there—words that said simply: "I am sorry. I should have known in the beginning that I had no chance with a girl who had loved and waited for someone else for so long. Jealousy is a terrible thing. Please forgive me— and, be happy."

Bill smiled faintly then. "You know, darling," he said. "I never should have come to Northwood. It was my coming—the possibility that I might buy the church and uncover its secrets—that precipitated the whole black business." He reached for the girl, drew her closer to him, softly spoke the rest into the soft warmth of her throat. "But now I'm here, I think I'll stay. Maybe we can buy the church after all—or pay off the debts on it—and give it to your father as a thank-you present when he—"

"Say it," she whispered. "Say it, Bill! Oh, I've waited so long!"

Bill said it. . . .

THE END

FLESH
FEEDER

By Paul Ernst

A strange tree it was, that hickory in Professor Xarno's back yard—a hungry-looking tree, whose strangely stunted limbs seemed to sway and reach eagerly for each passerby!

I WAS quite excited as I walked up the porch steps of Professor Andreas Xarno's combined home and laboratory. For over two years Xarno had been working on something the secret of which he had revealed to no one. Not even to me, one of his closest friends, had he given

a hint as to the nature of his experiment. But now he was going to let me in on his carefully guarded secret.

Whatever he was doing, was being done in the open air of his back yard. That was apparent because, just before he had started, he had walled in his yard with a fifteen foot high plank barrier along the top of which ran a live wire designed to give a discouraging shock to anybody who tried to peep over. But that was all any one knew.

Finally he had asked me to come over and see the fruits of his experiment. He had asked me casually, as though he did not know that I was consumed with curiosity. And I, of course, had dropped everything to come at once; "at once" being half past three in the sunny May afternoon.

I rang the door-bell.

Mrs. McCarthy, Zarno's housekeeper opened the door. At sight of her face my curiosity was fanned higher.

Mrs. McCarthy, I thought, looked a little worried, and more than a little pale. Usually the calmest of mortals, and with a high color on her fresh, middle-aged face, she seemed nervous and pallid now.

"The professor's in his study," she said. "He's phoning some of his friends and a few reporters to come here tomorrow mornin' and see the results of his last experiment. He says to go right out to the back yard and he'll be with you in a minute."

"What is his latest work with?" I asked. "He hasn't deserted bio-chemistry, has he?"

"I don't know the high-soundin' names for it," said Mrs. McCarthy. "I don't know anything about it."

Her lips parted, as if she were going to say more, then firmly closed—then reluctantly opened again.

"I will say this, though. 'Tis devilish, the thing he's made."

"But what has he made? What has—?"

"Go on out back," Mrs. McCarthy said. "The professor will be with you soon."

I WALKED through the downstairs hall of the house—which I hadn't seen in two years—and out the back door into the yard which Xarno had walled so secretively before starting his work on whatever it was I was to see.

I took three steps across the springy green grass of the yard, then stopped, while a most disquieting feeling took possession of me. I had no word for the emotion and I could see no reason why I was experiencing it, but it was most unpleasant.

A shudder tingled through me from head to foot. A slight moisture stood out on my hands. I felt the short hairs at the back of my neck crawl slightly, like the hackles of a dog in fright or anger.

I experienced this vague, instinctive feeling of unease only for a moment and, as I said, there seemed to be no reason for it.

More carefully, I looked around the yard.

It was about a hundred feet square, walled invulnerably by the high barricade, and absolutely empty save for a tree in its center. That was all. A tree, about eighteen feet high, in the center of a hundred-foot square of inoffensive looking grass. . . .

No longer shaken by the momentary feeling of vague and reasonless terror, I walked toward the tree. There was nothing else in the yard to occupy a man's attention. I would wait near it for the professor to get through with his long-distance telephoning.

I had dismissed the tree from my mind as an ordinary hickory, transplanted to the yard for whatever shade it might give. But as I neared the thing I began to notice slightly unusual details about it.

It had the leaves of a hickory, and the loose shags of bark on its trunk, but there all similarity ended.

The tree was rather sparsely leaved and branched. The limbs were thicker and stubbier than tree branches usually are; more like immensely attenuated, blunt-ended fingers than like the branches of a tree. The leaves looked uncommon, too. They were larger than hickory leaves ought to be, and thicker. Almost like pads. Fleshy looking, if you can apply that word to leaves. And the bark was peculiar. It had the oddest appearance, I saw as I got still closer! It looked—this was so fanciful that I grinned a little foolishly even describing it to myself—it looked more like gnarled and wrinkled skin than like bark.

There I began to get the key.

This tree, that from a distance looked like an ordinary hickory, gave out a subtle impression of being made, not of wood, but of some stuff softer than wood and harder than flesh. That was it! It had a distinctly fleshly appearance. The trunk looked like dry, tough animal tissue; the bark like horny, wrinkled hide.

Now I was within ten feet of the tree and I saw one more peculiar thing. That was, the color.

The whole tree, leaves and trunk and branches, had a reddish tinge. It was a dark, purplish red, almost of the color of venous blood, so imperceptible that it made me wonder if my eyesight was failing to register hues properly.

Then I blinked. In a twinkling the tree, by some trick of optical illusion, appeared an ordinary tree again—looking softened and slighty diseased, but otherwise normal. . . .

"Well," a voice at my shoulder made me jump, "what do you think of it?"

I TURNED. Xarno was beside me, having approached noiselessly over the smooth grass. His deep-set blue eyes were twinkling, and there were humor-corrugations on the broad forehead under his snow white hair.

"You mean what do I think of the tree?" I said. "It—it looks a little unhealthy, doesn't it?" I saw no reason to tell him the chimerical fancies I'd had on first seeing the thing.

He nodded his head, a bit grimly. "It is unhealthy, in a way," he replied enigmatically.

"Is that what you've been working on all this time?"

"That's it," he said. And his eyes began to glow as they always do when intricate and difficult work has turned out to his satisfaction.

"But it's an ordinary hickory—" I began.

"It was an ordinary hickory tree," he cut in. "It isn't now. It's like nothing else on earth. It's my own creation. For lack of a proper scientific name, I call it a blood tree."

"A blood tree!" Through some trick of the sunlight, or of association called up by the word, I noted again the peculiar, imperceptible reddish tinge of the tree—like impure, venous blood!

Xarno laughed at the expression on my face. "I don't know why I always pick you as the first to see a completed experiment," he said. "You know nothing of science. Perhaps because it's so amusing to watch your reactions when you observe something contrary to all the rules of nature. . . ."

I smiled faintly then, and he went on with his story. "It's like this:" he said. "For the last two years I have been working with porphyrin. Peculiar, marvelous stuff, porphyrin! You know I was the first to discover that it is the base of the red blood cells of animate life—and also that it is the base of chlorophyl, the coloring matter of plants, which they use to synthesize plant food from the energy of sunlight. That discovery suggested a train of thought which I have been following ever since."

I nodded, and would have mentioned that I understood so far, but the professor didn't give me a chance to speak. And from then on he became more scientifically complicated.

"There is only one difference between the porphyrin which is the base of blood, and the porphyrin which is the base of the green matter in plants. That is, that in the blood it is combined with iron—and the green kind contains magnesium. Otherwise the two porphyrins are chemically identical. The deduction is self-evident: Far back in evolution the chlorophyl of plants and the blood of animals originated from the same source.

"I have been turning the clock of evolution backward. I have been transposing the two essences."

I must have looked rather stupid at that, for he snapped his fingers impatiently.

"But it's simple! At least in the telling. The actual work has been delicate and complicated beyond belief. Porphyrin-iron is the blood of animals. Porphyrin-magnesium is the green of plants. Very well. I have been extracting the magnesium from the porphyrin of this tree and substituting iron in its place, by a control of the nutrition it ingests. In a word, I'm creating blood—startlingly similar to the blood of insects—in a hickory tree! I'm linking, to some slight extent, the animal and the vegetable kingdoms! What wierd plant-animal-thing do you suppose I could ultimately cultivate from this experiment?"

"What you'll ultimately get, in all probability," I said, "will be a dead tree."

The scientific enthusiasm died from his face. He sighed.

"In your blunt and unlearned fashion, you're perhaps right. The hickory does look diseased. And no wonder. As I've substituted iron for magnesium in its porphyrin, it has been less and less able to take nourishment as a plant should. And, speaking along that vein, I want to show you a peculiar thing."

He reached into his voluminous side pocket and took out a parcel about the size of my fist, wrapped in heavy brown paper. He unwrapped it. The thing revealed was a chunk of meat.

And at once the most amazing thing happened. . . .

THE tree began to stir restlessly, to move its branches. Like sluggish tentacles, the sparse, stubby limbs weaved, with the fleshy leaves twisting on their stems so that the undersides were all turned toward the professor. The whole tree seemed to lean a little toward him.

The professor stepped toward the tree. He touched the bit of meat against one of the lower branches.

Sluggishly the branch-tip curled around the meat. Several of the thick leaves pressed their undersides against it. The meat was soon hidden from sight.

"Good heaven!" I burst out. "That's monstrous!"

"Not at all," said Xarno, lifting his snowy eyebrows. "In the botanical catalogue are names of many plants which subside on flesh. The only unusual thing about it is that I have made an ordinary hickory tree into a thing able, with some difficulty and poor efficiency, to extract nourishment from meat. Well, now what do you think of my latest experiment?"

"I think as Mrs. McCarthy does," I said soberly. " 'Tis something develish you've made here. Tell me, why is the ground so cracked around the base of the tree?"

Xarno peered at the ground where I pointed. Then he put on his glasses—his sight is not of the best—and bent lower.

There were myriad cracks in the earth near the diseased-looking trunk. They radiated in all directions, quite sizable near the tree, hair-fine at their extremities.

"I hadn't noticed that before," said Xarno indifferently. "Perhaps, when the tree was transplanted, the roots were crowded and it has now pushed up the earth a little in their expansion back to normal. Tree-roots are immensely tough, you know. They can crack concrete in time . . . . What do you suppose would happen if I tried my experiment the other way round and began substituting magnesium for iron in the blood of, say, a dog? Quick and disappointing death of the dog, I presume. The animal kingdom is not as hardy as the vegetable. . . ."

That was Xarno. One of the great scientists of his day, but pursuing his profound research in the spirit of a child curiously taking an alarm clock to pieces.

But the idea of making a plant out of an animal was too absurd. I laughed and, after a moment, so did Xarno. We turned from the thing he had so fancifully named a blood tree, and walked toward the house.

But just before we went in from the yard, I experienced again that faint, deep-seated, instinctive feeling of unease, almost of horror. The sort of fright that seizes a horse when it senses a deadly reptile near and sweats and jerks in a panic inexplicable to its rider. In this case my subconscious was the horse and my brain the impatient and puzzled rider.

We went into the house together, and then after a little while I went home.

IT seems incredible to me now that I should not have realized sooner why I felt as I did in the yard, and why I should not have guessed more quickly at the single reason behind the several phenomena which presently came to my attention.

The first one was that I received no answer when I telephoned the professor after dinner to ask if I might come next morning with the rest of his guests and see the tree again.

The second was that my wife came back to the living room at nine-fifteen, after phoning a friend, and repeated the news that Mr. Grayson's team had run away a few minutes before, and had pitched Grayson out of his buckboard and onto his head. He was in the local hospital with a fractured skull, unconscious. The team had taken fright near Xarno's house.

The third one was that a neighbor dropped in at ten o'clock to say that he had just heard a wild cry from the woods which began about two hundred yards behind Xarno's property, and to ask if we knew who might have been wandering out there at this time of night.

An unanswered telephone, a runaway, an unexplained scream in the night—and these things happened within eight hours of my preview of Xarno's completed experiment!

Yet I did not connect them till after I had gone to bed at eleven and was tossing in a restlessness that forbade sleep. Even then I did not think consciously of them. It was only that my restless mind somehow insisted on mulling them over.

Curious that no one had answered my call to Xarno's house. Never before, as far as I knew, had both Xarno and Mrs. McCarthy left the place at the same time. Mrs. McCarthy only went out to market; and Xarno was always there, working interminably on some experiment.

Odd that Grayson's team, the steadiest pair of plugs in the countryside, should have bolted and nearly killed their owner. What had they seen near Xarno's house to frighten them?

Queer, that cry in the night from the woods behind the professor's property. Had some tramp frightened a woman passing nearby? But why would a woman be near the woods alone at ten of a cloudy night?

It was only then that a thought sprung me bolt upright in bed, made me sit with hands clenched and eyes staring unseeingly into the darkness.

"But it's impossible!" I said aloud. "Utterly impossible!"

My wife stirred.

"I can't sleep," I said. "I'm going to dress and take a walk."

CLOUDS hung low in the black sky with a hint of rain, and that was good, for we'd experienced a pitilessly dry spring and needed rain. But I wasn't thinking much of the weather. I was linking up the three peculiar incidents centering near Xarno's house—and walking faster as the total grew.

Three blocks from Xarno's place I saw two men in the badly lit street ahead of me. One seemed to be fighting the other.

They were Ferguson, our sheriff, and an old fellow by the name of Bristles, who is our town sot. No one knew his real name; he was always Bristles, because a three to five day stubble of grayish beard always roughened his face.

Sheriff Ferguson was wrestling exasperately with Bristles, who was trying to break away.

"Nothin' doin'," I heard Ferguson snort. "You can't get away. I'm going to put you in the lockup for the night. Drunk as you are, you might set fire to somebody's house or somethin'."

I saw old Bristles' face now, and in it I saw something far different from drunkenness. Terror! Pure and unadulterated! He was mad with fear, fighting with Ferguson.

"What's wrong?" I said, feeling my heart begin to pound heavily in my chest.

Ferguson snapped his rusty, seldom-used handcuffs over the old drunkard's wrists.

"Aw, he's tight again," he said. "Not only tight but nuts! Seein' things worse than pink elephants this time. Says he saw a tree moving! Ever hear of anything as crazy as that?"

I felt the sweat start on my forehead.

"I did see it," muttered Bristles, his voice broken and quavering, but not the voice of inebriation. "I did! I saw a tree—moving!"

"Sure," said Ferguson. "Moving in the wind. They all do."

"It wasn't in the wind! It was moving—going along over the ground back there about as fast as a slow walk!"

Ferguson grinned at me. "A tree, walking!" He winked. "Better than purple snakes, ain't it?"

"I did see it! And I ran and hid—"

"In the drain pipe beside the culvert there," Ferguson said to me. "I found him in two inches of drain water Had his death of pneumonia if I hadn't hauled him out. Now he talks about a tree walking."

I ran around Xarno's house to the back, and there I stopped, feeling as if a cold, damp wind were blowing against my clammy skin.

A large section of the fifteen foot fence near the rear of the back yard was down. It was a gaping space in the plank barricade, with the broken live wire trailing on either side.

Overhead, the moon soared free of the clouds and shed a white light on the yard within. And the middle of the yard was ripped and gouged so that it looked like a section of plowed field. In all directions the torn earth lay, as though sluggishly but powerfully heaved up by some force buried within itself. In the center of the area there was a yawning crater.

The blood tree was not there. . . .

I started running again, across the torn up yard and into Xarno's house. I shouted for Xarno, for Mrs. McCarthy. Neither was there. I ran from room to room of the house. In the kitchen a pot of vegetables burned on a neglected fire. In the dining room dinner was laid—

I raced out the front door and down the street, yelling for Sheriff Ferguson.

THE rest of that night is a memory that wakes me out of a sound sleep with a cry on my lips and with my body trembling as if with ague.

I caught Ferguson six blocks away, still dragging Bristles toward the lockup. I grabbed his shoulder.

"Come back to Xarno's house with me! Something's wrong there!"

Ferguson is a good sheriff, but slow. "Something wrong? What's wrong?"

"I don't know. But neither Xarno nor Mrs. McCarthy is in the house, and dinner's laid on the table stone cold. Something must have happened to them."

"They're probably just down to the movie—"

"Without eating? For heaven's sake, turn Bristles loose and come with me!"

Reluctantly Ferguson unfastened Bristles, who sped away in the darkness like a terrified animal.

"What could have happened to the professor? What am I supposed to do? Where am I supposed to look for him?"

In the midst of my fears, I had debated what to tell the sheriff. Certainly not my real apprehensions! He would have tried to put me in the lockup beside Bristles.

"The back yard looks as if there had been an explosion, and part of the fence is down. The fence is broken on the side toward the woodlot, and a neighbor of ours told us at ten o'clock that he'd heard somebody scream in the woods."

Ferguson fumed as he trotted back toward Xarno's house beside me.

"Why didn't your blamed neighbor go see who had screamed, or report it to me, or something?"

"He did look," I panted, "but in the darkness he couldn't see anything . . . Have you a flashlight?"

He grunted an affirmative, and when we reached the place he flashed his light over the ripped turf of the back yard. In the white beam it looked more chaotic than ever.

"It does look like an explosion!" he said. "But it looks more like . . . more like somebody had ripped a good-sized tree out by the roots."

We ran out the hole in the fence, with Ferguson cursing as he tripped over an end of the loose wire, and headed for the woodlet a few hundred yards away.

A clump of hickory trees grew at the side of the grove to our right, and, instinctively, I ran toward this. Ferguson pounded beside me, with his flashlight sending a jerky beam ahead.

The outer edge of the growth of hickory trees presented a curious appearance. The smaller trees were bent aside and the branches of the larger ones were broken back as if a giant had walked into the grove, smashing everything in his twenty-foot path.

We fellowed down this path, Ferguson rushing ahead, I trying to hold him back from a too-foolhardy pace without telling him why, lest he think me insane. And in the center of the hickory growth, we found it.

The blood tree!

There it stood, in the center of the hickory grove in a clear space, an eighteen foot tree canted slightly toward us on a great mass of tangled roots. . . .

YARDS and yards of roots! A spider-web tangle of roots, some as big as a man's leg, some as small as a man's little finger. Tendrils, coils, snarls of roots. And all of them were moving slowly, like lethargic blind worms, striped like zebras in the light of Ferguson's flash as it pierced the lower branches of the tree near which we stood.

A spiderweb of roots! And in it, like

flies in a web, three things that looked at first like bundles of old clothes!

I heard Ferguson gasp, but I paid no attention to him. I could only stand in horror and look at those three things buried in the yards and yards of rope-like roots.

One of them was in woman's garb—a gray dress (or at least it had been gray) with a torn white collar, beyond which I did not care to look—Mrs. McCarthy's dress, that she had worn that afternoon!

Next to this bundle was another—a tangle of men's clothes with the shoulder of the coat clasped in the clutch of something that projected from the right sleeve of the gray dress. The other bundle was off by itself—a dirty, tramp's costume that looked as if it might contain a mangled scarecrow.

Up every aperture of these bundles of clothes—sleeves and legs and collars—roots of the blood tree writhed slowly. And the tree itself, as I could see even in the white beam of the flashlight, had changed color completely. It was all red, now. A dark, purplish, red, of the hue of venous blood.

So much I saw, and then Ferguson's big hand found my arm in a grip that almost made me sink to my knees.

"My God," he whispered. "It—what's it doin' . . ."

The blood tree leaned toward us a little more, stubby branches writhing slowly like tentacles swaying in a sluggish tide, thick leaves rasping like dry hands being rubbed together.

"It's alive!" yelled Ferguson.

He dropped my arm and wrenched out his gun. Six times it spat flame and lead at the bulk of the monstrous thing that waved its blood-red branches sluggishly toward us.

Nothing much happened. Several smaller branches and a few fleshy looking leaves dropped, snicked off by the bullets. That was all.

And then the tree began to move toward us, seeming to flow slowly along on a myriad of legs as its roots coiled and writhed awkwardly over the ground. . . .

SHERIFF FERGUSON is a brave man. He did not run, as every fiber of my body urged me to do. He sidestepped to another part of the hickory grove, white-faced and tense but as ready to fight this weird creation as he was to fight anything threatening life or property in the district under his guardianship.

"What in heaven's name is it?" he whispered in awe. "Do you know?"

"It was once a tree," I said hoarsely. "But Professor Xarno made of it a kind of arboreal monster. . . ."

The tree stopped its first course. Its roots contracted and expanded. It moved lethargically, blindly in our present direction, as though in some way it sensed our new position. Perhaps the vibration of our voices reacted on it . . . . But I won't even guess at what senses and functions had been developed in that diabolical thing when Xarno made of it a link between the animal and the vegetable kingdoms.

"We've got to kill it somehow," breathed Ferguson as we slipped to another part of the grove, out of the thing's path. "Three it's got! The professor—that's his brown suit—his housekeeper, and I guess some poor hobo caught here in the woods. We've got to kill it. But how can you kill a tree?"

How indeed? Bullets were useless. A dozen men would not have dared attack with axes—not with those yards of roots curling and uncurling around every projection in reach (but still keeping tight hold of the three grisly bundles!) and with the branches overhead weaving hungrily like ropey, long fingers!

"We might burn it," whispered Ferguson, looking at the powder-dry twigs and leaves at our feet. I saw his eyes glint glassily in the reflected light of his flash. "The drought has made this stuff like tinder. But the damn thing can move! It could get out of the fire before it got hurt much. It don't look like it would burn easy, anyhow."

It didn't. Its trunk and limbs, softer than wood, tougher, stringier looking than animal tissue, were suffused with a plethora of red that looked too moist for easy burning.

It was then that I had a thought which later seemed absurdly complicated, though even now I can't think of a more effective method.

"Watch this thing," I whispered to Ferguson. "Don't let it leave the grove. I'll be back—with something to hold it still!"

I burst out of the woodlot and raced back toward Xarno's house. His car was in the garage. I got into it and rushed to the town hospital.

DOCTOR ARMSTRONG was there, chief surgeon of the staff, staying a little longer with Grayson and watching the man's fractured skull. Armstrong is a friend of mine, and a clever man.

"Doctor," I said, disregarding his look of surprise at seeing me rush hatless and breathless into the room where the night nurse had said I'd find him, "I want you to do something for me and ask about it later. No time . . . to explain now. Have you any tetanus germs in the place?"

He shook his head, staring at me as though I were mad.

"We have a little tetanine, a ptomaine derived from cultures of the tetanus microbe in meat—"

"Get me some," I interrupted. "And I want some meat from the hospital kitchen. Raw. Quick!"

I think any one else would have knocked me down and held me for the violent ward. But Armstrong, after one more glance at my white face and urgent gestures, turned and went from the room.

He was back in an incredibly short time. He had with him a slab of raw beef, and a little bottle half filled with a crystalline substance.

"Pretty strong stuff," he said. "Be careful. That would kill anything on two legs or four. It even induces a state of rigidity in plant tissue—"

At the hickory grove I found Ferguson in such a state of shattered nerves that he yelled and jumped as he heard my step behind him.

"That thing—" he said shakily. "That thing—I think it can *smell* a person! I haven't made a sound while you were gone, been moving all around. And everywhere I move, the tree starts coming my way. I don't know what we can do—"

I unwrapped the meat, and poured the crystals on it.

"This is what we'll do," I said. "We'll give it some tetanine in its food and see if that will cripple it."

"Tetan—tetan— You mean the stuff that gives you lockjaw?"

I threw the meat into the ghastly tangle of roots that supported the blood tree. Ferguson shuddered, and I turned away. The meat had chanced to land near the two limp bundles which were Professor Xarno's clothes and Mrs. McCarthy's.

The upper part of the tree seemed to shrink into itself as the branches strained downward toward the meat clamped in its roots. The roots themselves coiled around the meat like a great nest of snakes. A ton of tree required a lot of nourishing. . .

It was an hour before anything happened. I began to think my plan had been ill-founded, and that we'd have to round up all the men in town, with ropes and axes, and try the tremendously dangerous task of chipping the blood tree to bits. More lives would almost certainly be lost in such an attempt. . . .

But finally Ferguson clutched my shoulder with bone-crushing force. "It's—there's something wrong with it—"

I stared, trying to keep my gaze off the things convulsively held in its roots.

There was something wrong with it! Roots and branches were shuddering as though the whole tree were gripped in a deadly chill. Several of the fleshy leaves dropped off and thudded to the ground. Then the ptomaine crystals acted.

It began to thresh feebly. Then limb by limb, root by root, it froze into a strained rigidity, more like a tree carved from marble or cast in bronze than a living thing.

"And now," I said, in a voice I did not recognize as my own, "for the fire!"

We ringed the rigid blood tree with heaps of dry brush.

The flames leaped up as high as fire from a burning house. And sizzling in the center of the flames, still rigid as it was slowly consumed, stood the result of Professor Xarno's all too successful attempt to bridge the gulf between plant and animal life. And Xarno . . . What was left of Xarno, and his housekeeper and the unfortunate and unidentified stray human who had been a third victim of the blood tree, were cremated. . . .

I TOLD the assembled reporters and scientists at Xarno's house what had happened, next day. Some laughed, and some looked at each other in a manner with which I have grown familiar in the months that have passed since that night.

One of the scientists condescended to argue with me. It was impossible, he said, for such things to happen. Granting that iron could be substituted for magnesium in the porphyrin of a tree, thus creating within the tree a sort of synthetic blood, it would be entirely impossible for the tree to move as an animate thing. It had no muscles, no nervous system to guide it, no optical or other sensual apparatus to direct it.

I agreed—and repeated my story, not as one that could logically happen, but as what had actually occurred.

The coroner's jury formulated a theory.

Professor Xarno for some reason dug up a tree from the hickory grove. Mrs. McCarthy went to the grove to call him to dinner. A tramp killed both, motive being robbery, but was in turn killed by Xarno before he died. (The fact that Xarno never in life carried a gun or any other weapon that might have enabled him to perform such a feat, was ignored by the jury.) Ferguson and I went to the grove and saw the three bodies lying among the roots of the tree. We lost our heads and fired the woods.

But I know what happened. . . .

Xarno, near the tree at dinner time, was caught by the slow-weaving branches. Mrs. McCarthy, going out to call him, saw him in the tree's toils and, with a courage that undid her, rushed impulsively to his rescue. She was caught too. Perhaps the looping branches chanced to whip first around their throats, cutting off screams for help.

The tree, waxing in strength, ripped loose from the ground it had already cracked in its feeble efforts to free itself. It crashed through the fence and blindly teetered to its native grove, there to find a third victim. . . .

But any scientist will tell you that it would be impossible for a tree to move, even if made animate. So you can believe the theory of the coroner's jury if you like. I don't care much any more.

DEATH TEACHES

She knew only that the two before her who had taken that teaching post in desolate Death Hollow had vanished into the gloomy, threatening mountain silence. When she saw the faceless horror that was one of her predecessors, it was too late to draw back! For already death's red fingers were reaching from the crawling shadows—and the sons of death sat, row on row, before her!

DEATH HOLLOW! The name itself carried with it an ominous threat to Julia Winters as she paused hesitantly on the deserted station platform. And her chill sense of foreboding, of impending evil, was not less-

ened as she watched the grimy train that had carried her into this remote mountain fastness hastily pick up steam, as if anxious to be gone. The wind, rushing out of the encircling hills, was bitter with the dying breath of October. It whistled

SCHOOL

By Nat Schachner
(Author of "Death Takes a Bride, etc.)

*A Novelette of
Screaming
Fear!*

Where was the village? Surely those few rude, unlighted cabins, crouching against the ramparts of the engulfing hills, did not justify the job she had been so eager to accept. For the hundredth time she remembered the troubled, anxious face of the woman at the teachers' agency when she had offered Julia the position at Death Hollow.

"I'm tempted not to let you go, my dear," the woman had said. "You're the third I've sent up there in as many weeks. I haven't heard a word from the other

through her threadbare garments, whipped her skirt close to her slender legs, sent a shiver that was not entirely from the cold along the spine. The girl clutched her shabby handbag tightly to her and her frightened eyes peered through the deepening shadows.

two. Even though the telegram said it is urgent that I fill the vacancy before evening, and the salary is especially good, I really think—"

"Oh, please," Julia had begged. "I *must* get a job, at once. This is the first chance I've had since school, and—and my folks are dead. I've no place to go if I don't get it."

So her credentials and train fare had been given her. "But promise me one thing, my dear," the woman said to Julia before she left. "If you notice anything wrong, leave the place at once. I shall never forgive myself if anything happens—"

And now, recalling that last interview, blind panic swept through Julia. She turned instinctively toward the train she had just quitted as if that were her one refuge in a strange and horribly darkened world.

But it was too late. The lantern of the last car was only a red receding glow in the distance, the long, wailing note of the whistle made a hollow mockery in her ears. Then train and sound both disappeared, and she was alone.

Alone? It might have been better if she were alone. Another passenger had swung off the train just as it had started. He stood now at the farther end of the platform, a dim figure in the thickening gloom, the collar of his grey topcoat muffled against his face as he watched her with surreptitious glances.

Julia felt the blood in a cold mist around her heart. She was terribly afraid now—afraid of the threatening hills, of the shadowy cabins in which no lights appeared—of the strange passenger who made no move to depart, but eyed her with faceless stealth.

She shivered. Why hadn't she taken the kindly advice of the agency woman? Suppose she *had* been down to her last dime? Better to starve in the sight of crowded pavements and the every-day din of traffic than to face alone the half-hidden menace, the subtle yet unmistakable atmosphere of evil and peril of this Kentucky mountain hollow.

SHE bit her lip to keep from shrieking out her fear. Holding her bag convulsively, she edged farther and farther away from the shadowy figure of the man.

The telegram had promised that the school trustee who had hired her would be at the station. She tried to remember his name. Lemuel—Lemuel Fogg, that was it! Why hadn't he come? Why was she left on this lonely platform with a stranger who. . . .

Where had he disappeared to? She strained her eyes into the murky darkness. One tiny moment before he had been there, unmoving, sculptured out of shadows; now he was gone, vanished, and with no trace of his going. It seemed to the girl that the eerie twilight grew thick with leering shapes and vague, shifting forms, and whichever way she turned there were unearthly eyes that burned into her soul.

She started to run blindly down the rutted road that led into the hollow. Behind her the wind muttered with mocking voices, the pebbles rattled with the pursuing tread of unseen feet. She knew it was panic, yet she fled before her fears. Headlong, heart thumping, she ran on toward the refuge of the first dark and silent cabin. Perhaps it held people—rough, untutored people, they might be—but normal at least, with kindly faces and kindlier hearts. Tomorrow, she would telegraph the agency, collect, for funds to return, for—

What was that? She stopped her headlong, panting flight, frozen with new fears. This time there was no mistake about the sounds. Something was coming down the hollow toward her, making a noise like a horse's hoofs beating out a devil's tattoo, and dragging something crashing and banging behind.

There was no place to turn, to hide, before it was upon her. A horse and two-seater buggy raced out of the black shadows, swaying from side to side, bouncing and jouncing over the hard ruts.

"Whoa!" The horse slithered on his haunches, his flaring nostrils pitted with engorged blood; his flanks heaving. A man was seated in the buggy, pulling with powerful hands on the reins. In the dimness his massive, sculptured head seemed a frozen halo of white, shoulder-long hair and curling beard. He peered down at the shrinking girl.

"Be you the new school teacher?" he demanded. His voice was a deep, startling rumble. But it filled Julia with a thankful warmth, with blissful peace.

"Yes," she gasped, ashamed of her former unreasoned panic. "I'm Julia Winters. The Central Agency sent me. You're—"

"Lemuel Fogg," the man chuckled deeply. "Head o' the Death Holler School Board. I'm all-fired sorry I got here too late tuh meet the train, but I had a deal on with a feller t'other side o' the mountains, and it held me up a bit. Hope ye wasn't scared. Death Holler ain't a purty place at night, or in the daytime, nuther."

"I—I wasn't scared," she lied bravely. "Except there was a man got off the train with me, and he stood there on the platform, watching me. Then he seemed to vanish—just like smoke." She shuddered as she climbed into the vacant seat of the buggy.

The horse started forward so suddenly that she was thrown against her companion. He had jerked around to her, body rigid, deep-set eyes burning. Terror, stark, unashamed, stared out at her.

"A stranger, ye say, come tuh Death Holler?" he gasped. Then, seeing the girl's startled gesture, a mask dropped swiftly over his eyes, and he laughed. "And why not, Miss Winters? You're a stranger too, ain't ye?"

But his laugh was hollow and unconvincing. And suddenly it struck her that the man was afraid, afraid of hearing about that silent, shadowy figure she had seen. Once more, as they swayed and crashed over the bumpy road, the night became full of creeping fears and gibbering echoes.

LEMUEL FOGG must have sensed the frozen tenseness of the girl's body. He seemed to shrug off this terror with an effort. "Let's git down tuh brass tacks, miss. Ye mought be wonderin' about yer job, eh?"

"Well—that is, naturally, I—"

Why did he look at her sideways, she wondered, as the buggy rocked and careened over the frozen ruts. Why did that stealthy glance hold what seemed to be fear, sympathy, even warning? Why did he hesitate, as if reluctant to commence? In God's name, what was wrong with this job? School teaching was the same all over, wasn't it? Yet already, before Fogg began, the girl knew with dreadful certainty, with every fiber of her being, that this job in Death Hollow was different, that it held a sinister threat in its darkling folds.

"Wall, ye see, we pay a purty good salary," Fogg said irrevelantly.

"I know," she said very low. That was why she had come to this desolate place, in spite of warnings. Why didn't he look squarely at her, so she could read in his eyes what terror it was that lurked there? But he kept his face forward, intent on the broad, heaving rump of the horse, and holding the reins in his hands.

"Ye know science, eh?"

"Yes."

"Ah, but mebbe ye dont' know this here new-fangled business of evolution—

'bout man an' a monkey bein' first cousins?"

Strange! He sounded almost pleading, as if—as if he didn't want her to say yes, as if it would be an excuse not to hire her. Why then had he sent that urgent telegram? Why. . . .

She fought to keep her voice steady, determined. "Yes, I know all about that. I majored in biology at college."

"Waal!" There was genuine regret in his deep voice. "It's this-away. We ain't much on book-larnin' around these parts, and Death Holler ain't got more'n a few few people. We've been too busy with plantin' an' huntin' an' makin' a little corn likker to bother with schools an' sich-like. But there was a feller lived in Death Holler, who quit to go to the big city. Claimed we was a passel o' mossbacks. He died back a bit, name o' Ingersoll Greenway, an' left a heap o' money." Fogg rasped out a sudden chuckle. "What d'ye think the derned fool did?"

"I haven't the slightest idea," Julia acknowledged. The country through which the galloping horse was whirling them was getting wilder and wilder. The cabins of the hollow were behind them now, and deep night shrouded the closing hills. Where were they going?

"Here's what he done," Fogg rumbled on. "He left all his money—exceptin' a mite tuh his two nephews, Hugh an' Philip Elson—tuh Death Holler. That's what he done. Made a will what said we was benighted fools. No eddication, no science, with silly superstitions and a belief in hell-fires. He'd change all that, he said. So he pervided fer a school tuh teach Death Holler science an' evolution. Not the chillen, mind ye, but their pappies, what snickered at his wild talk when he was a younker here. That's the job; tuh teach 'em evenin's, after workin' hours."

A heavy weight rolled off Julia's heart.

"Why, I'd love that," she said impulsively. It sounded easy.

Lemuel Fogg stared straight ahead. Seconds passed while the thud of hoofs rolled with eerie thunder up the narrowing valley they had entered.

"Yup," he said finally. "Giddap, Dobbin." And he was silent.

They were jogging up a mountain road now. The trees were marching with them, keeping stealthy pace, it seemed, hemming them in with locked branches that looked horribly like bony, strangling fingers. The moon had risen, and poured a dead white light over rough-barked boles.

Then it was that Julia remembered. The bearded man's strained hesitation, his averted face, made the other a hideous, looming question in her mind. Once more fear squeezed her pumping heart dry, laid ice-cold fingers along her beating skull.

"Why did the other teachers leave?" she asked in a small, strangled voice. "What happened to them?"

Fogg did not answer. His body became a rigid ramrod beside her. He gulped, made rumbling noises in his throat, opened his mouth as if to speak, but no sound came. And Julia saw the reason.

CHAPTER TWO

The Faceless Horror

A GHASTLY figure had appeared suddenly in the narrow path directly before them. The moonlight encased it in a ghostly shroud. Its face, uplifted from a torn shirt, was a grinning mask of madness. Its long, blood-streaked arm, bare to the shoulder, was extended in horrid warning. A shrill, tuneless screaming came from its bloodless lips, sheared through shrinking flesh and bone, shredded each nerve-end with quivering torture.

"Go back! Go back!" it mouthed insanely.

The horse snorted and then, frightened, reared suddenly on his haunches, back from the apparition that blocked the road. Julia screamed and flung up her hand. A cold wind whistled over the slender nape of her neck, froze her blood to gelid ice. Lemuel Fogg flung himself back, crying an exclamation in a hoarse voice.

The reins lashed against the horse's lathered flanks. He plunged forward wildly, straight for the pallid vision of madness in his path. Julia was thrown to her knees as the buggy crashed into the trunks of the close-pressing trees, bounced with spine-jarring *bongs* on the iron-hard ruts, and careened after the flying horse up the mountain road, with Fogg's powerful arms jerking on the reins.

Julia cowered against the seat, hearing still the wild cackling, the shrill warnings behind her.

They had passed directly over the terrible Thing that had loomed in their path, yet there had been no jar, and his mad shrieks followed them with dreadful din up the mountain.

The horse, exhausted, its flanks heaving convulsively, slowed to a stumbling trot. Julia gasped: "Who—what was that?"

Lemuel Fogg's hands pulsed with jerking nerves. His massive, bearded face was drained as white as his hair. His eyes were flaming pits.

"That," he said in a strangely hushed voice, "that was Mister Pittman. He taught school in Death Holler—till las' night!"

"Oh, my God!" the girl moaned faintly. Ralph Pittman, whom the agency had sent only a week ago, transformed into that unrecognizable monster! What had been done to him; what hideous things had driven him, a shrieking, gibbering madman, into the mountains? Her skin was suddenly a contracting web of agony; she could not breathe, she could not speak.

Hammers pounded insanely in her brain, made a fiery torment of her thoughts.

The terrible shrilling had ceased. The Thing that had been Pittman was silent; had returned, perhaps, to the grave from which it had arisen. . . . But Fogg was talking and his deep voice had a grim catch to it.

"Ye mought as well know the truth, Miss Winters," he said. "No sense keepin' it longer from yuh. That 'ere school's got a curse on't. Preacher Maunders sez it's 'cause God's plumb disgusted with sech heathen teachin's as Greenway's pervided fer. That mought be, though Increase Maunders ain't got no call to talk thataway, seein' as he's executor o' Greenway's will. That 'ere was another o' Greenway's little jokes, makin' the Parson see to't thet the will's carried out, even though its pervisions is pizen tuh him. But Increase, he claims a dead man's commands is God's commands, whatever they mought be."

Julia forced open her frozen lips. "But Pittman," she panted, "what—what—?"

Fogg shook his grim, shaggy head. "I dunno. It started two weeks ago. One night, arter lessons, they found the fust teacher's body thrown out on the mountainside, all chewed up, like wolves done it. Only they ain't no wolves round here. Then this feller Pittman came. The class warn't much—couple o' the boys who thought 'twas a great joke. But it warn't no joke las' night. Pittman, they say, looked shaky an' blue in the face, but he was a game 'un. He kep' on teachin', an' thanked em' fer comin'. No one ain't seen hide or hair of 'im sence, till—till—"

HE FELL silent. Horror drew a black pall before Julia's eyes. She felt faint. Then she shrugged her slim body erect. Indignation forced the blood once more through her failing heart. Whiplash scorn edged her voice.

"And so all of you," she cried, "kept

quiet about it, to lure other poor devils to their death, or madness. Why? Because of a will? What's in back of this? What . . . .?"

Lemuel Fogg twisted his head. He looked shamefaced. "I'll tell ye. There's more tuh the will than that. It left a heap o' money tuh the village folk in Death Holler, pervided not a single night's teachin' was missed. One solitary night that there ain't some'un talkin' evolution in the schoolhouse, an' the hull passel o' money goes tuh his two nephews. An' Preacher Manders, he comes round investigatin' every night."

Julia choked with surging anger. "And you—Mr. Fogg, you permit this to go on!"

The man squirmed defensively. "After all," he muttered. "It saves taxes fer me, same's the rest of 'em. An' supposin' I should stop hiring new teachers, the folks around would go gunnin' fer me." He straightened his powerful shoulders determinedly. "But you're right, Miss. It ain't fair, lettin' you go on with it. I'd have ye on my conscience the rest o' my days. We'll turn right aroun' an' go back tuh Preacher Maunders. Tell 'im ye're quittin'. Let him tear up that fool will."

Julia sat up stiffly. Lemuel Fogg, for all of his craggy, bearded face, was human. He was willing to sacrifice his own interests to save her, and others, from the mysterious fate that overtook the teachers of Death Hollow. Some of her fear, her anger at him thawed under the warmth of that kindness. Then other thoughts shook her.

If she quit now she'd be penniless, without even money enough to return to the city. The future loomed dully before her. No job, no money, her clothes worn down to the last thin layer. Within a year, in this place, she could save what seemed to her starved eyes a fabulous sum. And besides there were the people of the Hollow, who, because of her cowardice, would lose

Greenway's fortune, would stagger once more under a heavy burden of taxes.

Perhaps, she argued with herself, trying to still the dread that clutched at her vitals, the fates of the other two had been mere accidents. Spells, curses, the wrath of God? She tried to laugh to herself at that. This was mere backwoods superstition, the very thing Greenway had endowed the teaching to eradicate. But the inward laugh froze to a lump of ice that stuck in her throat. Now, again, she was afraid, horribly afraid. . . .

She turned her fear-haunted eyes on Fogg. She held her voice steady only by sheer will. "I'll go through with the job," she said, very low.

The horse had stopped. The night shadows clustered around her body with chilling embrace. Fogg gulped noisily. She could not see his face in the dark.

"Yuh mean that," he gasped, "even when yuh know . . . .'."

"Yes," she answered. Never had she found it so difficult to talk.

"Well!" he exhaled. "Yo're a blame brave gal. An' seein' as how . . . ." He extended his arm forward from the carriage. "There's the schoolhouse, and ye kin start teachin' soon's ye git in. Old Greenway's will said that school would be in session 'tween the hours o' seven an' nine."

She had not seen the building before. In front, the trees retreated up the mountainside. The path widened into an upland clearing. In the very center straggled a long pine building. The groping moonlight made leprous scabs on its scaling sides, surged in a ghastly flood to meet the wavering yellow that streamed from its single window.

Julia's heart bounded. "Oh, then there are pupils in there, waiting."

Lemuel Fogg shook his head. "Nary a one. Ye couldin' pay folks from Death Holler to come here after dark, since Pittman was took las' night. That there lamp was lit 'fore sundown."

"You mean to say, I'm to teach, even if no one is here to listen?"

Fogg grunted. "The will didn' say nothin' 'bout pupils; only 'bout teachers."

"And you, Mr. Fogg?"

"Who, me?" The man spoke hurriedly, with labored breath. "Not me. I don' believe much in ghosts, but I ain't stayin'. I—I got some chores tuh do. I'll tell yuh what: I'll be here tuh pick yuh up at nine."

"Oh!" The girl said no more. But she forced her suddenly dragging limbs out of the carriage onto the ground. She could hardly hold herself erect. Unholy things scuttered in the depths of the muttering forest, sent shivers of sheer terror through her aching skull. Her clenched teeth held back the fear that whimpered in her throat. Again and again she said to herself: "Julia Winters, you are not afraid! You are not afraid!" Aloud she said: "Thank you, Mr. Fogg. I'll be expecting you."

"Good gal," he whispered. "I'll be back, don't ye fear." And without another word he swerved Dobbin's head around, and was off in a very fury of impatience. The buggy banged on the hard ground and the sound of its going died out with an eerie whisper in the distance.

SHE was alone—alone in this wild mountain clearing, with the ominous schoolhouse in front of her, dim-lit with the flickering yellow lantern light. She was to teach in there, where a girl had been done to a horrible death and a man had been metamorphosed into a shrieking, gibbering mad thing. She was to face, night after night, the ghastly mockery of rows of empty benches, knowing all the while that unseen shapes lurked in the shadows, waiting only to drag her down, to gouge her soft, white body with hideous teeth and snarling, bloody muzzles.

Shivers of dread coursed up and down her spine. It would be two hours before Lemuel Fogg would return. Two long, dreadful hours in which every second would be a shrieking agony, every minute a dragging horror, and each hour an eternity of waiting.

Waiting for what?

If only she knew, if only she could see the fate that awaited her embodied in tangible form, it would be bearable —yes, even if death or torture or madness lay at the end. That was it—that was what drained her veins of blood, made her face a set mask of taut, insensate skin—the awful feeling that she did not know what Things were even now waiting in gloating expectation of her teaching.

She forced her lead-heavy feet forward. She set her teeth to strangle her welling fear into silence. She *must* enter that black-looming door now. If she didn't go on she would, in another moment be flinging herself down the road, shrieking her dread to the gaunt mountains and to a desolate moon.

What was that?

That slight crackling sound that only ears, keyed to abnormal sensitivity, could have detected. Something, someone was creeping through the dark hemlocks behind her, stealthily, trying to make no noise.

Flogging her paralyzed limbs into movement, she whirled. Better to see it face to face than to imagine. . . .

Framed between the black boles of two tall trees she saw a head. The moon drenched it with corpse-white luminescence, etched out the startled, distorted expression on the youngish face as it emerged from the upturned collar of a grey topcoat. Then, like a shadow seen in a dream, it faded back into the shrouded dark of the woods and was gone.

But Julia had seen enough. For a second her heart stopped beating, then pounded furiously against the thin protection of her ribs. She spun around and flung for the heavy panelled door that led into the schoolroom. Anything, even the terrors that awaited her inside, was better than the open clearing with that figure lurking stealthily in the sinister forest. She had recognized him. He was the strange passenger who had followed her off the train, who had tracked her, unseen, unheard, to this lonely school in Death Hollow. The place accursed, where a girl had died and a man had turned to a mindless idiot.

Her slim hands pounded insanely on the door, her slender shoulder shoved with mad strength against the barricade. It opened with protesting, grating sound, as if reluctant to admit the sobbing girl.

With a little cry she stumbled inside, flung the heavy pine portal tight shut behind her, thrust the iron bolt into its socket. Thank Heavens for the lock! Perhaps now she would be safe from the creeping terrors of the wood.

She whirled, her shoulders taut against the door. Her knees were weak as flowing water, her eyes were wide with shadowed amazement; her hand was up clutching her throat. She had not expected this.

CHAPTER THREE

Satan's Gospel

SHE was in a long room, as long as the building itself. High overhead, out of reach of her slight form, hung a lantern. It swung with a slow rhythmic motion, as if fanned by invisible breezes. Its smoky, yellow flare cast a dim, wavering light over the unpainted, pine interior. The shadows danced on the damp, musty walls, and gathered into strange, terrifying lumps of darkness in the farther corners.

Near where she stood was a plain board desk, huge and flat. Its top was bare, and wan shadows crawled over its surface with each swing of the hanging lantern. A chair, overturned as if in a struggle, lay on its back beside it. But it was not that which held her gaze and brought warm moisture to her brow.

It was what lay beyond. The rear of the room was crowded with long, backed benches, arranged in parallel rows. The sooty yellow barely tinged the cavernous recess with faint color. But on the benches, like pallid blobs of modelled clay, dimly descried in the muttering darkness, were faces—rows of them, uplifted to her straining gaze, waiting patiently, motionlessly.

A great sob of thankfulness burst from the girl's tense throat. Thank God! Thank God! Lemuel Fogg had been wrong. The people of Death Hollow were not all victims of superstitious fears. There were some who laughed them to scorn, who wished to drink of the strange doctrines which clashed with their primitive beliefs.

She was not alone, but had an audience for her teaching. It was hard to distinguish them in that silent, waiting row, but they must be the gaunt, grim men of the hills — sufficient protection against the lurking terrors of the school. That was it! They had heard that she was coming; they knew of the dreadful fates that had befallen her predecessors, and they had congregated to see that no harm should come to her.

Her heart warmed to these kindly folk. She felt her knees firm again. She moved to the desk and said quite loud: "Good evening!"

The simple words of greeting flew like leather-winged bats around the room, and rebounded from the enclosing walls in eerie, mocking echoes.

There was no other sound. She had

greeted her class with friendly words, but they, her pupils, uttered no response. The lantern still kept up its rhythmic motion overhead, and cast its shifting light over the shadowy faces. It pricked them out with whitish-yellow glow; mere bodiless heads, dissociated from the darker shadows beneath, against which the light beat in vain. Then, as Julia strained her eyes to penetrate the murk, the wave of light passed on.

A tiny needle of fear slid painfully into Julia's consciousness. Why did they not answer her friendly gesture; why did they sit there, row on row, huddled, dim, unmoving? Why did those deep-socketed eyes, fixed on her with unwinking gaze, seem to burn searing holes in her skull?

JULIA shrugged her shoulders angrily. After all, she was there to teach, not to bandy social amenities. Besides, these were inarticulate simple folk, shy of their instructor from the city.

She cleared her throat nervously. It sounded startlingly loud. The little fear in her bosom was growing larger. She must start at once, to banish a queer choking sensation. She must not give way to silly thoughts.

The first words of the lecture she had hastily prepared on the long train ride came forth with a sense of strain. They sounded foreign to herself; they beat hollowly in her ears. They did not seem to be a part of her, to have any meaning. She knew that she must not foozle this job. If she failed. . . .

Determinedly she stilled the rapid beating of her heart, and concentrated all her attention on one pallid face in the front row. She would lecture only to that particular auditor; she would forget the rest. Thereby she would establish a bond of intimacy, and thus be able to talk freely,

naturally, interestingly, as she had always done at Normal School.

If only there were sufficient light, instead of that horrible swinging lantern. The face she peered at was a dark blur. She must see him closer, more plainly, if she were to establish that relationship so necessary to a lecturer. Of course, she could move away from her desk. She could ramble aimlessly across that emptiness between the flat table and the rows of benches, and see, face to face, these mountain pupils of hers.

In God's name, what was the matter with her?

The thought had been a normal, natural one. Why then did her hands, in sudden reflex, grip the edges of the desk with such convulsive tightness that their muscles ached in painful protest? Why did her blood shrink back from her skin to make it a dry sheath? Why did slimy maggots of fear go slithering through her skull?

She knew now, with the awful clarity of those condemned to die, that she would remain rooted to her desk; that nothing, *nothing* could force her to traverse that awful No Man's Land and meet her audience.

Why? Why? The thought pounded insanely in her aching skull, even as the words of her prepared lecture flowed mechanically from her lips. Ah, there it was! The thin flicker of light crawled slowly, inexorably across the floor, swung murkily over the first backed bench, empty of figures, shuddered hastily over the face on which she was so fiercely intent, and went skittering on.

God in Heaven! There was something wrong! There *must* be! That face! It had been that of a girl. A girl with grey, bloodless features and soulless, staring eyes. Blonde hair that was caked in a stiff mold. A glimpse of a dead grey throat speckled with red splotches. A sudden vision of sagging shoulders under the torn stuff of a mud-flecked dress. Then black shadows again, alive with horror.

A great shriek tried to pierce the unending flow of Julia's words. Every pounding vein in her body tried to tear loose, to scream out its shuddering terror. But the meaningless patter bubbled on. Her hands, white with strain, gripped the table more fiercely.

What were these strange people who had come to attend her school? Why was there no slightest sound from them; why did they sit in those queer, distorted positions, without the slightest shift or normal shufflings or casual clearings of throats? Why did those dark blobs that were eyes make her flesh crawl and her scalp become a squeezing horror?

On and on the words poured through her stiffened lips. She did not know what she was saying, but she *must* talk without pause, without ceasing. She *must* fill that dreadful void of silence with the sound of her voice. Let her stumble, let her but hesitate an instant, and those staring, rigid shapes would spring from their rooted seats and swarm over her pallid form with hideous mouthings.

She wanted to shriek out aloud, with all the outpouring of released fears. But she dared not. Cunning crept with sly edgings into her distorted mind. As long as she talked, as long as she let her voice echo around the dim emptiness, she held those Things, aching to spring at her throat, in thrall. For she knew now what they were.

They were the dead!

THEY were the mouldering corpses of the mountain cemeteries, risen from their graves in ghostly wrath against the sacrilege that had descended upon their native hollows. Had not their preachers thundered against the abominations of the doctrines that she dared to teach?

But that girl? That Thing in the second row, with caked, blonde hair and bloody grey throat—what was she doing in this stealthy throng? *She* was Nan Hackett, the first teacher from the Agency, who had been ripped to death as by wolves —when there were no wolves in Death Hollow!

Desperately Julia forced breathless, garbled words from her tightening throat. As long as she spoke. . . . Then her words grew faint, it required more effort to move the fear-stiffened muscles of her mouth and throat. A frozen wind stirred the tender hairs on the nape of her neck. The lantern dimmed, flickered unsteadily, then swung more violently. A thin creaking came to her fear-edged senses.

Behind her, the door through which she had entered—the very door that she had barred with a stout iron latch—was opening.

Dear God! she moaned to herself, don't let me faint! She felt as in a nightmare where bottomless pits yawn before racing feet, yet there can be no turning, no retreat; for greater horrors pursue with fetid breath.

In front of her lurked the gloating corpses, waiting for her to cease her babblings, waiting for her to come within reach of their skeleton hands. Behind her, borne on the icy breath of the mountains, came shuffling feet.

Ah, the window! She fought her trembling body erect, talking desperately all the while. She would hurl herself out of that window, and run—anywhere. Race on fear-driven feet through streams and whispering woods and slimy marshes, back to town, back to civilization, where the vengeful ghosts of the bigoted dead had no power over her.

Carefully she gathered up her **failing**

strength for that last dreadful lunge. The feet were louder now behind her. . . .

Her knees contracted and stiffened. Her eyes froze to the dead-gleaming oblong of window. The pale moonlight beat unsteadily on a peering face. Its nose was flattened to the grimy pane; its eyes were wide upon her with a grim intentness. It was the strange passenger of the train, the man who had watched her from the shelter of the darkling woods!

A shrill scream racketed from her lips and quavered down the long room. No longer could she fight against the encircling doom. She was lost; soon she would be a loathsome mangled Thing like Nan Hackett, or a mindless, shrieking monster like Ralph Pittman. It did not matter any more. . . .

A strange authoritative voice pierced her consciousness: "In the name of Almighty God, woman, cease that senseless squalling."

Julia stopped as if a slashing sword had cut off her breath. She flogged her stiffened limbs into similitude of life. Like an automaton she turned, holding with pressing fingers to the desk. No demon out of Hell, no gloating Thing from the grave, would have invoked the name of the Almighty!

THERE, in the wavering yellow light, stood a tall, bony man. So thin and lank was he that the lantern's flare seemed to flow around him without a perceptible break. His elongated face was gaunt and cadaverous, and a profusion of black, coarse hair hung like a horse's mane down over a sloping forehead. The fires of fanaticism burned in the hollow depths of his deep-socketed eyes; they blazed on the fear-swathed girl with almost hypnotic compulsion. Jet black clothing encased his lankness.

Julia forced a whisper from her parched throat. "Who—who are you?"

The man chuckled morosely. "You ought to know, woman. I am the instrument of the Lord's work in Death Hollow; the thankless keeper of its immortal souls. I am the Reverend Increase Maunders. And you," he thundered, "are the godless woman who preaches that Devil's gospel called *evolution!*"

Julia fell limply into the chair. A wave of faintness loosened the rigidity of her limbs. This then was the executor, the agent appointed under the will of Ingersoll Greenway. He had come as Lemuel Fogg had said he would, to make certain that the terms of the will were being adhered to.

The harshness of his speech slid unheeded over her numbed brain. Only one thought whirled before her in ceaseless circles. He was human, he was flesh and blood—he would protect her from that dreadful audience of the dead, from that peering face in the window.

"Save me!" she panted.

The mountain preacher surveyed her sternly. "How can those be saved," he demanded, "who deny God's handiwork? It is a bitter enough cross for me to fulfill the sneering wishes of that infidel and agnostic, Ingersoll Greenway. But God has given me this task to try my strength, and I obey, unworthy as I am. I have preached to my flock unweariedly, day and night, forbidding them under penalties of eternal hell-fires to attend this atheistic school." He raised a long, black-clothed arm on high. "I have succeeded," he shouted triumphantly. "No one in Death Hollow will ever come to hear your damnable doctrines; you waste your smooth, cozening speeches on the empty benches. Look about you and. . . ."

He stopped in mid-gesture. His bony jaw went agape. The flare of sooty light had gone shuddering over the shadowed row of benches. Face after face, staring, rigid, without motion, etched into startling relief, and faded back again into the enveloping murk.

For one dreadful moment the Reverend Increase Maunders was without speech, his skeleton-like finger extended, a frozen image. Then his face went black with wrath, and the floodgates loosened.

"Ye have mocked me, then," he thundered. "Ye have sworn on the Holy Book that ye would not attend, and now ye slink behind my back. I call down upon ye. . . ."

Julia shrank back from the fanatical preacher. He was mad! The flames that shot from his eyes were not those of a sane man. He was mouthing curses against a congregation of the Dead, against parishioners who had moldered in their graves for God knew how long.

Horror rose like frozen lead in the pit of her stomach. She leaned over the desk. . . .

SHE screamed again. The sound galvanized the moon-drenched figure at the window into action. The grim, tight lips drew back in a snarl. An arm raised and crashed against the pane. Glass shattered. A bloody fist thrust into the room, fumbled for the catch.

Maunders whirled and saw the staring face of the man. Grey, deadly eyes clashed with flaming black. For one instant they locked while Julia shrank moaning against the desk. Then the deep-set eyes of the preacher flared with lightning blasts.

"Hugh Elson!" he breathed. "I should have known." His voice raised to an insane fury. "Blast your rotten soul for this." His hand slid out of sight and came forth belching flame. The concussion blasted hideously against the leering corpses. Glass splintered into a thousand fragments; smoke swirled.

Julia felt herself going. Wildly she tried to hold on to her slipping senses.

Through a fire-shot haze she saw dimly the hand at the window jerk back, the face grin at her and fade suddenly from view; in a deeper daze she heard strangled cursings from the preacher, the thud of his long legs as he dashed through the open door into the white-glimmering clearing; the bang of wood behind him. Then suddenly she was alone, alone with those rows of waiting corpses.

They were coming for her! They had risen from their seats, they were swaying forward, grinning hideously, bony arms outstretched. The flesh fell away from their faces, the clothes rotted off their bodies. They were skeletons, menacing with bony laughter, white jawbones agape, dancing with slow, mincing steps toward the desk.

Then the kaleidoscope of lights in her brain exploded, and blackness overwhelmed her. . . .

CHAPTER FOUR

Flame to the Flesh!

SHE was cold. A bitter breeze slapped against her limbs, prickled them with new sensation. A nightmare weight lifted slowly from her chest. Blood started a sluggish flow in her veins. She opened her eyes, stared wildly about her.

Then memory that brought a new shriek bubbling to her pallid lips. Oh, God, hadn't she been through enough? Must there be more? The Reverend Maunders —where was he? Hugh Elson, the face at the window, the young man of the platform, whom he had shot at with a pistol; what had happened to him? She remembered that name. Lemuel Fogg had told her. He was one of the nephews to whom Greenway's fortune would revert if Death Hollow's school were closed.

Her own scream forced her eyes wide. Silence had followed, unbroken by any sound. She stared down the long room, straight at the shadowy dead Things on the benches. There they sat, in huddled rows, unstirring, blank eyes protruding from grisly faces in silent mockery.

She forced her weary body upright. She must get out of here before she went completely mad. Thank Heaven, it had been delirium that made those seated bodies seem to move toward her. They were dead for all eternity. She took a painful step toward the door, and froze in her tracks.

Something was rustling back there among the corpses. It was coming for her!

She tried to drive her limbs forward, but they seemed suddenly rooted. It was true then—that the dead were coming to life!

Closer and closer came the dread sound of muffled movement. Now it was upon her. Hot breath fanned her neck. With a frenzied scream Julia threw off her strange paralysis and plunged ahead.

But it was too late. Something caught her shoulder in a powerful grip and whirled her around. The white, flowing arms tightened, crushed her until bone and sinew seemed to merge in a gory mess. A gloating chuckle rasped her eardrums. Then something snapped in her mind.

SHE was being carried through the woods. That much her darkened senses told her. The night slithered pallid fingers along her cheek; her body hung in a limp arc over powerful shoulders. Branches whipped across her face; unseen things plucked at her hair.

Then the creature who held her stopped. Voices sprang out of the dark. As in a dream she heard them. One was the voice of the Reverend Increase Maunders. It boomed startlingly close; almost in her ear. The other was strange to her.

Desperately Julia tried to pierce the dully roaring haze that enveloped her, to hear what they were saying. But her head was a throbbing pulse, and her body a thing dissociated from her. She was held, bound in a paralysis of dread. Her muscles could not move; she opened her lips, but no sounds issued. And the voices were an indistinguishable confusion.

Then the voices ceased, and the crash of footsteps took their place. Farther and farther away, snapping dry branches beneath heavy shoes, until they were gone.

Once more Julia knew she was moving. Shoulders heaved beneath her flaccid form; the stinging wind slashed her flesh. How long this nightmare trek took she was never to know. In her half-conscious condition it seemed an eternity.

Then it was suddenly warm. Through the closed lids of her eyes bright sparkles darted. A thin hissing sound came to her. And she crashed sickeningly onto a hard surface.

The shock forced her senses into the groove of life again. She moaned.

She was lying on a wooden bunk in a rough log cabin. The bark of the walls was green with fungous slime, and little puffs of steam curled upward from the damp, untrimmed wood. Signs that the cabin had long been abandoned.

But now red flame glowed over the sizzling walls and danced with gloating shadows over the dark green mould. A furnace blast smote her frozen cheeks.

In the farther corner blazed a charcoal fire in a bed of brick. The blood-red sparks flew upward with insane glee; the leaping tongues of flame reached out from the flaring embers with a greedy hissing. Imbedded in their midst was a long iron rod, shaped at the end into a curious flat disk. It seared the eyeballs with its shimmering white heat. And to Julia there seemed something unutterably malign about that instrument.

Shuddering, she forced her eyes away. They strained upward at a sheeted figure. It loomed over her like a destroying demon. A long white shroud of coarse material enveloped it from head to foot. Two slits bored at her where eyes should be. Like a graven image it stood, soundless, unmoving. Like the corpses that had sat row on row in the school.

Insane thoughts hammered in her brain. She must make that shrouded Thing speak; she must force it to unlock its hidden lips.

The words barely trickled through fear-stiffened lips. "Who are you? What do you want of me?"

He did not answer; he did not move. He loomed over her like a tower of evil; he grew on her blurred vision until he seemed to fill the small confines of the cabin. She shrieked and babbled and flung her body forward.. Her nostrils were full with the stench of rotting flesh, of moldering earth. He would drag her down. . . . Down. . . .

But her limbs refused to move. She was tied hand and foot, helpless in the presence of this faceless horror.

THE shrouded figure flowed away from her. It made no sound as it stooped over the blazing charcoal, lifted the metal rod and stared intently at the white-glowing disk. Then, without a sound, the figure returned it back into the fire, as if it still were not hot enough. Julia closed her eyes in a spasm of dread. Already she felt the approach of that hellish brand; already she felt the tender flesh of her body scorch and sizzle under its burning embrace, stamping her tortured skin.

She tried to focus her crazed mind on what that brand might be. She narrowed her thoughts to that single hairline. What scarlet letter would the sizzling iron blazon on her for all the world to see? She must not think of anything else, or she would follow Ralph Pittman into the gibbering realms of madness. Only by concentration on a single thing, no matter what, could she save her reason. . . .

Curious what queer thoughts cluttered up her mind. Was it a symbol that proclaimed a sin, like Hester's, in *The Sarlet Letter?* Was it a device to prove ownership, as if she were some four-footed beast? Or was it something unutterably hideous, deforming, at the sight of which men would go mad and flee from her as from a monster unfit for earth?

Denial rasped madly from her throat, conjured by the compelling spell of her own imaginings. Fever burned her veins and her mouth became a kiln of lime and ashes. Then she opened heavy lids, afraid of what she would see. She gasped.

The sheeted figure was gone! The brand was blazing whiter and whiter in the embers—leering imps seemed to dance over the writhing iron—but the Thing had vanished. Hope flared momentarily in Julia's fuddled brain. She jerked madly at her bonds, and they cut into her soft, white body with razor edges.

Then she went limp, hopeless, sobbing in low, tearing tones. He was coming back for her, now. She could hear the thud of clumping feet on the ground outside; she heard the door latch lift and a gust of wind howl into the room. Someone came inside.

She dared not look up any more. This time the iron would be hot enough for even the fiendish desires of the sheeted Thing. Soon now the searing flame would be at her shrinking flesh; soon . . .

An exclamation of surprise broke in on the frenzied whirl of her thoughts. She lifted frightened lids. A man was staring at her wide-eyed. She had never seen him before. He was short and stocky, fleshed with good living, and his lips were thick and unnaturally red.

"Good Lord!" he stuttered. "I thought

. . ." He stopped and looked hastily around. His eyes seemed to pop out of his head. He had just seen the branding iron. His mouth gaped and his lower lip dropped as if it were pendulous on a hinge. He seemed to have forgotten all about the helpless girl.

"Please, save me!" Julia cried out frantically, writhing in her bonds. "Quick, before the Thing returns!"

The man swung back to her. He cast sidelong glances at the instrument of torture, licking his lips with stealthy, pointed tongue. It seemed to exercise a fearful fascination over him.

"Who are you?" he demanded. His voice was shrill and effeminate, and he made no move toward the girl.

"My name is Julia Winters and I'm the new school teacher in Death Hollow," she gasped. "What difference does that make? For the love of God, untie me before it is too late."

He disregarded her agonized appeal and sat down on a rickety chair. "So you're teaching evolution to Death Hollow, eh?" he said, surveying her with strange interest from under pasty lids. "That is interesting," he purred.

"Don't you understand?" she cried desperately, the pulses pounding like triphammers in her temples. "We're both lost if the Thing comes back. He'll kill us both."

The man started suddenly. "Why, bless my soul, did you say kill? You don't mean to say . . ."

The sound of steps outside cut him off.

"Too late," she moaned. "Oh God, it's too late."

CHAPTER FIVE

Mark of the Beast

THE man jumped to his feet. His over-red complexion went dirty grey. The chair slammed back with a crash.

The shrouded Thing filled the doorway, silent, ominous.

The man shrieked and cowered away. His pudgy hand flew over his eyes. "Don't you touch me," he screamed. "I—I have nothing to do with this girl. I swear it. came here to meet—"

The sheeted figure laughed hollowly. "You came to meet *me*," he intoned.

The shivering wretch stiffened. "Good Lord!" he cried. "*You!* What fool mummery is this?"

A low chuckle dripped through the sheet. It held a tone of sadistic gloating. "I aim to give value for money received. After tonight, when Death Hollow sees this gal with the brand of Cain on her forehead, there ain't going to be no more teachers coming. There won't be no teaching of evolution in the hills. That's what was wanted, wasn't it?"

The stocky man staggered. He turned his furtive eyes on the girl, swung them back to the hooded figure.

"Y-e-es," he admitted hesitantly. "But, man alive, I didn't expect this. I drove in tonight as we arranged, thinking everything was settled. I find you all dressed up in a nightshirt, and this girl . . . I won't have it!" he cried with a feeble access of energy. "Scare her out of the place, but don't mark her up. That—" he gulped heavily, "—would mean jail."

Julia trembled with new-found eagerness. "Yes, yes," she begged. "Let me go. I'll leave Death Hollow and never return. I swear I won't say anything. Please, please!" Her haunted eyes implored the newcomer.

The man's glance wavered over the slimness of her body, revealed in every contour by the tightness of the thongs. His reddish eyes gleamed lustfully.

"I'll take care of you," he promised with a smirk. "Now listen," he blustered to the shrouded man. "I'll take this girl with me. You make sure no one else takes her place for tomorrow night, and the deal is closed."

The sheeted figure straightened. He advanced threateningly on the shorter man.

"So that's what ye think to do, Philip Elson," he rumbled.

Elson made a quick, fluttering gesture with his hands. He shrank back from the ominous advance. "For God's sake, no names!" he squealed.

THE hooded man kept on coming. He laughed horribly. "Philip Elson, Philip Elson," he repeated. "You think you're smooth as silk. You think you could break the old man's will, an' get all his money without dirtying your hands. Or mebbe you thought you'd leave *me* holding the bag. Well, it ain't gonna work out that way. Folks in Death Hollow don't like sinful teachin's more'n I do, but they like the fortune that old Greenway left, right fine. You didn't think it was goin' to be easy when you made your proposition, did you?"

Philip Elson backed into the corner. "Why, I—I thought—" he gulped.

"You ain't got no right to think," the other thundered. "You told me yourself it was up to me to deliver the goods. Well, I'm delivering 'em, see, and you're in the same boat with me. Do you hear?" His voice rose to a great shriek, his hand clenched under the folds. "I killed the first teacher; I made a raving lunatic out of a second, and this one is goin' to be branded for everyone to see. After that, *nobody* will come here a-teachin', and Death Hollow'll be glad to give back old Greenway's money to ye."

Elson pressed his rounded body against the wall.

"You—you—killed someone," he stammered. "You're crazy; you're a lunatic. I'm through with you," he screamed.

The white-sheeted hand reached out

with lightning speed, caught Elson by the coat collar, and shook him as a terrier shakes a rat.

"So ye think ye'll run out on me, hey? Well, think again. Mebbe you don't know the law—you're an accomplice, an' you're in this with both feet. And mebbe you forget this gal knows your name?"

Elson sagged weakly against the wall as the other let him go. He stared at Julia as if he had never seen her before.

The girl listened with mounting horror to the strange colloquy. Hope alternated with grim despair, as the argument waxed hotter. The figure in the shroud was not a Thing risen from the grave, but a man! That gave her no comfort. He was a killer, a fiendish murderer who slaughtered for money, and because of the innate cruelty of his being. There was no mercy to be expected from him. But the other, Philip Elson, Greenway's nephew, who, in his greed for fortune, had instigated this monster to break the terms of the will—he was weak, yet he shrank from murder. Now, however, the madman's cunning phrases had instilled poison into his mind. It was his own skin that was in danger now.

"Don't listen to that vile Thing," she cried desperately. "I promise you, I swear I won't tell. I'll go far away—"

But Elson was shaking with a new dread. The hangman's rope loomed before his terrified gaze. This girl knew too much!

The monster chuckled gloatingly. "I see, Elson, ye understand. We'll brand her with the sign—an' then—to save your neck, we'll kill her an' throw her body out on the road."

Elson nodded. He was beyond words, beyond any pitying emotion. His own life was at stake.

THE hooded man moved with doomful tread to the fire. He took out the sizzling brand by its long handle and stared at its blazing disk. Then he swung around in a billow of robes, and came slowly toward the bunk on which Julia lay rigid with terror. Elson still crouched in his corner, eyes desperate and hunted.

Julia shrieked in an ecstacy of fear as the inexorable brand approached. Every fiber in her body ached with the anticipation of that dreadful iron. Her head was a bursting globe; her limbs seemed encased in a concrete mold as the hooded figure grew on her tear-drenched vision until he seemed gigantic, filling the universe with his frightful, torturing hate.

She threw herself again and again at the cords that held her in horrible embrace. She shredded her flesh into long red strips and did not even feel the pain.

Closer and closer came the blazing iron. The heat flared in her face, crisped her eyebrows into ashes. She tried to close her eyes, but some terrible power held them open. The white-hot disk flamed and shimmered with unholy glee.

Julia let out one last despairing shriek. She had seen the design! It was a grinning, leering, hideous ape! What distorted brain could have thought of that —to brand her with the Devil's sign for all Death Hollow to read and shudder?

The looming figure bent closer. The iron was stabbing down for her white forehead. She smelt the frizzling hair, the stench of hot iron. She went limp in dreadful anticipation. . . .

CHAPTER SIX

The Curse of Death Hollow

SOMEONE shouted. The next instant the flaming brand flew violently away, went sizzling and scorching across the cabin. The hooded madman staggered and went down with a crash.

Julia opened her eyes in a shiver of dread. Had the brand already etched its path into her forehead? What had happened? She saw the smoking iron bite deep into the rough wood of the floor; she saw the sheeted monster struggle furiously with a grey-coated man.

They rolled over and over, pounding each other with clenched fists. She caught glimpses of a rather good-looking young face, grim now and terrible with anger.

Julia's wracked heart gave a tremendous bound. It was the passenger from the train, the man in the forest, the face at the window. Hugh Elson, the Reverend Maunders had called him, and had shot at to kill. Why? He was Philip Elson's cousin, co-heir to Greenway's money. Had the conspirators fallen out —or was he really . . .

Philip Elson came out of his crouch with a mad shriek. "Hugh!" His eyes bulged in terror. "We'll split the money. Let him up. Don't—"

Hugh rolled like a cat on top of the cursing, gouging figure. His face bled freely from a long, raking slash. His sinewy fingers grappled in the folds of the sheet for an invisible throat.

"You can't bribe me, Philip," he panted.

The powerful figure beneath him heaved and thrust out with both knees. Hugh staggered, rolled off with a groan, and came back scrambling. But the shrouded man was already on his feet, rushing for him with a bull-like roar. They met with a crash in the center of the cabin. Hugh's fist flailed out, smashed with a heavy thud into the monster's muffled face. A mad, thick snarl answered the blow. And two long, snaky arms whipped out, caught the young man around the waist, and strained.

Hugh's face engorged with strangled blood. He tried desperately to free himself from that bone-crushing grip. He smashed his fist again and again into the billowing folds. But the madman only grunted and held on with a grip of death.

There was a sharp, sickening crack. Hugh went limp.

"Oh God!" Julia moaned. It was all over.

Then the monster let out a great cackle of triumph. He relaxed his guard for a fleeting instant, and in that moment Hugh acted. Using every last ounce of his failing strength, biting his lips with the agony of a final tremendous effort, he crashed his balled fist for the point where a chin should be.

There was a dull thud. The shrouded figure grunted, staggered and toppled to the floor. A horrible scream followed; there was the smell of burnt cloth, and a burst of flame enveloped him. He had been thrown directly across the still-blazing brand!

Hugh staggered wearily, held himself barely erect. He groped toward the bunk, swaying from side to side. His face was a drawn, taut mask of pain.

"Look out!" Julia shrieked.

Philip Elson, eyes glaring, thick lips drawn back in fiendish snarl, was crashing downward with a chair. He was too far immersed in this welter of blood and death now to withdraw. If Hugh lived, the hangman's noose dangled for his own fleshy neck.

Hugh put up a feeble hand to ward off the blow. The chair smashed down his guard, sent him writhing to the floor. Philip mouthed animal sounds, raised the chair again for the finishing blow. There was no light of reason in his face. The chair came down with horrible speed.

A film appeared suddenly over Philip's inflamed face. He seemed to stumble oddly. Then he went toppling headlong over the body of the cousin whom he had tried to kill.

JULIA'S skull squeezed with iron bands; she groaned and shook her head.

There, in the doorway, holding a still-smoking pistol, stood the gaunt, thin figure of the Reverend Increase Maunders, executor of the will of Ingersoll Greenway! His great holes of eyes burned in his cadaverous face as he swung his accusing gaze around the shambles of the cabin.

In one stride he was at the side of the flame-enswathed figure. His stamping feet pressed out the hungry filaments of fire. In the next instant he was with the fainting girl, loosening her pain-wracked limbs from their bonds. Then he thrust aside Philip Elson, dead with a bullet in his fear-crazed brain, and heaved at the limp man beneath.

Hugh stirred, opened his eyes, smiled weakly at Julia. Her heart thumped oddly at that smile. In spite of battered, blood-smeared features, it held a certain luminous, thrilling quality for her.

Maunders strode stiff-legged to the Thing that lay, oddly still, in the smoldering corpse cloths. He ripped away with strong fingers.

"I might have thought of him, instead of blaming Hugh Elson," he said. "But the Lord turned his vengeance on the bloody and the sinful."

The singed face that stared up sightlessly at Julia was still enhaloed with white, flowing hair and patriarchal beard. It was the face of Lemuel Fogg, head of the School Board of Death Hollow!

AFTERWARD, when wounds were bandaged, and the dead decently shrouded, came explanations.

Hugh held Julia's hand in a firm, warm grip. "I suspected something was wrong," he said, "when Philip came to me with the idea of trying to break our uncle's will. He had run through his own money, and was pretty desperate for funds. I refused. After all, Greenway had a right to dispose of his fortune as he saw fit. At the time Philip was pretty angry at me. But when I met him the following week, he seemed in high spirits. He had been to Death Hollow, he said, and everything was going along fine.

"I wondered what he meant, and decided to find out for myself. A telegram to the executor of the will, the Reverend Maunders, brought an answer I didn't expect. It spoke bitterly of the horrors that were taking place here."

He grinned down at the girl. "I went out to investigate the business myself, and saw you on the platform, frightened and alone. I trailed you to the school, to see what was up." His grin hardened. "I saw plenty through that window. I was just coming in to help you when Maunders took a pot shot at me. I had to run for it—he had a gun and I had none. By that time I was convinced Philip had bribed him to put on the act."

"And I," the preacher rumbled, "was sure that *you* were to blame. Your telegram—and your face at the window—"

"But what," Julia shuddered, moving a shade closer to Hugh, "were those awful corpses in the school room?"

Hugh smiled grimly. "I went back to find out when both of you disappeared. They were wax dummies, realistically smeared with blood. Fogg had thought first he could drive you mad—the way he did Pittman."

Maunders interrupted. "I was chasing Hugh through the woods, when I ran into Philip. He was coming along this trail, and seemed uneasy-like at meeting me. Made up some excuse about being here."

Then those were the voices she had heard while Fogg was carrying her, Julia thought.

"After he left me," the preacher went on, "I got to thinking. I remembered this old cabin along the trail that was supposed to be deserted, and thought I'd take a look at it."

"It was a good thing you did," Hugh agreed.

"And now," the Reverend Maunders rose and buttoned his clerical coat. "Don't ye both think it's time to put an end to this godless will of your uncle? The wages of sin is death and there has been enough of sin and death in Death Hollow for a good many years to come."

Hugh looked questioningly at the girl. She shuddered. "I don't ever want to teach in that horrible place again," she said hastily.

The young man pressed her fingers. "You won't have to," he whispered.

Somehow the words brought the blood once more to her pallid cheeks. She turned shyly to the preacher, but that gaunt savior of souls was on the threshold, back turned to them, staring out into the night.

THE END

THE DEAD MUST EAT!

By H. M. Appel

What terror lay behind that horribly baited ghoul trap? Was it food for a madman's dead mate? Would Mora Martin be the next grisly feast of the soul-bound dead?

"NOT for a million bucks!" The scrawny driver of the rural taxi shuddered. "Not even if you offered me two dollars, I wouldn't drive you out to no Doyle farm in the dark." With a glance toward the departing

lights of the train, he added prophetically: "You'll wish you'd stayed aboard Number 9 if you go messin' around that spooky place."

Neil Doyle repressed a smile. Evidently his Uncle Rafael, famous as the "Old

Master of Magic" before retiring from the stage, had been playing tricks upon the gullible villagers.

"I'm not afraid of ghosts if my uncle can live with them," he retorted. "It's only a mile, so I'll walk. Shame on you for letting the spooks beat you out of a fare."

"You're one of them Doyles?" The fellow eyed him sullenly. "Well, maybe you think it's a laughin' matter—murderin' girls and choppin' their bodies to bits. But"— he threw the car into gear— "tonight, folks hereabouts ain't thinkin' so much of laughin' as lynchin'."

Neil Doyle stared, astonished, as the man drove away, his lithe, well-tailored figure silhouetted against the yellow glare of station windows. With an exclamation of concern he set off through the ominously deserted village streets at a rapid pace, wondering whether the horrors mentioned were real or just some of his uncle's pranks.

Under the tutelage of Rafael Doyle he had, two years before, entered the theatrical world as a magician and quite competently maintained the prestige of the name he bore. Recently though, in connection with certain peculiarly difficult bits of "business" in a new act, he felt the need of further coaching. Arranging for a break in his booking at Cincinnati, he had come unannounced to this obscure Kentucky village near which the old Doyle estate had long been a refuge for retired generations of the clan.

Beyond the limits of the town his heels clumped hollowly upon the white rock pike as he bored into the moonless darkness. The route he well remembered from summers spent there as a boy. While he walked, disturbing thoughts plagued him. Could the recent death of his Aunt Carlotta have warped the old man's clever brain? Rafael Doyle had idolized his wife, and her passing would have shocked him deeply. Impatiently, Doyle put the idea aside, half-convinced that the "murder" would prove a hoax perpetrated by his uncle as an aid to privacy.

SHORTLY, his impetuous pace brought him to a grove of towering oaks which, by day, nearly hid the ancient Colonial mansion from the gaze of passersby. He approached the stone gateway with an instinctive feeling of dread, recalling the monstrous "front yard" dotted with tombstones which had frightened him as a youngster. The Doyles, no matter where they died, were all brought home for burial.

To his surprise, tight wooden doors had been fitted into the archway. Upon either hand, along the line of the low stone fence, stood a new barrier of woven wire. He found a bell-button, pushed it vigorously. But, though he waited long minutes, he heard no response, although far back amid the trees light gleamed in a window of the house.

Cursing nervously, he tossed his bag over the top of the gate. He managed to scramble up one column where he found the flat crown littered with broken glass to discourage trespassers. Dropping down upon the inner side, he felt his way along the dark, curving driveway, keeping to the grassy edge, suddenly cautious.

Startling him with its unexpectedness as he came into an open space among the dimly-seen headstones, he saw a large granite tomb illuminated with ghostly radiance. Creeping forward on tiptoe, nerves tingling with grisly fear, he repressed the cry of horror that leaped up in his throat.

One side of the mausoleum stood open. Upon a snowy bier within, the waxen face plainly recognizable as that of his Aunt Carlotta, lay a dead body clothed in a white shroud. As he stood transfixed, chills playing up and down his spine, a gaunt black shape was momentarily silhouetted against the luminous square. And then the light flicked out.

Into his mind flashed stories of ghouls who lust for flesh of the dead. With a hoarse cry of protest, he sprang forward. Echoing his shout, the scream of a girl made the night vibrate with terror. Running footsteps thudded upon the dry sod. He gave chase. Near the house he overtook the fugitive, threw himself ahead in a flying tackle, knew before they struck earth that the softly rounded form he clasped was feminine.

The girl's shrieks of fright blended with the angry exclamations of a man. A flashlight speared down at them briefly as they struggled. Then Neil Doyle was half-stunned by a blow on the temple. which his assailant dealt with the torch, and the voice of his Uncle Rafael commanded fiercely:

"Let go of her! Let go—or I'll beat your brains out!"

Catching the rain of blows upon his upraised arm, Doyle cried: "Wait! Stop, Uncle Rafe! This is Neil—"

"For the love of heaven! How came you here?" The flashlight had apparently been broken in the brief fight so the astonished speaker scratched a match, looked at Neil closely. "Why did you run after Mora?"

"Climbed over the gate," Doyle gasped, "when no one answered the bell. Then I came upon that open tomb—saw Aunt Carlotta—" He broke off, fingering his battered head. "There was some one prowling at the grave, and I heard a scream—"

"The tomb is not open. I was shutting off the light. Carlotta lies behind a wall of glass. But come inside. Help that poor girl whom you've frightened so. She is Mora Martin, your cousin."

Doyle lifted the trembling victim of his onslaught. "What were you doing out there?" he asked her curiously. "Why did you scream and run?"

In the light of the doorway, as his uncle entered, he saw the girl's pretty face, tearstained, beneath dark tresses that accentuated the pallor of her fear-whitened cheeks.

"Who wouldn't run?" she retorted, catching her breath jerkily. "When you came roaring at me in the dark—"

RAFAEL DOYLE dropped into a worn leather chair beside a library table. Tall and emaciated, his bloodless skin matched the snowy mustache and imperial, and his aged face seemed drawn with care.

"Sit down," he said. "This calls for explanation, else Neil may believe us mad." His black, piercing eyes sought the face of his nephew pleadingly. "She wanted it that way. I'm only carrying out the wishes of your dead aunt. Carlotta suffered from an awful fear of being buried alive."

Comprehension dawned in Neil Doyle's glance. "I can understand. Because of the trances? But it shocked me immeasurably to find her lying there—to see your dark shape blotting the lighted grave."

"Yes, the trances." His Uncle Rafael nodded sorrowfully. "Who knows but that they hastened her end—that I am to blame. And I loved her so—" Unashamed, he wiped away a tear. "You know she was always my subject in hypnotic acts. And Neil, for months before she died, she kept falling into sleep so deep that I scarcely could tell if she were alive. Not so many years ago, you'll remember, she went under the influence for thirty days, at the New York exhibition of suspended animation. I didn't want to use her then, but she insisted. Always she was my best subject, but I believe that hypnotism affected and dimmed her life force."

"Surely, you don't mean—" Neil Doyle was stirred by a feeling of horror. "Not that she may be alive . . . in that tomb?"

"Would to God she were," Rafael groaned. "But she is dead—she is gone—forever lost to me. And now I keep the deathbed promise. She begged to be buried unembalmed, in a glass tomb supplied with air, under my personal observation for at least sixty days. So that if life should be resumed—" The old man bowed his hoary head, unable to say more.

Mora Martin went to his side, placed her arms around his thin, trembling shoulders.

"Of course you must keep your promise, Uncle," She said soothingly. "I know what an ordeal it is—the hopeless watching. . . . Tonight, I worried about you. I stole out to see if you were all right, and then he shouted—" Her accusing eyes turned toward their visitor.

"If it were only the watching!" Rafael Doyle muttered. "God, if it were only that!"

"What do you mean?" Neil eyed him suspiciously. "What's this talk in the village about a murder out here? That's what set my nerves on edge. The taxi driver was afraid to come near the place. He even suggested that the townspeople have been roused to lynching pitch by some weird happenings."

Rafael jerked to his feet. "Stupid yokels!" he growled. "I've put up a gate to keep them out. They might do anything."

"Murder?" Mora Martin stood with slim fingers pressed to her distorted lips. "Why—what do you mean?"

"I wish you hadn't mentioned it," Rafael Doyle said regretfully. "Mora didn't know. There was no point in frightening her because of a terrible coincidence. Prying villagers were shocked by the manner of Carlotta's burial. They've protested, called me a 'heathen,' though it's none of their business. To make matters worse, a girl was savagely slain two nights ago, and pieces of her dismembered body strewn all about our graveyard. It was the work of a fiend."

"God!" Neil Doyle stared. "No wonder they went up in the air, when you reported that."

The old man's grey face was haggard when he hoarsely answered. "I had no chance to report it. Two boys, out hunting rabbits, discovered the butchered corpse yesterday morning. The superstitious village folk came to a dreadful conclusion so revolting that I dare not tell you what it was."

A splintering crash of boards outside sent all three wheeling toward the dark windows. They heard a babel of shouts and angry cries. The motor of a heavy truck thundered in the drive. White lights flooded the room.

"Come out!" echoed the strident command. "Rafe Doyle, come out! Or we'll come and get you—" Footsteps clattered upon the porch. Excited men hammered at the door.

Rafael exclaimed bitterly; "They've smashed the gates! They've come to repeat their horrible demands. But they shan't have her. I'll defend her with my life!"

FISTS clenched, brow knotted, Neil Doyle flung open the door. A noisy mob surged forward. Forcibly he pushed the foremost back.

"One at a time! Who is spokesman here? Let him come and the rest of you stay out."

His determined tone made them hesitate. A lean, dark-visaged man stepped up aggressively. His thin lips were curled in a sneer.

"Call me the leader. Blame me—whoever you are—for anything that happens if old Rafe refuses to do our bidding."

"Well, suppose you give yourself a name," Neil retorted. "I am Rafael Doyle's nephew. What do you want? Why do you come yelling about the house?"

"Ask him," the fellow grated. "I gave him his orders yesterday—"

"And if you come again—" Rafael hurried to Neil's side, a shotgun in his shaking hands—"I'll kill you, Otto Killian! Get out—all of you!" He pointed the weapon toward a ring of scowling faces beyond the door. "The first who lays a finger on her grave gets a charge of buckshot."

Killian seized the shotgun, wrenched it away. Neil Doyle, in turn, snatched it from the man's hands, drove his fist into the snarling face, covered the crowd as Killian staggered backward.

"You heard what he said—get out! Whatever you've got to say can wait till daylight."

"Murder won't wait!" some one shrilled, hysterically. "Another girl has been missing since dusk. Tomorrow we'll find her flesh among the tombs, unless he does as we say."

Harsh voices jangled. "String him up! Hang the old devil, and the young one, too. He's to blame for what she is doing—"

Harassed, Neil Doyle demanded: "What is it that you want done? That he refuses to do?"

"Burn the body! Destroy it by fire. Then our girls will be safe," Killian cried belligerently.

"You mean—" Neil's lips twisted in amazement. "You want Aunt Carlotta's body burned? Why, this is an outrage. You have no right—"

"Right!" yelped one of the mob. "With one girl slaughtered and another gone God knows where, we got a right to do more than that."

"But why?" cried Neil, bewildered. "What has her body to do with the girls?"

"I'll tell you." Killian faced him doggedly. "Because she is not dead—nor is she alive. *She is a ghoul!* But the poor woman can't help it. There stands the guilty one." He pointed a bony finger at Rafael Doyle. "With his infernal trafficking in black magic he has caught her soul in its flight and held it earthbound. Of course, it must have food. Every one knows that ghouls feed on human flesh."

"What utter rot." Neil Doyle grimaced helplessly. "You're old enough to know better—all of you. Because this old man was famous for illusions exhibited upon the stage, you listen to silly talk about 'black art.' Don't you know that all a magician's tricks are mere sleight-of-hand?"

"I know plenty!" Killian shook his fist at Rafael Doyle, blurting angrily: "I know that he put her soul under an evil spell. I know—"

"Enough of this," his patience exhausted, Neil broke in sharply. "You've broken into our home. Get out—now!—or I'll shoot the legs off every man in that doorway. And if one of you stops inside the grounds I'll let fly. I'm giving you just five seconds—"

"And we're giving you just one more chance," cried Killian. "Burn that body, or we'll come back and do worse."

As the sullen faces backed into the night, Neil Doyle slammed the door and turned to his uncle, while Mora Martin, pale of face and eyes dark with tears, strove to comfort him.

"They'll do it," Rafael groaned. "And she is not the one to blame. Ah, this is horrible—horrible—"

"Stop worrying," said Neil. "They won't come again tonight. Tomorrow, we'll decide what is to be done. . . ."

WITH the aid of Mora Martin, he got the old man off to bed. For hours, then, he loitered about the gloomy graveyard, guarding the tomb of his aunt from desecration. At last, deciding that the temper of the mob had cooled, he sought a couch in the library and slept soundly until dawnlight wakened him.

In the pale morning light he walked out among the spectral headstones that stood like grey ghosts beneath the somber oaks. He approached the glass window of the crypt and stared in at the sunken wasted face. For a moment he made no move. Then, suddenly, a sharp exclamation escaped him when a small, repulsive creature darted beneath the white shroud.

"A rat!" he muttered thickly. His distraught gaze centered upon a metal air pipe leading through the top of the tomb. Apparently that was their way of getting in. But how to get them out? Feverishly he fumbled with the glass window, found that it might be removed by loosening thumbscrews. A moment later, his frantic beating of graveclothes which clad the decaying form drove two grey rodents out of the horror place. With a gasp of relief he replaced the pane, turned his head aside, wiped his clammy brow, nauseated by the awful fetor which arose from the long-dead corpse.

"This can't go on," he gasped. "Burned or buried she must be without delay. If only I can convince him——"

He started violently, lids narrowing as he stared toward a grassy mound where the rats had vanished.

God in heaven! It couldn't be——But jerkily, he stepped forward a pace, retreated at what he saw. Flesh! Part of a body—the arm of a girl. . . .

Controlling an impulse to flee, he approached the gruesome thing, saw blood clotted upon the ragged end which had been brutally severed. The flesh, when he touched it, was firm and not like that within the crypt. And, as he stood there he thought of last night's visitors. They had said that the girl would be found here—ripped to pieces—

Fearfully, his eyes swept the surrounding graves. A moan of terror throbbed in his chest and his spine seemed to freeze. Upon a dozen mounds lay frightful pieces of a torn body. . . .

Neil Doyle glanced toward the house. Soon his uncle, and Mora Martin, would be risen. Far down the pike, creaking wheels marked the slow approach of a farmer's wagon. Suppose one of the militant villagers entered . . . and saw?

Hurriedly he ran toward a nearby outbuilding, searching for something in which he could hide the awful evidence of this second murder before people came to see. He approached the door of a windowless brick shed, seeking a sack, a box, anything in which the remnants of flesh might be gathered. But a heavy padlock halted him until he noted that it had not been securely fastened.

Stepping into the dimlit chamber he started backward, horrified. Upon a bench which ran the length of the room lay the severed head of a girl. The dead eyes were closed, blood hung in clotted strings from the stump of neck, gore splattered the floor and walls. And beside the blank white face was a long carving knife.

Crumpled in a corner he saw a large burlap bag, guessed that it had contained the entire body when the killer carried it here for dismemberment. Snatching up the fabric he ran outside, breath whistling across clenched teeth. Was Rafael Doyle mad with brooding over his dead wife? Suppose that *he* proved to be the "ghoul" whom the villagers feared?

Unnerved, Neil went about his revolting task, thrusting into the sack each bit of flesh that he could find. Then, dragging the heavy thing behind him, he flung it into the shed, snapped the lock tightly. For a moment he leaned against the door weakly waiting for his strength to return. He wiped cold sweat from his brow.

AN ANXIOUS voice brought him around galvanically. Mora Martin, looking fresh and sweet in a white, ruffled apron came down a path from the house.

"Neil!" she exclaimed. "Are you sick? You seem so pale and wan. Did you stay up all night—watching?"

"Yes, yes," he muttered thickly. "I'm just fagged out. Have to get some rest this morning."

He could not meet her eyes. She murmured sympathetically. Then her glance turned to the shed and she voiced a question curiously.

"I wonder what uncle keeps in there? I never knew it to be locked."

"Nothing! Nithing at all!" He saw that his vehemence surprised her and added more casually: "Just a store house, I suppose. Isn't it time for—" Doyle nearly gagged—"for breakfast?"

"Of course. I've got biscuits in the oven. Come on—" She seized his hand. "Why, Neil! You've cut yourself. You're bleeding—"

He pulled away roughly. "Just a scratch. I'll go wash it." Urging her toward the mansion, surreptitiously he rubbed upon his trousers the dark, clotted blood of the dead girl. It seemed to burn his skin like fire.

While he was removing the crimson stains at a kitchen sink, Rafael Doyle came bursting in from the lawn, his pallid face twisted in a terrifying expression. Neither Mora nor Neil had heard him come downstairs and go outside. "Uncle Rafe! What's happened?" the girl exclaimed.

"Killian was right!" he gasped, one hand pressed to his laboring heart. "Oh, I've known it for days—but I dared not tell you. *There is a ghoul!* It is consuming Carlotta's body—"

Neil caught the old man as he reeled and would have fallen. "Steady! I know what you saw. It is horrible—but not supernatural. There were rats in the crypt. I chased them out. Oh, we must bury her properly today, Uncle Rafe. Those awful vermin—"

"No, no!" Rafael pushed him aside violently, voicing angry protests. "You can't fool me with such talk. No rats could get in. The tomb is sealed. There is a ghoul!"

Mention of the air pipe as a way of entry did not convince the old man whose hysteria increased. It needed the combined efforts of Doyle and Mora Martin to get him upstairs and into bed. There he tossed and raved that he would defend, with his life, the body of his loved one against ghouls or villagers. They feared that but little life was left to him.

THROUGHOUT long morning hours Neil Doyle prowled around the house and grounds, ever on the alert for the mob's approach, tormented by the problem of the body in the shed, puzzled as to how he might disclose the truth to proper authorities without fanning the flaming superstitions of tense village folk.

Mora Martin, sensing his distress without comprehending the cause, went about her household tasks quietly, asking no questions, controlling her instinctive fears save on one occasion when Rafael Doyle's wild shouts brought Neil running in from the porch. Then she rushed into his arms, trembled in his quick embrace.

"Oh, I'm so glad you came!" she whispered. "What would I have done alone in the face of such awful trouble?"

Startled by the sudden realization that no girl ever had stirred him as did this lovely cousin, Doyle exclaimed, "You'll never again face trouble alone if I can help it."

After a luncheon that Mora prepared, but which neither touched, Neil considered telephoning to the sheriff at the county seat, but delayed such action. He thought that during the night to come he might find conclusive proof of the killer's identity. If Raphael Doyle was guilty, there would be the dangerous task of conveying him to an asylum beyond reach of the mob's vengeance. That the old man was insane, he no longer greatly doubted.

Toward evening, when shadows lengthened in the grove, Doyle could not restrain the uneasiness that possessed him. He felt a strong impulse to search for gruesome evidence of other killings, but was afraid to leave Mora alone.

"I'm getting nervous, just sitting around," he said. "Used to hunt squirrels about this old place. We could use a mess for dinner. Come with me."

"I'd like to." She eyed him thoughtfully. "No matter why you're going. Uncle Rafael has been quiet this past hour. I suppose he is sleeping."

They wandered through adjacent wooded patches, then extended their range toward a wilder area at the rear of the farm. Topping a brushy knoll, half a mile from house and highway, Neil Doyle paused to study the circling flight of buzzards that soared above some neighboring glade. The black birds of ill omen swooped to disappear amid the treetops. He saw none rise.

"Something dead over there," he muttered. "The carrion of a dead sheep or calf, maybe." He dared not voice his true thoughts.

Moving silently, he led the way down a hillside through the trees. Presently, a crackling of brush made him crouch with the girl at his side. Shielded by a patch of briars, he looked backward, saw a tall form appear upon the crest. "Uncle Raphael!" he whispered to the girl.

While they watched, the man stood gazing at the buzzards, frowning darkly. Then he strode toward the spot over which they circled.

Cautiously they stalked him to an open space mid a thick growth of trees. Raphael was staring upward, and they moved to the left a little way, so that they, too, might see. In the center of the clearing stood a bushy tree around the top of which buzzards were flopping and fighting. Neil could discern a white, dangling object at which they struck and pecked voraciously. Suddenly his eyes distended. Mora's moan of horror told him that she had recognized the thing. It was a half-picked skull, hanging by long hair.

With a shout of anger, Raphael Doyle disturbed the charnal feasting. He darted forward, a gruesome object swinging from one hand. Neil gasped.

"The dead girl's head—from the shed—"

Glancing at Mora's terror-stricken face, he knew that she might be the next scheduled for butchering. Rearing up, thrusting the barrel of his gun through a screen of brush, he cried hoarsely:

"Drop it! Raise your hands, or I'll shoot—"

Raphael Doyle whirled, moved with unexpected speed. A jerk of his arm sent the severed head spinning straight toward their hiding place. Neil ducked instinctively, at the moment of firing. He missed. Echoing the shotgun's blast came the spiteful crack of a pistol—and a bullet furrowed his temple.

THICK darkness shrouded the woods when Doyle's senses returned. His head throbbed with hammer strokes of pain. His hair matted beneath his groping fingers told him that he had lain as one dead for hours. Mora Martin was gone, and so was his gun.

Struggling to his feet he staggered through the trees, hurrying his pace, wild with anxiety for the fate of Mora. Had Uncle Raphael, leaving him for dead, spread her flesh to feed the ghouls in which he believed?

It seemed an endless time before Neil came to the fence which divided the pastures from the grounds about the house. Climbing over, his harassed eyes searched the black expanse for a glimmer of light. He stumbled forward among the scattered headstones. . . .

Then a shrill scream of terror made his heart leap sickeningly. It came from somewhere in rear of the dwelling. He began to run, heard the quavering cry again, was sure that it originated in the shed where he had found the mutilated remains.

Dashing over to the low brick structure, he shook the door. It was locked from within. He shouted hoarsely.

"Let her out! Don't harm her—or I'll kill you with my bare hands!"

"Neil!" Mora Martin shrieked. "Stay away—or he'll butcher you, too. Ah, God —don't! Don't cut me—" Her voice died on a note of stark fear.

Doyle sprang to a woodpile a few feet away, groped in the dark for an ax used there that day. He battered at the door. Swung the ax with all his wild strength.

"Don't touch her!" he howled. "I'll kill you! I'll—"

Splinters flew. Through a jagged opening, Doyle saw a flickering candle. The girl, bound hand and foot, lay stretched upon the bloody bench.

Bursting through the aperture he stumbled across the floor, missed the deadly sweep of a knife aimed at his breast, then collided with the bench and sent the candle toppling. In utter darkness he whirled to face the murderer.

Doyle heard Mora's frenzied moans. Springing forward, he bumped into the unseen, snarling man—felt a slashing blade graze his throat—winced as it sank into his arm. When he locked his wrists about the killer's neck, sharp teeth clamped upon his hand. Blurting an oath he jerked away, drove both fists into a body.

The knife swished past his face again, ripping one cheek painfully. Fearing its deadly sting, he closed with the man, crushing him in a tight embrace that might imprison the steel-fanged arm.

But as they wrestled and swayed, Doyle's foot slipped in a pool of blood. He was on top when they thudded to the floor. The man beneath breathed a gurgling sigh. Doyle was surprised when the sinewy form went limp in his arms. Hot gore spurted in his face.

"Fell on the knife," Doyle gasped. "I believe that settled him—" He was groping through the dark now toward the girl. "It's all right, Mora," he muttered. "I'll have you free in just a—"

WHITE light flashed through the doorway. Yells of an angry mob sent him whirling around. Once again, along the drive came a speeding truck. Men leaped into the glare waving guns.

"There's the young one," someone shouted. "Nail him, quick!"

"Wait!" Doyle ran out toward the approaching mob. "The guilty man is dead. I fought him and he fell on his knife. He was about to butcher Mora."

"A likely yarn," a sneering voice exclaimed. "Show us!"

"It's true!" Mora Martin called from inside the building. "He was going to cut me up and strew my flesh—"

Half-convinced, the crowd stared, edged closer.

"My uncle was mad," Doyle explained. "But he will murder no more girls."

"Oh, no!" Mora's shriek of protest cut the night. "Not Uncle Raphael—"

An angry mutter rose in the throats of the lynchers. The circle began to tighten around Neil Doyle. A man seized his arm.

"What kind of yarn you givin' us?"

Doyle jerked free, darted into the shed, the mob close on his heels. "Then, for God's sake, who was it?" he blurted.

Mora quavered: "Didn't you know? Oh, I thought you understood—"

Men tramped in as Neil knelt beside the body. In the light of a lantern, he saw a familiar face.

"Otto Killian!" Angry villagers stared down at the corpse. "You Doyles murdered him, too! Because he called the turn about your uncle bewitching the woman into a ghoul."

Mora, still writhing in her bonds, tried to explain to the townspeople.

"Killian was the murderer! I saw him! He wounded Neil, then shot Uncle Raphael down in cold blood. When I ran, he caught me and dragged me here—"

A faint voice from outside the shed cut her off. The mob swung toward it, stopped spell-bound.

"That's the truth. He got me through the back. Paralyzed my legs. I've been crawling . . . and crawling. . . ."

A pitiful figure slithered into view. The gaping mob gave way. Raphael Doyle dragged himself to the side of the corpse.

"I suspected him," he gasped, "when I found the first head in this shed. I was trying to get rid of a second one hidden here last night—trying to hide it with the other in a tree—when he got me. Killian was my lifelong enemy. You know how he loved Carlotta, but lost her to me years ago. He swore revenge on both of us if ever we came back here to live. And I guess—" the old man choked, rolled upon

his back, breath rattling—"I guess he made good the threat. . . ."

"Dead!" some one whispered. "That bullet must have busted his spine."

"But why," a gruff voice demanded curiously, "didn't Killian just shoot him right off and be done with it? Murderin' them girls don't make sense—"

"Oh, but he had a horrible plan," cried Mora Martin, as Neil loosened the ropes that bound her. "He told me—bragged about it—"

She stood up, reeling on numbed feet. Neil caught her in his arms. "Tell us," he said gently.

"First he thought to break uncle's heart," Mora exclaimed, "by inducing you people to burn Aunt Carlotta's body. Then, he intended to incite you to a lynching—to let you do the killing for him. He got the idea from an old book that he showed me. I think it's in his pocket—"

Neil Doyle searched the dead man's clothing, rose with a tattered pamphlet in his hand.

"Book of the Dead," he read aloud. "It's Black Magic. Maybe it will tell us something." The volume fell open at a turned-down page. His face whitened. "Listen to this." He read slowly.

" 'The soul of a loved one may be held earthbound by offerings of human flesh. He who would hold nightly converse with the departed must first lure the corpse from its tomb by baiting the surrounding graves with blood and bones of fresh-killed maidens—' "

Staring at the ring of horrified faces, he cried: "Had Killian shown you that, and told you the book belonged to Raphael Doyle, you'd have hung my uncle upon the nearest tree!"

Loathingly, he flung the revolting volume aside. And no one moved to halt him when he helped Mora to the house.

Death's Frozen Brides

By Ray Cummings
(Author of "The House of Doomed Brides," etc.)

*A Novelette of Wilderness
Horror*

There was no escaping, once Jack Hallen began to sense the hidden horrors of that honeymoon hotel— for already the irresistible fingers of a gloating lust were reaching from the shadows to take away the body and soul of his helpless bride!

THE trip was longer and more difficult than Jack Hallen had anticipated. In a single-horse sleigh, with his young bride beside him wrapped in bearskins against the cold, they had left Quebec City in early afternoon. The road, winding northward, had long since left the frozen valley of the St. Lawrence, where bleak grey-blue foothills of the Laurentians banked the snow-piled river. It was no more than a back road now, climbing steadily up into the mountain forests.

The short northern day had plunged into darkness by mid-afternoon. Snow was falling—huge occasional flakes, then a thick white torrent sifting down like a myriad feathers ripped by a Titan from the grey quilt of the sky. What few frozen tracks had been in the road soon were gone. In the gullies the flakes floated gently down; but when, at intervals, the road came into the open of the frozen uplands, the north wind whipped and surged the snow into a turgid white maelstrom, blinding, so that the patient horse leaned into it and Jack and Glora huddled down deeper into the bearskins.

Out of a long silence Jack laughed grimly. "Well, we wanted an adventure —we're getting it." The wind tore at his words and flung them through the naked trees. He turned his head, and in the white blur of gloom he could just distinguish the snow-bloated figure of the girl beside him.

"Not too cold, Glora? Lord, I should

think we'd be nearly there by this time."

"You don't suppose we've missed our way?"

"How could we? No road but this since we left the main valley. He said it was only fourteen miles from the fork. Heavens, what a desolate country . . ."

For an hour the tumbled mountains and forest had been unbroken—no light; no sign of human habitation in all that white wilderness. The road had become so deeply buried by new snow, Jack barely touched the reins, but let the horse pick the easiest path by instinct. And though Jack did not voice it, a vague fear was coming to him. To be lost up here in this blizzard . . .

Abruptly the horse stopped. His head was flung up, his ears pointed.

"What the devil—?" Jack gasped.

Glora gripped him through the furs. "What is it?"

Ahead there was a crashing of frozen twigs—the plunging of a rushing animal. Then silence, with only the howl of the wind through the crags that stood like white headstones here above the road.

Jack laughed. "Just a moose crossing."

THE horse relaxed. Jack flipped the reins and they started forward again. Certainly this Honeymoon Inn must be close at hand now. They had heard of it quite by accident in Quebec City. Married only a week, they had come from New York to Canada for their honeymoon. And yesterday, with other American tourists they had met an Indian guide, a romantic looking fellow in his furs and parka, who had introduced himself to them. Pierre Lemieux, he had called himself. Quebecois; habitant. And smiling at Glora, he had murmured to Jack his suggestion for a real honeymoon adventure—a trip to a little known inn, high in the fastnesses of the Laurentian moun-

tains. None but honeymooners were welcome—and at this winter season, a visit there was an adventure indeed.

Jack and Glora, new to this Canadian winter, were young and adventurous—as the guide had surmised. They had started out. . . .

"Must be nearly six o'clock, Glora. Wish we'd get there—"

He wished already that they had not come. The cold was eating into them. Both were hungry. What fools they were to have embarked upon a thing like this . . !

Then the horse quickened his pace, and in the smother of darkness ahead, they saw the inn. The road here at its end wound circuitously up a rocky defile. The inn was a low two-story building of frame and stone, perched upon a little cliff-top. A wide veranda fronted it, beyond the rail of which was a sheer drop of perhaps a hundred feet to the tumbled crags of the canyon.

Only the building outlines were at first discernible; with the rectangles of windows like little disembodied yellow lights in the murk of the storm. An eyrie perched up there, clinging it seemed, precariously on the edge of the abyss. Then, as the road mounted, they came level with the inn, saw that it was a quadrangular structure, with a small inner courtyard. A few outside lights—quavering candles, for there was no electric current here in the wilds—struggled with the gloom of the storm.

The road turned to the rear of the building where a small level space held a ramshackle stable. They came to the driveway entrance of the Inn, and stopped. The door was closed, with a glow behind its red curtain. The snow was piled thick everywhere here. The wind howled past the overhead gables; but except for that, there was only silence.

No voices; no movement—no attendants to welcome these arriving guests.

Jack helped his bride from the sleigh. They were both stiff and chilled. The tired horse stood drooping, shivering. . . . The heavy wooden door had a huge knocker. Jack pounded it. The sound echoed back into silence. Honeymoon Inn! One might have fancied that there would be a spirit of gayety within—but Jack, standing there with his bride, felt the premonitory chill of something evil. As though, even through these closed portals, the sinister spirit of the place already had laid its eager finger upon these visitors.

And Glora felt it. "Jack, if only we hadn't come," she murmured.

But there could be no withdrawal now. The storm was upon them . . . If one, even for a moment, might lift the silver veil of the future! If then they could have envisaged the terror that was here! This bride of warm and youthful beauty —if she and her young husband could only have realized—

FOOTSTEPS came. The door swung aside. By flickering candlelight, suddenly dimmed as the wind surged in with a gust, Jack and Glora saw a bare hallway. A man had opened the door. He recognized them, and said:

"Ah, it is you. That is good. *En'tre m'sieur. Madame—*

It was Pierre Lemieux, the guide who yesterday had directed them here. Romantic fellow, they had thought him yesterday, in the civilization of Quebec as he had stood enveloped in furs, with the parka framing his face. But he was that no longer. They saw him now as a tall and stalwart Indian—a swarthy halfbreed with high-bridged nose and a wide mouth spread with a smile of welcome. He was dressed in corduroy trousers, a woolen blouse of vivid colors, with the thick braids of his black hair falling to his shoulders. He stood for a moment gazing upon Glora's pale beauty, her ash-blonde hair wet from the melting snow. . . .

"Madame—you are welcome," the Indian said. His lean hands lingered on her shoulders to help her off with her coat.

Jack pushed him away. "Someone must put up our horse. . . ."

"*Oui, m'sieur,* I shall do it. Ah, here is Mrs. Poltz. . . ."

A woman was approaching. The Indian opened the door and was gone. The woman said, "Mr. and Mrs. Hallen. We are glad to haf you."

Her thin, cracked voice seemed to have a mid-European accent—German or Austrian perhaps. She came hurrying with soundless tread down the empty hallway —and Jack suddenly was aware of the abnormal silence here. Were there no other guests? No talking? No laughter of honeymooners?

The woman was small and thin; sunken-cheeked. Her smile displayed uneven broken teeth. Her black dress had a white apron tied around it. Her white hair straggled from under an incongruously youthful maid's cap. She smiled crookedly.

"My dear—I am glad you haf come," she said softly. "Pierre told me of you."

She stood peering at Glora's beauty— Glora, with fur coat off now, revealed so slim and tall, pale and slender as a lily.

Jack said, "We would like to go to our room. And dinner—"

"Yes, young sir—of course. I am the housekeeper. My son—you will meet him —he is master here. . . ."

She gathered up their coats and led them along the hall, past a few public rooms, dim and empty. A log fire burned in one of them, cheerless, with a row of empty seats before it. To Jack it was suddenly as though this place were peopled only by what had been; as though here were invisible guests talking with muted voices. . . .

On the creaking wooden stairs, Jack paused.

"Are we your only visitors?" he asked curiously.

The woman turned her head and bared her yellowed teeth. Like a female dog, with a grin that could have been a snarl.

"Yes—just now—this bad weather. We hope to haf others yet tonight—one more party if the storm does not turn them back. . . . You will be comfortable here in this room—"

The bedroom seemed cozy enough—a bed piled with heavy covers; a rug on the floor; a single draped window. Jack peered with cupped hands through its frosted pane. It faced front, with the snow-piled veranda roof directly outside it, and the dark abyss of the canyon beyond the frozen gutter.

They prepared for dinner and in a few moments were downstairs again. The woman and the Indian were not around. The small front living room with its log fire, held only the disconsolate row of empty seats.

Then a guttural voice broke the silence. "Mr. and Mrs. Hallen? I am Dr. Poltz."

They turned, startled. The man had, of course, followed them in from the hall. But they had not been aware of it. He stood materialized close beside them —stood smiling at Glora, while she and Jack, transfixed, stricken, stared at the strange man who was master of this strange and sinister hostelry. He was, in height, no taller than Glora. A man of forty possibly, with a massive head set low between high thick shoulders almost as though without a neck. His chest bulged like a barrel; his thick arms hung gorilla-like almost to his knees.

Yet of his aspect, his face was most ar-resting. Like a gargoyle—a face of amazing ugliness. Protruding pointed chin; huge nose upturned like a snout, and little dark pig eyes gleaming from deep sockets under heavy black brows. A shock of short black hair bristled above the retreating forehead. It was a travesty of human features—grotesque, so that the fellow's semi-formal evening clothes seemed utterly incongruous.

A human gargoyle. A thing astounding to see here in flesh and blood when it should have been carved and set upon the cornice of some edifice. He stood, with thick knobby hand fingering a black eye-glass ribbon which dangled down the white bosom of his dress shirt—stood peering at Glora's pale slender beauty. And somehow there seemed in his aspect something expectant, as though he anticipated the shock of his ugliness upon this woman.

Jack found his voice. "Oh—Dr. Poltz? You are proprietor here?"

And Glora, staring with a terrified fascination, murmured, "How do you do?"

"Yes—proprietor," he answered shortly. He stood and gazed at this bride's blond, slim beauty; and as though his parted lips were dry, the red tip of his tongue came licking out.

"Why, my dear, you are beautiful." His guttural voice mouthed it, as though the words were for himself alone. "Beautiful —Pierre told me—but I had no idea—" He broke off. His gaze swung to Jack, and he added, "My mother has the dinner ready. This informality—we haf no other guests just now. I will dine with you, if I may? Informal—"

He led them down the dim and silent hallway. The stalwart Jack bent over Glora as he walked gripping her arm.

"By God—we'll get out of here tomorrow," he murmured to her. "Can't tonight—this storm—"

He tried to tell himself that the nameless fear gripping at him was idiotic. . . .

THE empty board tables and chairs of the bleak dining hall seemed still to hold the shades of guests who had been here, but now were gone. Honeymoon Inn! Jack shuddered. A disconsolateness was here. More than that—something aggressively sinister haunted the place.

"—and is it not so, Mr. Hallen?"

Jack became aware that Dr. Poltz was addressing him. They sat among the empty tables, and the old woman served them.

"Oh yes, of course," Jack said.

Dr. Poltz sat hunched in his chair, massive like a ape trained to sit at table and mimic human ways.

"This storm, when it comes out of the north and west this way—a full sweep from the lower tip of James Bay—it could last a week—"

His eyes seemed never to leave Glora. She could not meet his gaze now, but sat reddened, eating her food, and with an occasional sidewise glance at her husband.

"I suppose that road is all but impassable—?" Jack said rather stiffly.

"Tomorrow it will be wholly so. But that iss goot. Snowbound! An experience for you honeymooners. Snowbound at Honeymoon Inn."

Snowbound! It brought no excitement of romance to Jack—only a vague thrill of apprehension. . . And Poltz added, with his gargoyle gaze still upon Glora. "A honeymoon couple, snowbound, can make their own pleasures. Iss it not so, my dear?"

There was an amazing lewdness in his look—and something else, something of irrationality? Was it that?

Jack pushed back his chair with a rasp. "You'll excuse us—my wife is very tired. And cold—we'll go upstairs—"

"Cold? A bride who iss cold. That must be remedied—"

The Indian stood in the kitchen door. "M'sieur Poltz—the other party is arriving."

It was a welcome diversion. Poltz and the Indian hurried away. Glora and Jack hastily finished their meal. In the hall outside they heard the voices; and when they left the dining room they encountered these other arriving guests as Poltz was ushering them in. Poltz introduced them. Robert Fitzgerald, a stalwart dark-haired man of forty. Thomas Fitzgerald, his younger brother. He shook Jack's hand. A thin, sandy-haired fellow who looked ill.

"Glad to meet you." He smiled. "This is my wife."

Rita Fitzgerald was a small dark-haired girl, beautiful in a fashion characteristically Latin.

"She iss beautiful, Mr. Hallen," Dr. Poltz said. "Would you not say so? And so different from your wife. A lily, and a rose—Both so fragrant—"

Jack and Glora stood together. The party proceeded into the dining room. Rita Fitzgerald contrived to be last. And as she went past, they saw terror in her dark eyes. She hesitated just an instant. And she murmured swiftly.

"I need help! Oh please—I must talk with you—tonight or tomorrow—"

She hurried on to join the others in the dining room. . . .

CHAPTER TWO

The Terror of Night

"YOU'RE going to try and talk to her tonight, Jack?" Glora asked as they stood before the glowing fire in the main room.

"Yes, of course. That was an appeal, Glora—that girl looked as though she was frightened out of her wits!"

"Something more than just the sinister atmosphere of this place? Something more than just her repulsion at sight of the gargoyle Dr. Poltz?"

"I'm sure it's more than that," Jack said softly. "Something that she knows, maybe—and we don't know. . . ."

Frightening words! They seemed so pregnant with a myriad sinister possibilities. . . In the drab and silent living room, chill now with the languishing unattended log fire, Jack and Glora sat waiting. The Fitzgeralds were in the dining room; but when they came out, they went directly upstairs. The storm seemed to have increased in fury. The wind roared outside; and the beat of the frozen snow against the windows was a steady tattoo.

Dr. Poltz entered. "Ah, you are here." He stood before them, swaying on his thick, crooked legs with one arm dangling almost to his knee, and the other hand toying with his eye-glass ribbon. He gazed steadily at Glora.

"But you must go to bed now. Of an evening we haf no downstairs pleasure, here at Honeymoon Inn."

They felt strange relief when they reached the seclusion of their bedroom. There was no lock on the door. And Jack was unarmed. Crazy thoughts! He tried to tell himself so. This Poltz was a man obsessed by lewd thoughts of honeymooners—but he was nothing more than that. . .

"Guess I'll shove the bureau up to it, Glora."

"Yes. That man—he terrifies me. . . ."

"It's his ugliness. Lord, did you ever see such a face? But he's harmless enough."

They shoved the bureau against the door nevertheless. And presently, with the lamp extinguished, they were in bed.

"Oh Jack, I'm so frightened."

"Nonsense, darling." He held his bride close in his arms, warm and fragrant under the heavy covers in the chilling room.

"Don't shudder like that, Glora. It's just got your goat—this damn place. We'll get out of here—soon as the storm is over."

In the silence the pounding of the blizzard was more apparent than ever. . . Horrible silence here in the room. Jack lay tense, holding his shuddering bride. But this fear was all imagination, of course, and he tried to convince himself that this was all very romantic, being snowbound up here in the Canadian wilderness upon the fringe of the Arctic.

"You asleep, Glora?"

"No."

"I was thinking—that Rita Fitzgerald —wonder what she's frightened about?"

"Something weird, Jack—something— oh, if only we knew! She said that she needed help. . . ."

Jack tried to laugh. "She's got a husband. But he looked sick, didn't he?"

"Yes."

"And a brother-in-law. He looked husky enough. You go to sleep, darling."

"I can't. I—all I can see when I shut my eyes is that gargoyle face—"

THEN presently it seemed that she was asleep. Jack lay listening to the beat of the storm. Would they be able to get back to Quebec tomorrow? He thought of that narrow mountain road winding up through the canyons. A blizzard like this might make it impassable for days. . . Impassable, certainly, until the wind and snow let up.

Then he realized that he had been asleep. He had been dreaming of something here in the darkness, peering at him and Glora as they lay in the bed. . . Or was it still a dream? He was conscious of Glora's fragrant warmth against him. Half awake, he lay puzzled, with the sweat of fear bathing him. He had memory of having heard a noise—A dim scraping sound. No! That was not a memory!

Something here in the darkness, was scraping. For a moment Jack struggled to wake himself up, but the chains of sleep still held him. The bureau which he and Glora had pushed against the door —it was moving inward now. Someone— something—was coming into the room. The scraping stopped; but there was some other dim sound. A breathing? Something with panting breath was here in the solid darkness?

Jack was at last fully awake, but for another instant he did not move. Something here, peering? . . . Then he heard a dim and distant wailing cry. Something outside the room, mumbling with a gibbering, gruesome voice.

And Jack felt Glora lunge and stiffen in his arms. Her voice split the silence with a scream of terror.

He held her close. "Glora—Glora—"

The panting breath here at the bedside receded. Muffled, receding footsteps? A padding as something fled? There was only silence here now; but out in the hall that eerie distant mumbling continued. . . .

Glora lay trembling. "Oh Jack—I thought something touched me—"

He murmured, "Nonsense." He held her close, with her face against his chest, caressing her.

"But something did touch me—a hand on my face—it woke me up." And now she heard the distant cry. It had risen louder; and it clarified into a man's voice. A groan—then a shout. . . .

"Let me out! My God, let me out, I tell you!"

"Good Lord, listen to it!" Jack gasped. He leaped out of bed, fumbled for matches, lighted the lamp. The shouting, pleading man's voice merged into a commotion. Footsteps sounded in the upper hall. Poltz' voice came to them.

"What iss this? What iss the trouble here?"

OTHER voices joined in the turmoil. Jack saw now that the bureau had been moved, and that the bedroom door was a-jar. But Glora seemed not to notice, and he did not mention it. Clad in dressing gowns and slippers, they rushed into the hall. Poltz, his mother and the Indian, were there. From a nearby bedroom Robert Fitzgerald appeared; and from another came Rita and her sickly husband. All the occupants of the Inn, aroused now by this shouting voice. It came from a bedroom near the end of the small hall.

Poltz said, "He iss worse tonight." He strode down the hall, with the Indian beside him and the others following. Jack noticed that the guests were all in dressing gowns over their night clothes; but that Poltz, the Indian and the woman were fully clad, as though they expected some midnight alarm.

Poltz unbarred the bedroom door, flung it open. "You fool! Haf you no sense to make a shouting like this?"

With the others, Jack crowded forward. In the bedroom a man of perhaps fifty sat in pajamas on the side of the rumpled bed. He wailed:

"You let me out! I don't want any more of your medicine. I want my wife. . . . You've taken my wife!"

Poltz swung back. "I am sorry—all this noise." His gargoyle face was twisted into a fantastic travesty of smile; his voice was deprecating, apologetic. "I haf this man like a prisoner here since three days. I try to quiet him, with drugs—"

Out of the silence, Jack asked. "Why?"

The man was evidently half drugged. "I want my wife," he wailed. "They took my wife—"

"He iss crazy," Poltz said. "We did not know it at first. He came alone—a week ago."

"I did not! I came with my young wife —we just got married—I want the police —I want—"

"Delusions," Poltz said. "When this storm is past I shall send him to the Quebec authorities. He came here alone. For two days he said he was waiting for his wife to come. And she did not—and then suddenly he began raving that she was taken from him. I shall gif him another sedative—"

"I don't want it! I'll fight—"

"Pierre—my medicene case—the hypodermic iss in my office."

The housekeeper tried to herd them away. "If you will all please go to bed—" She urged.

Robert Fitzgerald laughed. "A nut. Crazy as a bedbug. Come on, Tom— you'll take cold. You and Rita get to bed."

Rita stood pale, her black hair tumbling to make a frame for her lovely face. Her husband, shivering in the cold of the hallway, drew her away. Again she flung Jack and Glora a glance—mutely terrified.

Jack hesitated. Then as Poltz slammed the door shut upon himself and the protesting prisoner, Jack murmured, "Come on, Glora. Nothing we can do—not now, anyway."

They went back to their bedroom. Glora was shivering with fright and cold as he put her back into bed.

"Jack, don't blow out the light—please."

"All right. I won't."

He closed the door, climbed in beside Glora, held her close to warm her.

"I want—want to get out of this place," she murmured.

"Good Lord, so do I. If we can—tomorrow—"

Out in the hall they heard Tom Fitzgerald's voice. "Well, if he's crazy, why don't they 'phone and have the authorities come up and get him?"

And Robert Fitzgerald answered, "Nobody could get up that road in a storm like this. Besides, there's no telephone here. We're marooned—you two get to bed."

THE voices died away. The commotion had quieted. With the lamplight illumining the little bedroom, Jack and Glora lay silent. He thought she was asleep; but she suddenly murmured, "I didn't know that man—that Poltz, was a doctor."

"That's a fact—hadn't thought of it— he called himself Dr. Poltz. You go to sleep, Glora."

"I don't—don't believe that man he's got locked up is insane. A guest—like us—"

A guest—like them—with his wife, his bride, stolen from him in this damnable Honeymoon Inn?

"You go to sleep," Jack insisted. "Don't be frightened, dear—I'm going to stay awake."

Not for all the world could he imagine himself closing his eyes again this night. . . . At last, Glora was asleep. And Jack lay quiet, staring at the lamplight. It seemed to hypnotize him and once he felt that he was dozing off. He started upright in bed, decided that it would be safer to get up.

For a time he sat shivering in a chair by the lamp; sat gazing at Glora's pale beautiful face on the pillow with the glinting tresses of her ash-blonde hair about her. She was sleeping peacefully.

The house was wholly quiet now. Upon impulse, Jack moved to the door, noiselessly opened it and stood listening. All quiet. Then he heard very faint, distant voices from downstairs. The narrow stairway head was near at hand. He went there, cautiously, still keeping an eye on his bedroom door. Then he peered down the steep narrow staircase. The lower hall was dimly lighted, and he could see a segment of it plainly. The voices had stopped; but now there was the sound of heavy, labored footsteps.

Then Poltz' voice: "Easy, Pierre! It iss heavy."

"*Mon Dieu*, yes!"

Into Jack's line of vision came Poltz and the Indian, slowly moving along the lower hall. They were carrying a heavy oblong six-foot box. A coffin? They struggled with its weight, passed the bottom of the staircase, and vanished. In a moment their staggering tread and low voices had died into silence.

Jack went back to his bedroom. Glora was still sleeping peacefully. He sat at the window, shivering through the long night hours until the daylight came—turgid grey dawn at last coming to illumine the grey blur of the canyon and the crags, all blurred by the white smothering murk of the driving storm. . . .

CHAPTER THREE

The Living Death

THE road was gone. The canyon was piled with a white mound. All day the North wind howled and the shroud of falling flakes eddied and swirled and piled against the casements of the inn. To have tried descending that road in such a storm would have been suicide. . . .

Jack, after breakfast, contemplated the possibility of a trip out of here. It was manifestly impossible. Sight of the trackless blur where the road had been, made that obvious.

No one ventured beyond the thresholds of the building that day, save the Indian crossing the narrow backyard to the barn

to care for the horses. And by daylight, Jack's fears took on a different aspect from the darkness and silence of the night. He talked of it with Glora, as they sat watching the fury of the storm through the windows of the front sitting room where the disconsolate fire again was languishing. This was indeed an adventure; unpleasant, but nothing much more than that.

In the flat morning daylight Glora found that she could laugh. "This wouldn't be so bad, Jack if we were all alone here. It's that man Poltz—"

But he was not in evidence this morning. The prisoner in the bedroom upstairs was quiet. Jack asked the Indian about him; and Pierre said readily that the fellow seemed better, and was resigned to being taken to Quebec as soon as the storm was passed.

But there was that coffin—if it were a coffin—which Jack had seen being carried along the lower hall. He did not mention it to Glora. Nor the fact that the bureau of their bedroom had been shoved aside in the night. . . And there was this other honeymoon party—this Rita Fitzgerald with her dark Spanish beauty; her sick husband, and her stalwart, older brother-in-law. They did not appear until nearly noon. The girl again flashed Jack and Glora an appealing significant glance; but it was not until late afternoon that she found the opportunity of talking with them alone.

Jack had bundled Glora in her fur coat and taken her for a promenade on the front veranda. The wind had died; the storm was slackening—a few soft huge flakes sifted gently down. Darkness already had come—but it seemed likely that by tomorrow, with clear daylight, the outward trip might be made.

They paced the snow-piled boards of the veranda, beating a track through the drifts. Beside them was the low rail with its hundred-foot drop down to the crags of the little canyon. The darkness made it all a blur.

With the coming of another night, Jack felt his fears returning. And Glora began shuddering, clinging to him now as they paced back and forth. Then abruptly the front door of the inn opened. By the slanting yellow light from the front windows they saw the small fur-clad figure of Rita Fitzgerald. She came and joined them, pacing with them. . . .

"I had to see you. I—I'm so frightened." She clutched at Glora as she spoke. "There's no one out here but you? You don't think anyone can hear us?"

"No," Jack said. "What is it?"

Why would she come to them—strangers—when she had a husband and a brother-in-law? She seemed to answer his thoughts.

"It's Tom—my husband—I'm so afraid for him."

"He's ill," Jack said. "He looks sick."

"He is. He had a nervous breakdown. I married him without waiting for him to get well. I—we've waited so long—"

But this was nothing frightening. He seems better today," Jack said. "You mustn't be worried."

"You need help," Glora added practically. "What did you mean by that, dear? How can we—"

The girl sucked in her breath. "That's it—help. But I don't know—I'm just terrified, that's all. This place here—and Tom's brother, Robert—"

They were standing in the snowy darkness. "Keep walking," Jack said sharply. "It looks better. Tell us—"

With a low, swift burst she went on. "I'm afraid of my brother-in-law. Oh maybe I'm all wrong. Maybe it's just imagination."

"Afraid of what?" Jack demanded.

"Afraid for Tom. He—Robert—he wanted to marry me, but I chose Tom. And Robert is rich—he persuaded us to come up here—for Tom's health. We'd never heard of this place. And now I think—I don't know what I think!"

Tremendous relief seemed to sweep Jack. This was just an hysterical, fanciful girl. All the nameless fears of things unspeakable which had been crowding him, now were dropping away. This was nothing to do with that sinister menace which had seemed hanging here in the Inn.

"You're not very coherent," he said, smiling. "You're afraid for Tom? What does that mean?"

"I think," she said; and her voice held stark terror, "I think now that Robert brought us up here to—do away with Tom!"

Glora gave a little cry. Jack gasped, "Murder him?"

"Yes. Oh, I know it's fantastic. I guess I'm all wrong. You couldn't help me anyway."

Jack laughed grimly. "I can suggest that you and Tom get out of here. We're going tomorrow—if we possibly can."

"Yes, of course. I want to do that. I'm afraid of this place."

"So are we," Glora said fervently.

"Have you told Tom about this?" Jack asked.

"No. How could I? It would shock him—make him nervous—and angry. He'd tell me I'm crazy. He likes Robert—he's always thought Robert was wonderful."

"You think," Jack said, "that your brother-in-law has offered this fellow Poltz money to kill your husband?"

The words drove her into a panic. "Yes, that's what I think! But I don't know anything definite. I've always been afraid of Robert since that day last year when I told him I didn't love him—the look on his face—but you can't help me.

"You can't very well accuse him of planning a murder."

"Not very well," Jack said. "In fact, I don't see what—" He checked himself; then added hastily, "Someone coming! We'll talk more later. Anyway, you and Tom bar your door tonight. I'm not going to sleep—I'll do what I can to—"

"Oh, here you are, Rita." It was Robert Fitzgerald. He joined them. "Looks as though the storm was about over, doesn't it? Romantic place, this. Don't you like it, Mrs. Hallen?"

THEY had no opportunity of talking to Rita Fitzgerald again. The supper and the short evening were soon passed. . .

To Jack and Glora their little lamplit bedroom was at once a haven and a place of seige. As they entered it now they closed its door and stood by the lamp gazing at each other with the feeling of embattled fugitives making a last desperate stand here.

Yet by what were they menaced? Jack could name nothing tangible; and the very nameless quality made him feel a greater apprehension.

"I don't want to get undressed," Glora said.

He shrugged. There was no use admitting how he really felt, and thus intensify her own fears. "All right, dear," he said.

"I just want to sit up—to get through this night." She flung herself abruptly into his arms. "Oh Jack, I really am horribly frightened."

They sat by the table and he tried to comfort her. She made him shove the bureau again against the door; and this time they also moved the bed, bracing it against the bureau. He had planned not to do anything like this tonight. The bedroom of Tom and Rita Fitzgerald was only a few doors away. If any alarm came he wanted to be free to dash quickly

out to them. But he barricaded the door unprotestingly when Glora insisted.

The house was deadly quiet by ten o'clock—more quiet than last night for the storm outside had lulled. Occasionally they talked in whispers. Were Rita Fitzgerald's fears truly founded? Was this a place where one might bring a victim, and, for a price, have him murdered? That supposedly demented prisoner—if he was not demented . . . Had someone paid these villains to murder his wife?

Was this a house of murder? But if that, why had Jack and Glora been sought out to come here? Surely no one desired the murder of either of them.

He put her to bed with all her clothes on, and covered her up. She was extremely drowsy and he felt sleepy himself. Unnaturally so. The thought shocked him. Was something in their food or drink making them unable to keep awake now? He sat by the lamp, fighting the drowsiness.

His head nodded on his hand; he teetered in his chair and recovered himself with a start. An hour! Was it only eleven o'clock now? It seemed several hours at least that he had been sitting here, thinking vague drifting thoughts, and listening to the silence. This interminable night! This silence, not empty, but seeming pregnant with a myriad things of horror. . . .

Good God! He had been asleep! He found himself slumped in the chair, stiff and cold with his head on his arms, resting upon the table. Had Glora also slept? He fumbled for his watch. Three o'clock! Well, that was a blessing—the night was well advanced; soon it would be dawn.

He rose, stretching himself. The lamplight gleamed on the room; on the bed—

He froze. He stood frozen, as though all his blood were ice, and his brain numbed beyond any capability of thinking. The covers of the bed were thrown back. Glora was gone! . . .

PERHAPS it was only a moment he stood there. Then action came to him. He swung around, shoved the bed and the bureau away from the door. How they still could have been close against the door and Glora gone, never occurred to him. He dashed into the silent dim hallway. He saw, at its end, a door standing wide. The bedroom of the demented prisoner. Jack rushed to it. On the bed lay the man. Sleeping? Jack touched him. The face was cold. Dead? He bent down, listened at the mouth. No breathing. . . .

Dead. Murdered!

The room had a lighted lamp. Jack saw no wound on the body. No blood, certainly. And suddenly he was aware of a strange smell here in the room. Very vague—hardly more than the air. . . .

Glora was gone, and he was lingering here! He fled back. He saw that the bedroom door of Tom and Rita Fitzgerald was a jar. He pushed it open. The strange air inside rushed at him. Almost perfumed air. Or was it poisoned? On the bed lay Tom Fitzgerald. Dead. Not wounded. Just dead. And his young bride gone. . . .

Jack's whirling brain was suddenly struck by the realization that this queer air was affecting him. His cheeks burned. An exhilaration was upon him. An intoxication. He felt suddenly extraordinarily strong. A wild sense of lightness— of physical power. They had stolen Glora? Why damn them—he'd catch them now and wring their necks! His heart was racing with the thought of it. He dashed back to the hall. All silent. Was everybody dead in this accursed place?

Again he was in his bedroom. The sight of the rumpled empty bed sobered him. Or was it that now again he was breathing normal air?

And what was this? Something he had not noticed before; or was it something that had just occured now? A little three-foot segment of the board room-wall was slid aside. He stooped and peered into the darkness of the hole. And then he saw a narrow, descending stairway. This was where Glora had been taken. This, of course, was how the prowling fiend had entered. . . .

The weird intoxication was gone from Jack now. He was alert; cautious. He squeezed into the dark little passage. Carefully he descended the stairs. One flight down to the ground level—then another flight—down underground.

It was solid darkness now. Heavy dank air was imprisoned here in this little-used passage. He felt his way along a small descending tunnel.

He stood listening to the silence; the only sound was his own pounding heart. Then he started forward again; came to a blank wall. A dead-end passage. But his fumbling hands struck a knob. He pushed, wrenched; tried to turn it. A door yielded with a slow onward swing. He saw a glow of light; heard the distant murmur of a mumbling voice.

And as he moved forward, something stabbed his arm. A tiny thrust through his sleeve like the stab of a long pin. He swung to whirl upon some antagonist but there was no one here—only a small panel which slid rapidly closed in the wall beside his arm. Some mechanical device which had stabbed him. . . God, already in this instant he felt queer! Ice in his veins! His muscles stiffening. . . .

With leaden feet, and a fearful effort of his will, he staggered forward. The drug in his veins was gripping his muscles. . . He came to the top of another stairway where he saw lights and a subterranean room below. . . . Like a statue he stood paralyzed. Numb. Rigid. As though turned to stone, he was standing with wide planted feet and a hand and arm outstretched to rest on a stone ledge at his waist level. A peering statue, insensible to feeling. A catalepsy. He knew that he was no longer more than barely breathing; his heart was stilled to the faintest of fluttering. But still he could hear, and see—and think. And move his eyeballs and his eyelids just a little. . . .

A living death. . . .

He stood gazing at the strange scene in the room beneath him. . . .

CHAPTER FOUR

Brides of the Fiend

IT WAS a low-vaulted subterranean chamber of stone, clearly lighted by a row of lamps upon a table.

Glora! Jack saw her, fully dressed as she had been in the bed upstairs. With wrists and ankles lashed now by rope, she huddled upon a broad low couch of black bearskins. Around the lower part of her face, and in her mouth, was a white rag for a gag. Her terrified eyes above it roved the room. Her body twisted and jerked at her bonds; her pale hair, gleaming in the lamplight.

And there were two others here. Jack's numbed gaze swung across the room to where, upon a stone pedestal, the figure of a young woman lay poised, her head supported by one hand and elbow under her. A life-size, carved image? In aspect it could have been that. A nude figure carved in pink-white marble. But with a rush of horror Jack realized that it was a young woman—like himself stricken into catalepsy. . . . The vanished bride of the prisoner in the bedroom upstairs— the man who now lay dead up there?

And upon another low stone dais lay Rita Fitzgerald; stiffened, stricken. . . . The figure of Poltz moved around the dais. He was removing the garments. Carefully lifting the stiffened figure, as one might move a fragile thing of art—unveiling it—laying the clothing aside. . . .

It was a silent, weird scene, save for Poltz. There were his muffled, mumbling gloating words; his footsteps; the sound of his panting breathing. And Jack saw the gleam of his little animal eyes. The dementia which before was submerged, was rampant now. . . .

Suddenly Jack was aware that Poltz had glanced up and had seen him. Surprise swept the gargoyle face. Then pleasure. He slid the last silken garment from Rita's stiffened form, and came up the stone stairway.

"So?" he gloated, "I thought my medicine would make you sleep. My device in the corridor caught you?"

His red tongue licked his wide slit of mouth. His hands lifted Jack; carried him down the stairs. It was a gruesome sensation. There was only the vaguest feeling in Jack's arms where Poltz' powerful hands gripped him. And Jack was aware that his rigid body held its pose as he was carried, so that now Poltz set him upright with his feet planted wide, and one arm jutting out.

"There! Your feet will hold you—"

He steadied Jack, and then drew away, regarding him.

"You look—just mildly, a little startled. Amusing? My drugged needle caught you almost before you could show fear? That iss gut—"

BEYOND the madman's hideous, grinning face, Jack saw Glora twisting on the couch, the terror in her eyes intensified by sight of him.

"Your brain iss working?" Poltz said

to him. "You can understand me? If you haf clear thoughts, close your eyes."

With an effort, Jack drew down his eyelids; raised them again to the grinning gargoyle face.

"That iss correct. Now I will explain how you can help me. This bride of yours has not the look of love. A woman with passion on her face is very beautiful. She iss afraid of me. But you can bring to her face that look of love—"

He swung suddenly around. A lower door here in the room burst open. The housekeeper and the Indian rushed in; they stopped, stood gazing at the scene—. the Indian with surprised annoyance, the old woman with apprehension.

And Poltz swung to them. "How dare you intrude. I am busy—go away."

The old woman gasped, "Artur! You should not do this tonight. We haf other things, important—"

She stood wringing her hands, the helpless dupe of this madman son. And she wailed: Dead people here—upstairs the two men Pierre has killed. We kill so many, it cannot last. We will be caught—"

The Indian shoved her away. "The oxygen killed them upstairs. Bodies without a trace of violence. Poltz, *Mon Dieu,* we have no time tonight for this madness of yours with women. Fitzgerald is ready to arrange the money payment. He wants the body of the man—and he wants the living woman—"

Poltz screamed, "You go away, I tell you!" Then the stalwart Indian clutched at him; shook him.

"Have your senses, man. The money I am after—"

"You take the money—let me alone!"

The swift interchange made Jack aware of many things. A murder house indeed, was this Honeymoon Inn. Rita's fears had been only too well founded. Her husband lay dead upstairs; her dastardly brother-in-law was somewhere here,

waiting to arrange to take Tom's body —and to take Rita—back with him to Quebec. . . .

Death by oxygen! It was a huge cylinder of compressed oxygen which, the previous night, Jack had seen Poltz and Pierre carrying along the lower hallway. The queer air in the bedrooms upstairs— that was an abnormal oxygen content. The exhilaration—the intoxication Jack had felt—that was his breathing of too much oxygen. It was a weird murder weapon. The unknown prisoner and Tom Fitzgerald—both had breathed pure oxygen as they slept—over-stimulating the heart —killing them, and leaving no trace! Within a few hours it would all be evaporated from the blood, so that an autopsy would show nothing. . . .

Poltz was screaming, "Get out of here —I haf my brides—"

Then abruptly Robert Fitzgerald burst into the room. He stood amazed. He gasped, "Why, my God—what—?"

And Poltz had jerked away from the Indian. With a wild scream, more animal than human, he leaped upon his new intruder. In his hand a knife-blade flashed. Fitzgerald fell with the steel in his chest.

"Artur! Artur—"

The frenzied Poltz swung upon the old woman.

"Artur! Artur—wait—" Her thin voice rose into a wail as the knife plunged into her heart—wailed and gurgled and died as she fell clutching at Poltz' ankles. But he leaped back, and the blood upon the knife and his hand inflamed him further.

The unarmed Indian made a leap to escape, but with incredible agility the madman caught him and thrust the dripping blade into his back. . . .

THE writhing half-breed at last lay motionless, weltering in a crimson pool. The panting fiend cast away the knife; came back, wiping his bloody hands on his jacket. On the bearskin couch Glora still lay bound, with only her twisting limbs, her pallid face and widened eyes to mark her terror. And on the two stone dais the beautiful nude figures lay transfixed, while in the center of the room, Jack stood as before. The charnel combat had raged around him, but miraculously he had not been toppled.

Then Poltz again stood before him. "We can haf our pleasure now."

He lifted Jack; gripped him at the waist, carried him as one would carry a stiffened child; and set him again on his feet before one of the platforms.

"You see? This was once the bride of that fellow in the bedroom upstairs. I caught her—like this—one night. My drugged needle struck her—as you yourself are stricken. Imprisoned the love upon her face—you see how she loved that old husband of hers?"

The girl was bobbed-haired; her flaring curly tresses gave her an elfin look. And upon her waxen face was the same elfin quality. A half-smile. A teasing, impish look in her eyes. . . . And suddenly Jack realized that she was dead. The strange unknown drug of the madman had flung her into catalepsy. But that was days ago. . . . Slowly she had died; still rigid; her rounded young body outwardly unchanged, save for a waxen look that had crept into the pink smoothness of her flesh. But there was that glazed vacancy to her eyes. . . .

Poltz was saying, "That iss interesting —that look of her. But it iss not what I want in my bride. Now this one—she iss very different. . . . I will lift you."

He set Jack before the stricken Rita. She lay reclining upon one hip, her shoulders raised by an elbow crooked under her. The mass of her black hair fell to shroud her bosom and framed her sol-

emn, beautiful face. Quite evidently she had been lying propped up in bed regarding her ill and sleeping husband as the fiend crept upon her. And there was a look of almost maternal anxiousness imprisoned on her face.

Jack searched her eyes. Yes, she was still alive. The lids fluttered; and in the deep dark pools he thought he could see the horrible terror that was striking at her now—surging within her, yet she could not show it. . . . In his own eyes, Jack knew, there must be a look like that.

"You see?" Poltz said. "The body is amazingly beautiful. But here is a woman thinking only of a sick man—I haf no use to haf a woman gaze at me like this. But Glora will be different." His heavy guttural voice was vibrant with his maniacal passion.

He lifted Jack again; set him before the bearskin couch where Glora's terrified eyes stared up at him.

"My dear—we haf a plan," Poltz said softly to her. "I do not want you so frightened. Wait—I take off that gag so you can talk with us. If you scream now there is no matter. Only us and the dead are here."

He untied the rag and tossed it away.

Then Glora gasped, "Jack! Oh—he has killed you!"

"No," Poltz said. "He iss not dead, my dear. Not yet! Maybe nefer—if you do what I tell you. Will you?"

It wrung Jack to hear her swift, unhesitating answer. "Oh, yes—yes, I will! Only please don't kill him! What—what do you want me to do?"

He stooped; untied her ankles and hands. "My dear—you are so beautiful. So pale and slender—smooth and white like a lily—" She shrank away. And at once he sprang erect, and whirled on Jack.

"You see? All my life it iss like this!

But no longer! I want her to look at me as a bride should look—love on her face, for me! I am a man. Artur Poltz. A man like any other man." His voice rose again into wildness as the mania swept him. "I want to catch that look. Imprison it—so that nefer can it change. I want to sit and stare at it. Look of love from a woman—for me. I want to see it. I want to sit and see it for hours and hours—all alone to be with it and gloat over it—all mine—mine—"

He stood panting. He gasped at the shuddering Glora, "If you want me not to kill him, then you help me to see that look. I will show you how to get it!"

The frozen, poised Jack could only stand and stare. The madman had leaped to Glora, stripping her clothes from her. She screamed once. She struggled only a little. Within Jack it seemed as though the torrent of his impotent rage and terror must burst its unnatural bondage—burst and rend him. With all his force of will he strove to move, to release himself; but there were only his quivering eyelids, his eyeballs sluggishly rolling, and tears of baffled anger oozing. . . .

Then Poltz stood aside, gazing, and Jack himself was gazing—at the pink-white beauty of Glora huddling, shuddering upon the black bearskin of the couch. . . .

CHAPTER FIVE

Mates for a Madman

"STILL you look frightened," Poltz said petulantly. "You want your husband not to die?"

"Yes—yes, of course! Oh, please—"

"Then stop looking so frightened. I haf no idea to hurt you. I only want to capture that look. Not fright. Not a woman who is an imp to tease an old man. Not a woman to be worried be-cause her husband iss sick. You wait—I get my hypodermics."

He turned aside; came quickly back with two hypodermics in his hand. Jack eyed them. Why two? And Glora gasped, "What are those?"

He grimaced; but it was meant to be a reassuring smile. The madman was apparently so gentle now, a human fiend whose diabolical purpose made it necessary for him to keep his victim from being terrified. But Jack knew that only death was in store for him and Glora. Death—like the slow death which had come to that smiling, impish girl frozen on the dais across the room.

"Nothing to fear, my dear," Poltz was saying. "An injection of this—" He gestured. "With this I can capture the beauty of you—hold it— And with this—" He indicated the other hypodermic. "This is release, for you and for your husband."

Release—for her husband. The urge of it made Glora strive anew to master her terror and revulsion.

She sat up. "What must I do?"

He stood regarding her with his burning, maniacal gaze. His red tongue licked at his lips. "Stand up, my dear. You lof your husband. Put your arms around his neck. Look into his face—caress him. I want to see the look of your lof. Careful that you do not knock him ofer—"

It seemed to Jack that he could almost feel the pressure of her encircling arms. Her face was against his; and into his ear she suddenly murmured,

"Oh, Jack—can't you move at all?"

There was no way he could answer her, save the fluttering of his eyelids. He saw, rather than felt, the caress of her arms; her cheek against his, with the gloating eager madman moving around them, hypodermic poised. . . .

There was amazing courage in this young bride! For Glora turned to the doctor and said, "This is not right. You must release him a little, so that he can sit with me on the couch. Standing like this—"

"Why, of course!" Poltz cried. "I haf not thought of that."

It sent an inward thrill through the numbed and rigid Jack. If only now they could trick this fiend—

Poltz raised the hypodermic to Jack's outstretched arm. "She iss right. Just a little—" Jack saw the needle go into his wrist, but he could not feel it. . . . Ah, now he felt something—a vague sense of warmth coursing within him. Glora stood aside; her nudity forgotten, she stood tensely watching. And she murmured, "A little more. He must drop that arm. He must bend his knees to sit down with me. I cannot caress a man of stone."

"Can you drop your arm?" Poltz demanded.

Jack could feel the weight of his extended arm now. The strength of his muscle was voluntarily holding it up. He made no move save to swing his eyes and blink. Strength was coming to him. . . .

"A little more," Glora urged.

Jack could feel the needle-prick.

"Enough," said Poltz. "It iss hard for me to gauge it—efery person has a different reaction—" He seized Jack's outstretched arm; tested its rigidity; Jack resisted a little as Poltz drew the arm forcibly down.

"That iss gut. Now—"

Jack's knees bent. He sat, rigid, bolt upright. But every moment he could feel the blessed strength coming to him.

Poltz bent over him, gave the girl her orders. "Now my dear, you sit by him. I want to see your face as you caress him—lily bride—so pale and beautiful—but you haf the fire within—"

She sat beside Jack on the couch, and flung her hair over his shoulder, and slid a hand caressingly around his neck. And her lips murmured against his ear:

"Can't you move yet?"

"Yes! I'm—almost all right! Keep it up—just a minute longer."

She murmured, louder so that Poltz might hear: "And I love you— Oh, I love you—"

Jack eyed the madman. Poltz was ready to thrust his other needle into Glora. He came closer, panting, peering, his hideous gargoyle face eager with this promise of satisfaction.

"Gut! This iss better! You are so beautiful. You lof him. Or iss it me you lof? A bride like a lily, with love on her face—"

HE LUNGED with the needle. But Jack suddenly lurched. He felt Glora roll away; and with a blow of his fist Jack knocked the hypodermic clattering to the floor. The effort flung him off the couch. He still was somewhat rigid.

Poltz screamed like a frightened animal. He stood a second; then turned and ran with Jack leaping after him. Like chains dropping away, his paralysis left him. He saw the distant Poltz stooping at a little low table which held a lamp. The action seemed like the last desperate move of this demented fiend, who always had been sane enough to know that some time retribution would strike him. So he had prepared for it, his end, here with the bodies of his victims around him.

But he seized the little lamp now, and raised it. The oncoming Jack checked himself, poised ready to dodge the missile. Then Poltz let out a wild eerie cry and flung the lamp—not at Jack, but to the stone floor in the room corner. The lamp burst with a splattering of flame. The fire caught a train of gunpowder which

Poltz had placed there. The powder flashed with its blue-white glare—a giant fuse rushing to ignite hidden explosives!

Vaguely Jack was aware of having leaped back to Glora. There was a muffled detonation near at hand; a chaos of surging, tearing rock; the clatter and crash of falling walls. . . .

THEN: "Glora—"

"Oh, Jack—darling—"

He held her, trying to protect her. The splintered segment of a rafter hit his shoulder; pinned him, with Glora under it. But it seemed to protect them. Then darkness, save for the flickering lurid light of burning lamp-oil, and choking, blinding fumes, settled over them.

But still they were alive. The clattering cataract of sound presently was stilled.

"Glora—are you—are you all right?"

"Yes. Yes, Jack—"

"I'll try and dig us out. Something pinning us—"

Jack heaved at the rafter. He was battered and bruised. But he had his normal strength back again.

He stood in the wreckage with the shuddering, choking Glora in his arms. Except for them, none but the dead were here in the littered room. The old woman, the Indian, the dastard Fitzgerald. . .

"Got to—get out of here, Glora. Choking—let's—try this way—"

The impish unknown bride by some miracle still lay unscathed on her dais; the broken head of Rita Fitzgerald showed beneath a pile of rock.

"This way, Glora. We'll have to climb —I'll hold you—"

A great chunk of jagged boulder pinned Poltz' body to the floor. Flames of burning oil licked at the mangled face of the broken gargoyle. . . .

Out of the charnel house Jack and Glora fought their way. They found the passage and closed the stone doors behind them upon the dying flames.

Back into their second-floor bedroom, he wrapped her shivering body in blankets. The dawn had almost come. So they sat by the window, he with his arms around her—watching for the daylight. It came at last, illumining the blue-white, frosty mountains. A day of brilliant Northern sunshine.

THE END

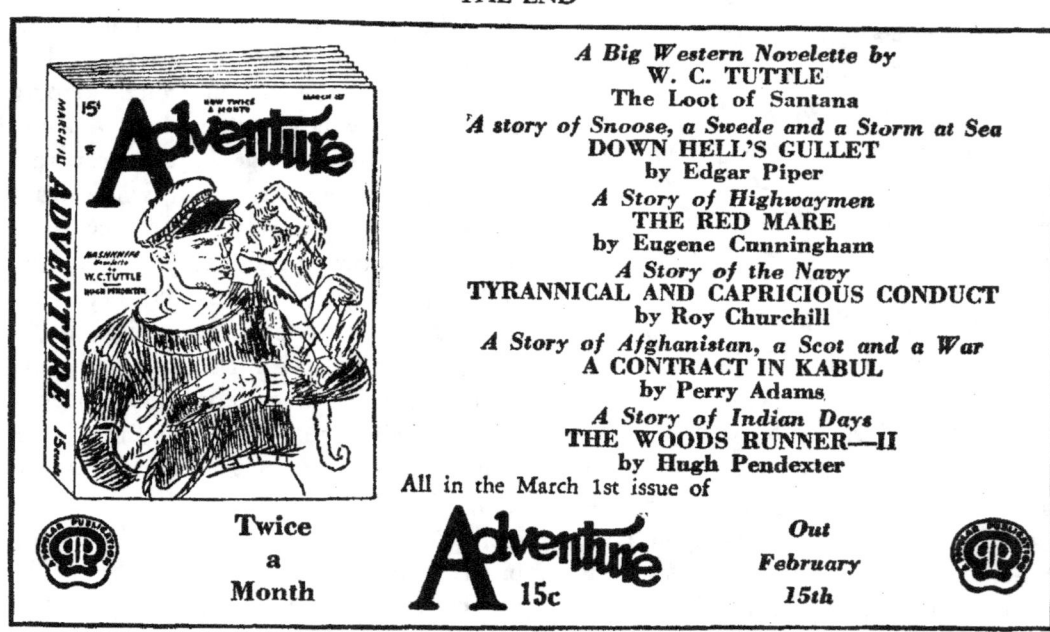

HOUSE OF HATE

By G. T. Fleming-Roberts

(Author of "Blood on Black Knoll," etc.)

The wolves howled their gnawing hunger outside, while strange silent death stalked the shadowed corridors of that rambling terror house. Too late did Rose Trent find that she was hopelessly trapped between the fangs of the starving wolf pack —and the evil lust of a miser's horribly eccentric household.

WINTER had invaded the prairie, stripping it of color and beauty. Nothing remained but the stern husks of summer that held no prediction of the spring to follow. And the bitterly cold wind from the northwest flattened dead brown grass in passing and left it quivering, fearful of the coming snow that the formless grey clouds foretold.

Nor did the icy wind spare the girl anymore than it spared the simple, dead things of nature. It whipped her grey woolen skirt about her legs; it pierced the fur of her short jacket; it needled burning beauty in the soft flesh of her cheeks.

Yet Rose Trent thought there was something kindly about the wind she determinedly faced; it seemed so intent on pushing her back towards the comfortable fireside from whence she had come. Ahead of her in that grey, sinister, prison-like house that was the only sign of human habitation for miles around, lived Gregory Planchard—hard-bitten, tight-fisted, dyspeptic old Gregory Planchard, who kept living, it was said, because hell would not have him. She was going to ask Gregory Planchard for money—but it was not to be pride-cutting begging; it was to be a demand. The Trents never begged. They had been a fighting crew, the Trents, and every ounce of Rose's petite little body was hard with the old Trent fight. There was about her face the so-serious attitude of a little girl playing grown-up—an expression that gave the lie to the frivolous wave of her long-bobbed, brown hair.

And Rose was resolved to take money from Gregory Planchard! The situation was not without a touch of absurd humor, she knew, as she compared her task of getting money from old Planchard to pulling the teeth of a rabid mastiff!

When she struck the beaten path, rough and frozen to stone hardness, she turned to glance back over her shoulder and saw a lank and angular figure following at some distance behind her. A more timid woman might have been frightened, for Rose was utterly alone and darkness was impending. But she stood there quietly watching him. And as he came on she saw that there was some-thing moody and sullen in the gait of the man, or boy—for he appeared to be about nineteen. A great, unkept shock of black hair lowered the boy's forehead and shadowed deep sockets where dark eyes dwelt. His nose was thin, cold-pinched—and there seemed to be something of the hang-dog about his thick, drooping lips. His khaki-colored trousers were splotched with blood obviously from two dead rabbits which hung at his belt. He carried no gun but idly swung a fork-handled sling shot in his right hand.

Rose felt nearly naked beneath the youth's bold stare when he caught up to her. She tugged the collar of her jacket more closely about her throat.

"Hello," she said, and there was a timid quiver in her voice that was altogether inexplicable.

His reply was gruff, his deep voice quite unlike what she would have expected from so young a person.

"Been hunting?" she asked. Silly question! But somehow she feared the silence—silence and the lonely prairie and this coarse-featured, strong, early-old boy.

He nodded. "Whar to?" he asked. "Thar?" He jerked his flat-topped head in the direction of the stern Planchard house.

"Yes, I'm going to see Mr. Planchard. You live there, don't you? I mean, you're Hunk, the—the—" What could she call the nameless waif who slaved for Gregory Planchard?

"Yump. I'm Hunk, the hired hand, only you can't exactly call it 'hired' when you work for the old man."

ROSE turned and continued down the path. She scarcely knew what to say to the strange youth. She could feel his bold, stripping eyes upon her. She stopped suddenly, stepped out of the path and said to the boy: "You walk ahead. We're nearly there now."

He shrugged, passed her, the dangling, dead rabbits making an ugly thudding noise as they bumped against his legs.

Hunk lead her around to the back of the house, opened a door that was solidly framed in the cement block wall, and walked ahead of her into the kitchen. She passed the threshold, looking back through the narrow aperture, loath to trade the grey gloom of the dying day for the dusky shadows within the house. Rose was seized with a sudden desire to cry out, to stop the door that slowly, inevitably swung back into place. She fought back her desire and met the sullen stare of Hunk.

"Well, where will I find Mr. Planchard, if you please?" she asked sharply.

"In his room," Hunk grumbled.

Rose turned towards the door that lead from the kitchen. She stopped as she heard a startling, cold, metallic click and glanced in fright over her shoulder. Hunk was locking the door, muttering to himself like, "Tonight, the wolves—" And the rest of his words were lost in a shudder that caused his lean shoulders to crawl and his voice to whisper unsteadily.

"What are you doing?" demanded Rose angrily.

Hunk fixed her with his beetling stare. He walked silently past her, picked up an oil lamp, and said: "Come."

Rose hurried her steps to follow the youth up a short flight of groaning stairs. Not since babyhood had Rose Trent been particularly conscious of shadows that peopled dusky hallways. But shadows were upon her now, held at bay only by the low-turned wick of the lamp. It seemed that the slightest breath of air would engulf her in smothering, terrible dark.

Hunk stopped in front of a forbidding, brass-bound door. He put down the lamp on a taboret. From behind the door came a man's voice, a mere whisper that sounded like dead leaves scuffed along the gutter by the wind. His words were unintelligible.

"The old man's thar now, talkin' to that son of his," said Hunk. "You can paddle your own canoe when he gets through. I don't want to be around when he meets Brian Trent's daughter. He won't be in no milk-and-honey mind after talkin' with Jules. I gotta go." Hunk started back the way he had come, but at the fringe of the yellow lamp light, he paused. Half in the shadow, his dull features took on an almost threatening aspect. "If you were a wise gal, you'd get back there whar you come from!"

And Hunk was gone, a grey shadow moving among deeper shadows.

For nearly a minute, Rose Trent waited. Then from Gregory Planchard's room again came the whisper of voices. The old man's voice mounted, trembling with fury. His whisper broke and fell back into crackling huskiness. But the intensity of his rage caused him to speak distinctly. "Go to jail and be damned to ye! But if ye touch the red-eyes, I'll kill ye with my own hands. I told ye the last time was the last. I'm a man of my word! Get out!"

The door flung open and a man stood for a moment on the threshold, looking back into the room. His small piggish eyes gleamed venomously from fleshy sacks of eyelids. His thin hand clenched on the door knob as though he wished it were a knife. "A fine father!" he whispered bitterly. "Damn you!"

A crackling chuckle came from old Planchard's room. "That's a lovin' son for ye! Well, we're both damned then. Good night, sir!"

Jules Planchard turned and saw Rose. His pasty face flushed suddenly. His scowl melted slowly and a thick-lipped grin replaced it. "Eavesdropping, miss? Then if either my father or I are found dead with a knife in the back, you'll know the killer. If *one* of us dies . . ." He broke into an ugly laugh that was brought to an end by a sound from outside the house.

A howl that started in a low register and mounted to a yelp that chilled, sounded from out on the prairie. Jules Planchard's face became again the color of raw dough. "God!" he whispered. "What was that?"

"Wolves, my dear son," came in the voice of Gregory Planchard from within the room. "Hungry wolves. The cold forces 'em here, looking for food. Go join the pack and howl outside my door. You'll not get in, nor do ye get a crumb from my table! Get out!"

Again Jules Planchard smiled at Rose. The girl was undecided as to the meaning of his ugly leer. He couldn't help the shape of his mouth, she supposed; and maybe there wasn't anything presuming in that smile. It might have been only a nervous twitch of the lips that were set to mask the real fear that she was sure lurked in the heart of Jules Planchard. Was it fear of his father, the iron-willed Gregory; or the unnamable fear that chills the heart at the howl of a prairie wolf?

ROSE TRENT stepped to the open door and stood there, the toe of one small shoe hesitatingly poised back of the heel of its mate.

Shadows, wolves, Jules Planchard, everything except old Gregory and his strange surroundings melted from her mind. The room was a veritable curio shop. Here and there lamp light found the glint of red and gold lacquer beneath the dust that filmed the cabinets and other furniture that she was certain was of Oriental workmanship. Old Gregory himself was the most repulsive human being she had ever seen. His head was turtle-like—oval, entirely hairless, and covered with skin that was like wrinkled, russet leather. His nose was a thin beak that drooped down nearly to his mouth. She could not determine the color of his eyes for they were merely dark slits between squinted, wrinkled eyelids, and if he had any eyebrows or eyelashes at all, they were so nearly the color of his skin as to be invisible.

Mounted on a T-perch back of old Gregory's chair was an ominous black shadow of a bird. It was Gregory's pet crow, Rose knew, and she remembered the rumor that the bird could talk better than most parrots. It regarded her intently through beady black eyes.

Rose knew she was staring rudely. She moistened dry lips and began to speak. "I'm Rose Trent. I would like to talk to you."

Old Gregory neither moved or spoke but stared back at her with fixed eyes that she could scarcely meet.

"I—I want the fifty thousand dollars you swindled from my father. He's sick with worry. I—you—" she faltered. Then hating herself for her timidity, she stepped to Gregory's chair, seized the old man by the shoulder, and shook him. "Can't you talk? Can't you even be civil?" The old man's head wobbled back and forth as if it were on a spring. His eyelids opened slowly.

Rose sprang back. A little cry escaped her. Her white teeth gnawed at the heel of her hand. Dear God! *He was dead.* Gregory Planchard was dead! He had been killed by a small knife whose hilt protruded from the folds of his smoking jacket.

But seconds ago, Gregory Planchard had spoken to his son. Was it possible that Jules . . .

The black crow walked restlessly back and forth on its perch. There was something accusative in the beady stare of his eyes as they rested upon her. Suddenly, Rose realized her position. Why, she might have killed Gregory Planchard, herself! No one else had entered that room since Jules had left. She had motive enough, some prosecutor could readily prove. But so had Jules!

Her eyes were on the old man's pet crow. The bird suddenly spread its black wings and screamed: "Peck out her eyes!" It launched itself straight at Rose Trent. Her hands came up, masking her face. She felt the breath of air as the bird flew close to her cheek; smelled the odor of carrion as it passed through the door. Then she followed it with her eyes. Could the bird talk sense, certainly it would be able to tell who had killed Gregory Planchard. It had seen everything!

She clenched her small hands until fingernails bit into her palms. She snatched one fearful look at the body and fled from the room into the hall where shadows lurked. A dark figure loomed ahead of her. She drew up, gasping. Big hands closed over her arms, gripped her flesh until it hurt. Hot, liquor-tainted breath fanned her cheek as she stared in terror into the bloated face of Jules Planchard. He was smiling now, only there was no mistaking the lasciviousness of his leer.

"The old man frighten you, Miss Trent?" His voice had the honeyed qualities that must be mistrusted. "He's a bit gruff, I know."

"Gruff?" she panted, struggling against his grasp. "He's—he's—" She bit her lip. How easily she could be framed for killing the old man!

"You and I, Miss Trent," Jules whispered, "might fix up a little deal. I mean, I need the money damned bad. From what I heard, you need some too. And somewhere in this house, the old man has the Stones of St. Stephen, the red-eyes,

he calls them. They're worth fifty grand. If you'd help me—"

"No—no!" she replied hurriedly. "Let me go! You—you're hurting me!"

His grip on her arms tightened. His low chuckle was actually insinuating. "It might be well to be on my side, little lady. There's a blizzard outside. The doors are locked—against the wolves—"

Jules Planchard ducked his head. Terror gleamed for a moment in his eyes. Again Rose felt the air about her beaten by black wings as the crow dropped like a small cloud. Its talons tangled in Jules' hair. Its wings flapped furiously. Jules cursed, released the girl, and fought off the bird. Then the crow was gone with an eerie flapping of wings, a thin line of blood, like a dark scar against Jules' pasty cheek, crawled from his forehead to his chin.

Impulsively, Rose raised her hand and pointed accusingly. "It knows you killed him! You threatened him! You—"

Jules Planchard threw himself upon her. His hulk of a body smothered her. His arms tightened about her with a pressure that was back-breaking. She tried to scream; and the hard toes of her shoes kicked at his ankles. He uttered a coarse, drunken laugh, then smothered her screams with a smear of a kiss.

Suddenly, he recoiled. The soul of passion fled from his eyes; his embracing arms relaxed. She pulled one arm free and pounded his back with her clenched fist. The hold of his fingers tightened desperately, pinching her flesh painfully. His lips peeled back from grinding teeth. Rose felt his great body begin to sag. Then her pounding hand met something and clung to it as Jules fell backwards to the floor. And Rose Trent, wide-eyed with horror, muscles quivering with terror-chill, stared at the thing in her hand —a knife, its long keen blade from point to hilt drenched in gore!

SHE gazed fixedly at the horror on the floor—Jules Planchard squirming in a welter of blood. Then her eyes darted down the hall. Anything might be lurking in those shadows beyond the lamp light. The sound of footsteps—footsteps coming ever closer. Up the stairs? From the back of the hall? How could she tell? There was no place of retreat save the room where Gregory Planchard lay dead with a knife in his heart; and outside the house, the wail of wind was broken by sharp, snarling yelps—wolves lashed to fury by hunger and cold.

There was a spurt of flame directly ahead of her. Rose fell back against the wall. An uncontrollable scream wrenched from her throat. Then her cry subsided into a sob of relief.

The light had come from a cigarette lighter held in the hand of a young man who looked more rational than anyone else she had met in the Planchard house. The flame from his lighter found nothing evil in his regular, clean-cut features. But his eyes were staring at her in a horror fixation.

"Don't stare so," Rose faltered. "I'm human!" She laughed headily.

"B-but, lady," he stuttered, "this—" he waved his hand towards the corpse of Jules Planchard, "—and you—that frog sticker in your hand—"

Rose's eyes darted to her right hand. Her fingers were still tightly clenched over the hilt of the dagger that she had pulled from Jules Planchard's back. She gasped. Her fingers sprang apart. The knife thudded point foremost into the floor where it stood upright, quivering. Impulsively she fled straight towards the bewildered young man with the lighter, flung herself upon him, clutched the lapels of his coat, and hung there, sobbing out her story. God! If he would only believe!

"He—Jules tried to kiss me. I fought—"

The man's head jerked. "I know Jules Planchard! You had to defend yourself. But, Lord! Did you have to kill him?"

She pushed away from him and glared wrathfully. "Then you don't believe! You think I killed him!"

The young man wagged his head bewilderedly. "You haven't denied it yet." His mouth made a little grimace. "I came out here to buy an antique for my aunt and I run into this. Oh, it's plenty bad!"

"Like a man!" Rose snapped. "Thinking of self!"

He uttered a dry little laugh. "Well, after all, lady—"

"Don't keep calling me 'lady'!"

He stared at her a moment. "Well, I'm sorry, but you looked like one. But I can't figure out why you'd come here."

"I came on account of my father. His business was going to ruin. I knew that old Gregory Planchard had swindled him out of fifty thousand dollars and I came here to get it back. I'm Rose Trent."

The man's jaw sagged. "Why, I'm Milt Draven. I work for your father! I'm supe at his plant. And I came here to buy that old wood carving of St. Stephen that old Planchard has. Wanted it for my aunt. She's—"

"Oh, you don't think I killed him? You couldn't!" Rose pleaded.

Milt Draven flung an arm about her shoulder and led her towards the lamp that stood in front of Gregory Planchard's door. "I'd hate to think that you did," he whispered. "Not that I blame you."

"But I didn't!" Rose persisted. "Why, I thought that Jules killed old Gregory—"

"Gregory?" Draven gasped. "He's dead, too? Say, what is this? I'd pay plenty to see that wood carving of St. Stephen right now! Stephen, you know, was the first Christian martyr. And legend has it that this old carving of Gregory's comes to life sometimes to avenge the wrongs and evil deeds of the wicked. But say, has anyone called the sheriff?"

Rose shook her head. "You see, nobody knows about it but me. I discovered the body—oh, you've got to believe that, too!" she added hastily as she saw the look of suspicion that crept into his eyes. "Come to Gregory's room. You'll see!" Rose Trent led the way back to the door of Gregory's room. There she hesitated. She had more than ordinary grit, but she wasn't anxious to enter that room again. "I—I'll wait here," she murmured.

MILT DRAVEN shrugged, pushed open the door and entered the room. Rose, crowding close to the lighted lamp, waited impatiently. She couldn't be too sure of Draven. He *looked* nice enough, but his explanation of how he happened to be there sounded pretty thin. A wood carving of St. Stephen, eh? And why couldn't Draven be after the famous rubies associated with the saint? The story had it that the stones by which Stephen suffered his martyrdom had been changed to rare jewels by contact with his blood. Value enough there to tempt the collector or even a common burglar! He might—

Her chain of thought was suddenly interrupted by a harsh squawk coming from down the hall. It was Gregory's pet crow again, but there was a quality of terror in its scream. The shadows beyond the lamp were disturbed by a frantic fluttering of black wings. Something flapped along the floor nearly to Rose's feet, and as she followed it with her eyes, she shrank back in horror, nearly upsetting the lamp on the taboret at her side. Her scream was shrill, unrestrained.

Milt Draven hurried back through the door. "See here, Miss Trent, you shouldn't do that! Why, wh-what . . ." He came to a stumbling stop beside her.

He seized her shoulders between his big hands. "Steady, there!"

Rose shook her head. She wanted to tell him that she wasn't going to faint, but could only point her finger at the shapeless object on the floor and at the red shadow that crawled from beneath it. It was Gregory Planchard's pet crow. And the thin, silvery blade of a knife had pierced the bird's breast and protruded from the dull black surface of its feathered back.

"See," she husked, "the murderer, somewhere out there in the shadows, knew that the bird had seen Gregory and Jules killed! The bird could talk—"

Draven moistened his lips. "Yeah," he whispered. "The killer could have stabbed Gregory by getting in through the window in the old man's room. It's not far from the roof of the summer kitchen. The bird could have seen it all. But you say the killer's down there?" he pointed towards the shadowy end of the hall.

"Must be. How could he have stabbed the bird? You're not afraid?" Rose asked fearfully.

Draven grimaced. "Nope. This just isn't my idea of a picnic! But here goes. Stick around. I'm goin' after the killer!"

And in spite of Rose's protestations, Milt Draven was off, running silently down the hall.

FOR dragging minutes, Rose stood, listening intently for sounds conjured up by her own imagination. Then, when Draven didn't come back, she called him softly, but heard no answer. She picked up the lamp from the taboret. Her teeth closed over her crimson lower lip. She would catch any more startled screams before utterance, she vowed.

Rose walked slowly down the hall, passing the body of Jules Planchard, her eyes averted. When she came upon the bloody knife she had dropped, she stared as one fascinated. Where had it come from? Her hand had closed so naturally upon the hilt. Could it be that she was mad? Could it be that she had unknowingly killed Jules? That knife—a queer thing with notches along its gore-stained blade. Didn't some killers out of sheer bravado notch their weapons for each man killed?

She hurried on, for she was afraid of standing still lest some unnamable horror steal up behind her. Se turned abruptly to the right and came upon a rusty iron door framed in the wall. Perhaps Draven had gone through there. She took the brass door knob, squirmed at the chill of the metal, and creaked open the door. Apparently, this was but a continuation of the hall but built along slightly smaller dimensions.

She hurried down the narrow hall, then stopped suddenly, bit her lip again. Something shadowy waved slowly back and forth in front of her. Only a curtain? But beneath that swaying curtain was a yellow snake of light. Rose approached on tiptoe, breath bated.

Something, *someone*, was beyond that curtain. She could see a shadow, tall, gaunt, and irregular—the shadow of someone standing as still as stone, waiting, perhaps, for her entrance. She glanced apprehensively back over her shoulder. Was there someone in the passage behind her, slowly, remorselessly crowding her into that curtained room? But the person behind the curtain, whoever it was, would face her in the light. She would throw back the drape, meet the man who stood there waiting. Anything was better than the awful uncertainty of the shadows behind her. Rose drew a long breath, slipped one hand through the curtains, and lifted them slightly.

Lip-biting checked her scream, reduced it to a little choking sound. For the thing that fostered the shadow was not a man. It wasn't even human. It was no living thing!

Antique, ecclesiastic candlesticks held guttering tapers that threw moving, fantastic shadows upon the walls of the narrow, cement-walled chamber. And the thing in the center that she had mistaken for a man was a statue—a crude, wooden thing, lacking in proportion, stiff because it had evidently been made before the discovery of artistic foreshortening. It was a more than life-size figure of a holy man, anciently garbed. There was something of real artistry in the face, for crudely carved though it was there was an expression of kindliness and piety about it. The wooden folds of its gown were gathered in front and held by one wooden hand. In this little nest formed in carved folds, were a number of small pebbles. Then she understood; this was the ancient wood carving of the martyred St. Stephen that Draven had told her about!

She thought that she heard a sound down the passage behind her. Could it be mere imaginings? Or had she really been followed. Rose stepped quickly within the room and dropped the curtains back in place. There was a small door leading through one wall ahead of her. She listened again for the repetition of the noise in the hall. But everything was silent now save for the moan of the wind and the howl of restless wolves outside the house.

ROSE turned again to the wooden statue of St. Stephen. She noticed that one of the brown pebbles that lay in the hollow of the statue's robe, glinted oddly. St. Stephen's stones! The legend said that the stones that had killed Stephen had been changed to rubies. Was she witnessing a miracle, or had Gregory hidden—

Rose reached out and timidly touched one of the brown pebbles. She picked it up, moistened her finger, and rubbed the smooth surface. Those brown pebbles had been painted! She scraped away brown paint with her fingernail and beneath she could see the live, red fire of a perfect ruby.

Rose hesitated only a moment. Stealing? She couldn't call it that. The St. Stephen rubies were worth just fifty thousand dollars, the amount that Gregory had stolen from her father. She picked up every one of the brown-covered stones, knotted them in her handkerchief, and dropped them in the bosom of her dress. Precious stones! They meant her father's return to health!

Rose took a step towards the curtained doorway. Again came the sound from the hall outside the door—a soft, sinister shuffling noise. Rose turned, ran to the other side of the room, and seized the handle of the second door. She tugged at it, found it stuck! She could not open it! She turned, moved stealthily towards the center of the room. If she could hide behind the statue—

"Stop!" The command came from behind the curtains. A hand was thrust between the curtain folds. Its fingers were locked upon the butt of an automatic. "Stand where you are. Toss them sparklers you stole under the curtain!"

"I—I don't know what you're talking about!" Rose whispered. The rubies— they meant so much! She dared not lose them now.

"Don't you, eh? Well, you'll stay there until you do. Don't move! I'll shoot!"

The curtains rustled slightly. Still there was the brown hand sticking between the folds. That hand—where had she seen it before? It was the color of old mahogany; it had gnarled, prominent knuckles. Good God! It was the hand of Gregory Planchard! Yet she had seen Gregory

Planchard with a knife in his heart! Was it true then, as folk said, that Gregory was too mean for hell to hold? Was he really some soulless thing from beyond the grave, something invulnerable?

The door at the other side of the room opened. But Rose's eyes remained fixed on the brown hand that trained the automatic on her. It was not until the door closed with a crash that she sent a hasty glance over her shoulder. It was Hunk, the youth who worked for the Planchards, who had entered. "Be careful," she whispered to him. She nodded towards the curtains.

A sensation of nausea surpassing anything she had experienced that night came upon her. Her brain seemed caught in a whirlpool. For the hand that held the automatic, the brown hand that she was sure belonged to Gregory Planchard, sagged slowly until the muzzle of the gun drooped. Then—then, the hand tore away, thudded to the floor, a dead, dismembered thing, cut cleanly through every bone and sinew at the wrist!

Rose Trent collapsed to the floor. The black curtain of oblivion descended upon her.

HARSH words accompanied by someone shaking her vigorously brought Rose to her senses. She was bitter cold and her knees were knocking together. She stared into a face that was masked with a piece of dirty brown cloth. Her lips parted, silently screaming.

"Look around, woman. Get where you are," commanded the masked man.

Rose needed only one look! She was outdoors, bound in a chair with her feet and ankles hidden in cold, fluffy snow. Not ten feet from her was another chair with somebody strapped in it, too. About them was a circle of lanterns. But beyond, beyond this circle of light, was a sinister circle of moving, flaming eyes and slinking, shadowy forms.

"Wolves," whispered the masked man. "And there's just enough oil in those lanterns to keep them wolves off from ye. The light will last about five minutes. When the lanterns goes out, the wolves won't be scared no more—get that? You or that Draven feller knows where them sparklers are. One or the other is goin' to tell me or ye both get chawed by the wolves. I'm gettin' square. And I'm gettin' what's owed me! I want them jewels!"

Rose raised her chin. "Never!" she whipped out. "You'll hang for this. Take off that mask, Hunk! I know you killed Gregory and Jules Planchard! I know because there was only one way for anyone to do it. You shot them with your sling shot! You made notches in your knives so that you could throw the knives in your sling shot even from a distance. You cut off the hand of old Gregory and taped that gun to the fingers of the severed hand and then attached the hand to the curtain after I entered the room where the St. Stephen statue stood. You did that just to trap me in that room while you came around through the other door to cut off my escape. I know all about you—"

"Nobody else is goin' to know!" Hunk snarled. "I'm takin' a light and goin' back to the house. You got just five minutes to decide to tell me where you've hid those stones. If you don't come across, I'm goin' to watch you get tore apart by the wolves!" And with a deep chuckle, Hunk picked up a stick of wood, kindled an oil-soaked swab at the end of it, and with this torch started for the house.

When he was gone the man who was tied to the other chair spoke. "We're in for a time!" It was Milt Draven's cheerful voice. "You better tell him where the rubies are. He means business!"

"Never!" Rose's lips were quivering with cold and something even more chilling. One of the lanterns had flickered out. The wolf pack, silent and watchful, concentrated near this breach in the protecting circle of light. She bit her lips.

"I think you'd better give up the rubies," said Draven gently. "It'll give us a spell for breathin'. Maybe, with a little time, we can get out of this mess. The kid's crazy. I suspected him from the first and went out hunting him. But when I did find him, he was behind me with a club! Lucky he thought I had the rubies or he might have knifed me. Hunk must have hated the Planchards. He was Gregory's son by a past liaison. Gregory wouldn't give the boy his name, slaved him to death, embittered him. So he killed them to even up— But say, we've lost another lantern. Only four left."

Rose was thinking of Milt Draven. She hadn't any right to keep him in such a spot. She drew a long, freezing breath, and called, "Come out, Hunk. I've got the rubies!"

THE door of the house sprang open and Hunk raced out, waving his lighted stick above his head. His dull face had taken on a look of insane cruelty. "Where are they?" he asked as he ran up to Rose. "You got just a few minutes."

"I can't get them unless you untie me," Rose sobbed. "They're—"

Hunk threw down his torch, seized the collar of Rose's jacket, and ripped it open. "I'll get 'em," he chuckled gleefully. "I know where you've got 'em!"

Rose writhed beneath the loathsome touch of his blunt fingers that clutched madly at the cloth of her dress; that pulled and ripped, baring her flesh.

Then something cracked like a small rifle. Beyond Hunk, Rose saw that Milt Draven's chair had collapsed. He had managed to crash its rounds against the frozen earth. He was on his feet now, stumbling towards her, fragments of the chair dragging behind him from the straps that still clung to his legs. In the ever dimming light, she saw the fury that blazed in his eyes. His arms were swinging like twin windmills.

With a snarl of rage, Hunk turned to meet Draven. Hunk snatched out a knife, but Draven's driving fist knocked it from his hand. A fast-moving upper-cut connected with Hunk's chin. The lanky youth went down in a heap.

Draven already had his pocket knife out. He bent over Rose. "Got to clear out, lady. Get to my car," he panted as he slashed through the cords that bound her. "Too numb to run?" Draven lifted her like a sack of grain and slung her across his broad shoulder. Rose clung to the back of his coat with one hand while the other clutched at her breast where lay the sack of rubies.

Draven nearly fell in picking up one of the lanterns that was still burning. But he succeeded in getting the lantern bail over his wrist and then ran towards the lane. He stopped. "Down you go." He dumped her, rather than set her down in his haste. He yanked at the handle of the door of his sedan, swung the door open, and lifted her in.

Behind Milt, Rose saw three gaunt shadows loping towards him. She screamed. Draven flung the light straight at the head of the foremost brute. The lantern burst open. What little oil remained, flared up. Draven swung back the door and leaped in beside her just as wolf crashed against the car door.

Then Draven turned on the headlights and plugged at the starter. As the motor turned, he glanced back towards the house. He cursed softly. "The lights," he whispered, "the lanterns have all gone out!"

Towards the house, headlamps of the car picked out the moving, racing shadows. Wolves! And at the head of the pack they could see the lank form of Hunk. Rose saw the crazed youth reach the door of the house and tug frantically at the door knob.

"Good Lord!" breathed Draven. "He's locked himself out!"

The yelping, snarling pack was upon Hunk. Sheer weight of a dozen brutes dragged him shrieking to the ground.

And Rose closed her eyes while the roar of Draven's motor drowned out some of the hideous, hungry animal din. She thanked God that Milt Draven was taking her away, out of the night the wolves were fed. . . .

EATER OF SOULS

By Arthur J. Burks

(Author of "Six Doors To Horror," etc.)

A Novelette of Swamp Spawned Terror

They said that those corpse-candles, those heathen beacons that filled the swamp with their ghastly glow, were the souls of girls who had died for love. Could Maria Tejada call on their occult power to help her snare the heart of the man she wanted? Could she summon the dead to infect her loved-one's betrothed with the silver plague . . . ?

I had been several months in El Gran Estero. It was almost home to me by now! When my job of reclamation was finished I intended to bring Lora Jaynes here from New York as my wife.

What ailed me, then? I had actually, in that moment, broken into a cold sweat. I stared down the jungle aisles in the direction of the chanting. I got the chill impression that some nameless terror, as though the very spirit of sullen Gran Estero were coming to me on the wind with the primeval chanting of the Haitians.

Belema Llansal and Divue Cerimarie, my foremen, were returning with my new laborers, that was all. . . .

And yet I wouldn't have been surprised to see a black cloud, filled with strange menace, floating above the trees through

IT WAS dusk. Night was settling like a black mantle over El Gran Estero, that vast Dominican swamp which I intended to turn into a Garden of Eden. I don't know what ailed me at the moment, for I was suddenly terrified beyond all reason. Maybe it was the chanting of my new Haitian laborers, coming to me through the gloom from Sanchez. But it couldn't be that, I thought, for I had heard Haitians chanting for months on end.

which they approached, still out of sight.

Then they came out from the jungle, and I saw them. My heart stood still for a moment, then began to pound like a trip-hammer. For in the midst of the long line of blacks, an orchid in a coal pile, was Lora Jaynes! This was her answer to my suggestion that she wait until I was ready. She had come to me in Gran Estero!

Then I looked at the other woman with her, and my racing heart missed a beat.

She was a Dominican, beautiful as a young Dominican girl can be. But her eyes! Just to look into them made me think again of the unreasoning terror which had gripped me a few moments before. In them I saw that Hell which many white men have seen in the eyes of quadroons of the deep jungle. But something else lurked there, too! I couldn't tell what it was. But it made me think of sullen pools in Gran Estero, from which witches' fires rose at midnight. I shivered as with the ague.

I noticed that the Haitians looked askance at her when they thought no one noticed, and I knew that they felt something, too—something strange, something distinctly *other*. I couldn't help what I next did. I stared down at the girl's brown legs and bare feet—she carried her shoes over her shoulders—and I wouldn't have been surprised to discover that she walked, not on the ground, *but above it!*

Nothing had ever given me such a turn. Hell, she was just a native woman, no more. And yet, something else caught at my throat as I remembered: wild oxen couldn't have induced the average Dominican woman to enter El Gran Estero at all, to say nothing of coming in when it was obvious she must spend many nights in the heart of the sullen quagmire.

Yet this girl wasn't afraid!

Her lips even twisted in a mocking smile, as though she read my thoughts. It made my flesh crawl—and I hated myself because I suddenly hated this girl. I hated her because I was so completely, and for no reason I could think of, afraid of her! Yes, both for myself and for Lora. I felt that she was something evil, out of the slimy depths of the swamp.

"You shouldn't have come," I heard myself telling Lora, after I had kissed her. "I'd send you back at once, but I need my men and you'd never get back alone."

"It's all right, dear," she said. "I've brought a chaperone, Maria Tejeda. My maid, Maria."

I GLANCED at the Dominican girl again in spite of myself. It was fortunate that Lora was not staring at her at the moment, for with a shock I made an awful discovery. Maria Tejeda had looked at me and found me desirable—and was instantly jealous of Lora. It wasn't a new situation at all. Dominican young women are hotblooded; when they see a man they want they believe in letting him know it. White men might recognize racial barriers, Dominican women never. Maria lowered her eyes, her olive cheek flushing delicately, when I frowned.

But—I confess it with shame—my heart's beat jumped swiftly into high speed. If Lora had not been there. . . .

But she was, and I loved her more than ever. Looking back at her I tried to forget Maria Tejeda.

I gave orders to the Haitians. Lora, myself and Maria went into the cabin. There was a lean-to behind it which would serve as quarters for Maria. Lora and I would have to occupy the main room, with a blanket on a pole between us to serve as a partition.

The party had arrived just in time. Shadowed always, even at midday, the swamp was a place of gloom at dusk, an ebon immensity at night.

I lighted the kerosene lamp and looked into Lora's face.

"I may seem brave, Jim," said Lora softly, as I took her in my arms again," but I'm not, really. I'll keep so close to you that people will think I'm your shadow."

"There aren't any people," I said, "except the Haitians, and they aren't really people. But there's nothing to be afraid of."

She shuddered. "I can't help it," she said. "Those gloomy aisles through the endless jungle, festooned with ghostly Spanish moss. Sullen black water into which one might sink endlessly, to right and left, before and behind. You wonder how the guides can find their way through, ahead. You look back and wonder how you have come so far. And all the way Maria kept telling me horrible things about El Gran Estero. She frightened me, for in the jungle she seemed strange, unearthly. In Santiago she was just a native girl. But the minute we reached the swamp she spoke *gloatingly* about the things!"

"Yes? What things?"

"About the creeping snakes, the queer butterflies, the shrieking bats, and witches' fires. The will-o'-the-wisps, she told me, were the souls of Dominican girls who had died for love in Gran Estero. They come forth at night and flit through the gloomy, whispering aisles, moaning for their lost loves, bewailing the fact that they lost them utterly by dying. Ugh! She gave me the creeps. But I learned a lot from her. Native women seem born with so much knowledge of men. She told me how to get and keep my husband, that a woman must be all things to her man. Come to think of it, she didn't say 'husband'."

"She wouldn't," I said ruefully. "You mustn't listen to such tripe, Lora. I'll speak to Maria about filling you with such tales."

"Don't. I encouraged her. But her tales filled the whole swamp area with terrors, and made her seem like its dark angel! I heard sighs of despair in the swinging moss, whispers of defeat in the the slithering sounds the green snakes made, and the death rattle of doomed men in the skeleton-like sound of the land crabs. . . ."

She shivered. Her face was very white. I held her tightly and, feeling her suddenly stiffen, drew back my head to look at her. Then I whirled. Standing in the door between our room and the lean-to was Maria Tejeda. Her black eyes were glowing, deep fires down in their depths. There was a challenge in her face. She addressed me boldly, in Spanish.

"You would have been wiser to have selected a woman who could endure El Gran Estero," she said. "A woman like. . . ."

"I know," I answered grimly. "A woman like Maria Tejeda. Listen, Maria, in this house you are a servant, a hewer of wood and carrier of water, no more, and if you make yourself obnoxious I shall send you out again at once."

She smiled. "I don't know the way. Can you spare a guide?"

SHE knew I couldn't send her out, not, at least, for another two weeks. The light in her eyes was a mocking one. Damn her! I knew what native women could do to men's souls, even those of white men who hated them.

"But she speaks English," protested Lora, "and I know no Spanish. If there are secrets between you. . . ."

"There are none," I said hastily. "I have the habit of speaking Spanish to Dominicans, Haitian *patois* to the blacks, that's all. They understand orders in their own tongues better. You'd better learn Spanish as fast as Maria can teach it to you."

"I like you," said Maria boldly," and the time will come when you will like

Maria Tejeda, very much indeed, and wish that this pale-faced weakling had never come here !"

That Spanish was machine-gun fast. Even if Lora had known the tongue she couldn't have understood it. I lost my temper in my mounting terror. I hurled myself at Maria, grasped her by her arms, gritted my teeth and snarled into her face.

"Any more of that," I began, "and I send you into the swamp, to find your way out alone !"

Lora was pulling me back. She was shocked by my exhibition of temper. Maria was smiling with infinite knowledge. I knew that she understood perfectly what had happened to me ; that while I was holding her arms in a firm grip, the treacherous thought had come to me :

"If Lora were not here I would kiss her fiercely !"

It wasn't love, but a murky, crawling horror, deep down inside me, which gripped at my very vitals. I hurled the girl from me. I knew how one could hate a native girl—yet grovel for her favors ! Maria still grinned. She knew, too, and smiled. But Lora was very angry. I turned my back on Maria, muttering.

"You have to put Dominican servants in their place. She was insolent."

"There's no reason why you should manhandle her ! Jim, let's don't quarrel the minute we get together. I haven't seen you for five months, do you realize that ?"

I caught Lora roughly and kissed her. Behind us I heard the low, amused laughter of Maria Tejeda. And something inside me turned over. I was suddenly more afraid than I had ever been before. I almost forgot that I wished to make a Garden of Eden of El Gran Estero. I forgot everything except that I should flee this place, with Lora, as though it were the abode of pestilence. But to do so would entail explanations that I could not make, because to make them would mean an ad-

mission I would not make even to myself.

"Make supper, Maria," I said over my shoulder. "Come, Lora, at least the chairs are comfortable."

We sat down, facing each other at a small table where for weeks I had amused myself by playing solitaire, and looked into each others eyes. From outside came the whispering of the wind through the quagmire. We could both hear the chuckling sound of the swamp as it seemed to shift and sigh, and turn over to sleep.

Maria rummaged, found my cooking utensils, my store of food. She set two places at the table. Now she seemed to have become the perfect servant, and I knew that Lora had selected her with care. She came to the table with the black coffee, flavored with *raspidura,* which I had grown to regard as nectar of the gods. But, when she was about to set it down she froze, staring. Both Lora and I followed her frozen, wide-eyed glance.

Just outside the window, rising and falling, flitting back and forth, was a solitary corpse candle, looking like a big single eye, dancing eerily in space. I shot a glance back at Maria. Her veiled eyes were fixed. Not on the will-o'-the-wisp, but on Lora and me. Lora's face was white.

And I hoped that my face did not look as cold as my heart felt at that awful moment. . . .

CHAPTER TWO

Terror of the Swamp

LORA smothered a little scream, sticking the back of her hand into her mouth to do it. Her eyes were wide. I reached across the table, caught her hand.

"It's only a will-o'-the-wisp," I said. "Phosphorescent bubble from the ooze."

"I was remembering . . . ." said Lora, her voice thin, and reedy with a sudden trembling she fought hard to control.

"I know. Maria's tales. You've got a touch of fever, that's all. I've got plenty of quinine. This place is full of malaria, you know. Maybe I shouldn't allow you to stay after tomorrow."

Instantly her face became cold. She shot a glance at Maria, and in that moment I knew that she had sensed the truth; that if she went out, and Maria went with her, Maria would come back. Lora didn't say a word, for she was too proud, but I knew that the last hope of sending her out, unless all of us went, had departed.

Maria's black eyes blazed. There was an almost fanatical light in them.

"It is a young girl's soul," she half chanted. "I know. I have lived all my life on the edge of El Gran Estero. A young girl killed herself for the loss of her man's love. She drowned herself in the swamp, and now she peers in through your window, to see if you are her man!"

"Maria!" I snapped at her. "I won't stand for any more of this nonsense. Finish with supper and get back to your quarters."

The girl had deliberately spoken English. God knew where she had learned it; from some white man to whom she had been mistress, probably. Some Dominican women would barter their souls for white men, and I knew that Maria Tejeda was one such. She would lie, cheat, steal, even murder—for love. She would even go into the swamp and die if she could not have the man she wanted. I knew. It wasn't a blinding flash of revelation; I had known it from the beginning.

"Let her be," said Lora quietly. "She can serve us as we eat."

Lora had suddenly become quite calm, although her face was deadly pale. I knew that she had calmly accepted the mute challenge Maria had given her. I adored her more than ever as I pulled back the chair for her. Had Maria been there with me alone, she would have pulled back *my*

chair, and gloried in the least menial service. I refused to look at her.

BUT as we ate I kept glancing at the windows, tightly closed to keep out mosquitoes, watching for the reappearance of the corpse candle. It didn't come back. And Lora didn't look at the window again. I knew that she was afraid to look. She knew that I knew. I could see that her jaws were grimly set.

Then, when we had finished, and Maria, with the catlike tread of her kind, was clearing off the rough table, Lora raised her head. "I refuse to be afraid, Jim," she said. "I won't let this swamp beat me."

I knew she didn't mean the swamp, but Maria. I merely looked at her, and felt miserable.

"Let's sit in chairs outside, and savor El Gran Estero," she whispered, every word a distinct effort. "You can tell me about it."

"But mosquitoes will fill you with malaria!"

"You have quinine," she said.

I shrugged. I took up two chairs, carried them outside. The mosquitoes immediately attacked with their usual savage vigor. I placed the chairs with their backs against the rough-hewn logs of the cabin. We two seemed instantly to have been set down in the heart of a block of ebony. All around us the swamp, thickly set with trees of many kinds, reached away for miles. I had cleared a small space around my cabin, whose floor was raised several feet to get out of the dampness which permeated even the spot of ground. But ahead of us the tree-wall blotted out the sky, a sky that was black now with a sullenness promising rain. I was relieved at that, for rain, I thought, would keep down the witches' fires. I hadn't minded them. I was too materialistic to pay any heed to foolish superstitions. But now

Lora's fear gripped me too, because she was afraid.

I could see, in my mind's eye, down the dim aisles which stretched away from us in all directions, the huge trunks of *ceiba* and *guayacan*, the former as white as the garments of a ghost. Among those trees the sun was blotted out as though there had been no sun, and the moon did not even seek to penetrate. I knew the places of the Spanish moss, the pools of reptiles and crabs, of frogs, snakes—the gloomy clearings where bats played. And for the first time, I who had spent so much time here alone, was afraid of the sprawling monster which was El Gran Estero. For right now it held in its heart my most precious possession.

I captured Lora's hand and held it.

Somewhere behind us I heard a low laugh and knew that Maria, with eyes that might, for all I knew, be able to see in the dark, was watching us.

I felt Lora tremble.

Off to my right I saw several fireflies dart through the trees, and shifted so that Lora could not see them. They looked so much like the headlights of an automobile that one instinctively listened for the sound of the motor. Lora hadn't seen. I could feel her tense, knew that she was looking in the opposite direction entirely.

"Jim," she whispered, "they *do* give me the creeps! I'm sorry, but I can't seem to help it."

Now I saw them too, several of them, the weird, silent, dancing globules of fire, off to our left among the trees that looked, up to now, like a black wall hemming us in. They might have been toy balloons, the sport of every vagrant breeze, with fireflies inside them. As a child I had used fireflies for lanterns, which made me remember them as I saw the will-o'-the-wisps.

UTTER silence suddenly possessed all Gran Estero. Side by side Lora and I watched the *ignis fatuus*. They were like a company of nameless creatures, blindly seeking a way through the jungle. They seemed to be following an aisle of their own, though I knew that in that direction there was no aisle at all, but only the sullen black water. Now two of them vanished, and I knew a big tree trunk had intervened. Then the two came into view again, one from the right, one from the left. It was as though they had separated to circle the tree, and now came on again.

"Jim," whispered Lora. "Jim. They're coming this way!"

"Maybe," damn it. I was whispering to myself, "for what breeze there is—and God knows we need one to blow the mosquitoes away—comes from that direction. That's all. They come from there because that is the swamp."

"But Maria said that they had died because they had lost their lovers, and would *kill* to get other lovers in their places!"

"Nonsense!" but I had to admit that my own voice lacked conviction, despite the fact that every night for weeks I had sat just here, smoking *anduga* to keep off the mosquitoes—wasted effort!—and seen thrice this number of the will-o'-the-wisps all around the cabin. Then they hadn't frightened me. But now they were the shadows which forecast coming horrors!

I found myself listening for Maria Tejeda. But no sound came from the cabin or the lean-to. It was a relief to look around, though, and know that the light still burned inside.

The globules of eerie light came on, reached my clearing. Then, caught by some breath of wind, they rose in a body and vanished against the sky.

"See," I whispered, "they have burst. That ends *that!*"

"But I could have sworn I heard someone *sighing,* in my ear," answered Lora. "It's my imagination, a touch of the fever as you said, perhaps, but I thought the sigh consisted of words, words in Spanish! I can't understand them, but I'll never forget them. Silly, isn't it?"

"Yes, very," but I couldn't help adding, "what did the words sound like?"

"Donde está mi vida!!"

Lora, who knew no Spanish, pronounced the words so plainly that even a novice at the tongue could not have mistaken them or their meaning. Interpreted—though I would never interpret them for Lora!—they meant:

"Where is the light of my life?"

But I didn't tell Lora that.

"Gibberish," I said. "Utter gibberish, having no meaning."

INSTANTLY I knew the lie wasted. Maria would teach Lora Spanish. Even now all she had to do was to ask Maria the meaning of the words and the girl would tell her.

"They came from the direction of the will-o'-the-wisps," persisted Lora, "just as they rose into the night sky and vanished!"

I confess that the swamp suddenly seemed as cold as the tomb; that its sprawling immensity had become a vast antedeluvian monster, enwrapping us in its folds. This morning I had been happy here, I should have been delirious with joy now because Lora was here—and I felt, really, as though I stood in utter darkness on the brink of a vast abyss, ready to topple into eerie, endless space at a touch. It might be a word, a look, a whisper that would do it. . . .

"Jim," whispered Lora again. "Look there! What is it?"

I looked and gasped. I saw a shadow, dimly white, further to the the left, moving straight into the blackness of the trees. I knew, with a queer tightening about my heart, that the shadow was Maria Tejeda, wearing little or nothing at all, going straight into the swamp from the lean-to.

"Maria!" whispered Lora. "Call her back! She'll sink into the swamp."

"I hope so!" I said fierely—and I knew that I lied! I lifted my voice in a savage shout. "Maria! Maria Tejeda! Where the devil are you going? There's nothing but swamp, quagmire, in that direction!"

Did I imagine it, or did a low laugh come from the shadow just as it vanished, almost as completely and strangely as had the will-o'-the-wisps?

"No use following her," I mumbled. "Natives can find their way in the dark. Strange that she isn't afraid of the swamp. No, it isn't strange, either, if she has lived all her life on its edge. Let's go in. I'm cold."

Lora didn't answer, but she looked at me queerly as she turned, inside the cabin, to stare as I stood on the threshold, looking out into the night toward the spot where Maria Tejeda had vanished.

"Shut the door, dear," said Lora. "You're letting the mosquitoes in."

I flirted the damp sweat from my forehead with a trembling hand. "Touch of fever," I muttered.

But now I had something to do. Lora held the door open while I used a blanket for a swatter and drove out as many mosquitoes as I could, and shut the door. I looked into Maria's quarters, where she had made a pallet on a pile of boughs, She was gone, of course. But a strange, Dominican odor came out of the place. I smelled charcoal, and knew that Maria had been brewing something in her quarters, something with a smell which was as much a part of the swamp as was the swamp itself.

"The sun will drive away the vapors," I said. "We must sleep."

I arranged the blanket partition, with myself between Maria's quarters and

Lora's bed. We kissed, parted. I heard Lora's gentle breathing as she slept. Then, though I didn't expect it, I slept, too, and I though I heard Maria come back and lie down on her pallet just as I dozed off.

I wakened to find the room filled with an eerie radiance. The blanket was down between us, and Lora was sitting bolt upright in bed, her face a white mask in the misty moonlight from the west window. . . .

CHAPTER THREE

Souls of Dead Maidens

I THOUGHT it was all some ghastly nightmare. The room was filled with will-o'-the-wisps! Moonlight touched them and was absorbed by them. They seemed to glow with an eerie radiance of their own, too. They rose when they floated into breezes which seeped through cracks in the wall. They dropped as though dragged down with an invisible weight as they passed into shadow.

"It's only phosphorescence," I told myself.

And yet, I didn't even believe myself. For the will-o'-the-wisps seemed to have a sigh, a sort of whisper of their own.

"Donde esta mi vida? Mi vida! Mi vida!"

"Where is the light of my life? Light of my life! Light of my life!"

That's not the exact translation, but rather the meaning of the Spanish words whispered by the will-o'-the-wisps, so many of which floated there in the room with Lora and me. The place was deathly silent save for the eerie whispers which seemed to come from everywhere and nowhere. There is no personality to a whisper. A man might whisper like a woman, a woman like a man. And that night it was all as impersonal and detached as the corpse candles themselves.

Corpse candles! The very words carry grim meaning. I knew what the things were, or thought I did. Mere explosions of gas from under the sullen waters, looking like fire because of phosphorus. That was all. And yet so many superstitions had risen about them. Such stories as that one about being peoples' souls—the souls of young girls.

Dominican girls! How well I knew them! Ardent, passionate, all-possessive. They did all sorts of things in the name of love. They brewed love potions whose ingredients, if known to the lovers to whom they were given, would have caused the desired ones from sheer horror to slay them. And, who knew? Perhaps many of the dead in Gran Estero had been slain by their men because of those drugs. . . .

In Maria's quarters had been the odor of something brewed! She had come back just before I fell asleep. Maybe I should have questioned her then as to why she had gone into the swamp. But Lora slept, and I was afraid that if I got up and went to Maria Lora might not understand. Neither would Maria.

And I had been afraid besides—afraid of what I would do and say when I saw the girl.

But I had dreamed during my brief sleep—perhaps because Maria was the last thing in my mind—that the dusky native had come to me as I slept, bending over my rough couch, and that she had crooned a love song to me. Her arms had reached down to me; her hands, redolent with the odor of woodsmoke, had slipped through my hair, had caressed my cheeks. It had driven me mad and I had caught her tightly in my arms. . . .

Lora's scream had wakened me. The look of her face, so white and frightened, would never leave me again, would go with me always, I knew. She had been staring at me when I had snapped awake. But my first impressions were confused in all things save one: that the room was filled with the will-o'-the-wisps. And I began to wonder how they had gotten into the place? The windows were screened, and the globules would surely have burst on contact with the mesh. The door was still closed—so there were only the cracks, and the glowing lights could never have come through those.

How, then?

And whence came the whispering sighs?

I stared at Lora. Her lips moved as though she spoke, yet no words came forth that I could hear. Her eyes swerved from me to the will-o'-the-wisps, and she shrank back from them in unholy horror. I seemed to be rooted to the spot with nameless fear myself. It was as though I were still in the throes of some strange dream.

How had the blanket come down?

Had Lora pulled it down between us? Had Maria? If either had, why?

But now I watched the will-o'-the-wisps in utter fascination. They moved as though directed by some strange will of their own, or as though all were guided by some intelligence whose corporeal substance, if any, I could not see. They seemed to be concentrating on Lora!

She struck at one with her hand. A little scream came from her lips, oddly like that of a mouse that has just felt the jaws of a trap close over it. Her hand broke the globule, which made a little popping sound. Then she struck again and again at the things as if the striking fascinated her. Of course it must have been the wind of her hand through the close atmosphere of the place that caused it, but . . . .

The will-o'-the-wisps moved toward her, almost all of them. She slashed out at many. And horror gripped me as I saw two of them strike her head and burst. . . .

SHE flopped back on her couch. I jumped to my feet, caught up the fallen blanket with which I had driven out the mosquitoes, and struck savagely at the harmless phosphorescent globules until not one remained.

Then, spent and panting, perspiring as I seldom had, even while working hard in the heat of the suffocating swamp, I sat down on the edge of Lora's bed.

"Where in the world did they come from?" I asked hoarsely.

"What was *she* doing?" asked Lora, her voice scarcely audible.

"She? Who?"

"Maria. Maria Tejeda," she repeated the name as though not sure that I would know whom she meant. "I saw the globules first. Then I saw that the blanket was down. Maria was bending over you. She was running her hand through your hair—both hands! She was almost reclining on your chest. She was crooning to you!" Again came that hurt sound, like that of a newly trapped mouse. "And Jim, you took her in your arms, and she laughed! I screamed then. She vanished without sound and you sat up. What is happening to us, Jim? What is that girl to you?"

"Lora, before God I never saw her before she came here with you? I know nothing about her. But I'll find out what she meant by what she did. I had a dream . . . ."

But suddenly I couldn't tell her of the dream. It would have shown my own guilt which, now that I was awake, filled me with such foreboding and sensation of guilt. I did love Lora, with all my heart! I couldn't hurt her.

I walked to the door leading into Maria's quarters, and I held the lamp high. Maria was gone. The outer door stood ajar. Again I caught that faint, indefinable odor as of something having recently been brewed.

I walked to the door, looked about. Plainly, in the soft soil outside the door, I saw the imprint of bare feet. And beside Maria's pallet on the floor were her clothes, the simple things that a native woman wore. I turned back to Lora.

"Her footprints lead, this time, westward into the swamp, Lora," I said. "I'm going to find out what all this is about. Don't be afraid about the will-o'-the-wisps. They're natural phenomena. Or real ones are. Real ones couldn't have got in here through the closed door, or through the screens, or cracks between the logs. Maria had something to do with it."

"But how? Jim, they couldn't get in; but they did . . . ."

"Maria knows, Lora," I said. "Native women do strange things. I won't rest, and you can't, until we know the truth. I'm going after Maria. If she can find firm footing in the swamp, so can I. I'll follow her tracks, bring her back, and force her to explain the will-o'-the-wisps in the cabin. You stay here. Keep the doors barred. Don't let anyone in until you hear my voice."

"I'm going with you!"

"I may have to travel fast. Just . . . just don't be afraid, Lora."

I DRESSED quickly, pushing my feet into hip boots as a guard against crawling things, though there was nothing poisonous—that was real and alive—in the swamp. Lora's white face stared after me as I went through Maria's door, and then I stayed outside until I heard the bar fall heavily into place, making me think of the clanking door of a tomb! I cursed and started to follow Maria's footprints, using a flashlight to show me the way.

I had a guilty sense of relief as I hurried. Somewhere at the end of this eerie trail into the swamp, I would find this girl who so plainly wanted me. I panted as I followed. I was dazed. I couldn't for the life of me have explained my unease, my desire for speed. That dream in which I had clasped Maria in my arms was very real. It seemed to dance ahead of me in the beam of my flash, as though it too had been a will-o'-the-wisp. So real was it that I finally had to forcibly banish it or I would have walked into some sullen pool whose bottom was quicksand.

Far away behind me, to the east, I heard the booming of the Atlantic's surf against the barrier which shut off El Gran Estero. It was a touch of realness in a situation that couldn't possibly be real. It made me step along faster.

I was drawn two ways—to Maria the strange, and back to the girl, Lora, who must by now have been holding her breath for very fear.

Had Maria begun on me already? Had there been something in my food tonight which had induced the dream of her? But no, for Lora had seen her beside my bed, and Lora had not been dreaming. How could I tell her that, going to the door the first time, I had seen damp footprints on the floor beside my bed? I had carefully obliterated them, smeared them with my own, before she could have seen them when she followed me to bar the door.

I knew now whither the muddy trail of bare feet was leading me. I knew that hole which oozed forth the will-o'-the-wisps as Maria could not have known it.

I came to the edge of a clearing.

I saw the sullen, slimy pool. Maria stood beside it, her back almost turned toward me. She wore a filmy slip which was gauzy and unreal in the moonlight. She was a figure in bronze, standing there on the very lip of the pool, so close that a push would have sent her in. Her hands were held over the sullen black water as though she administered some queer incantation or benediction.

I halted, listened. What in God's name was she saying?

"Thy soul will show me how to take and hold him!

"Thy soul will show me how to make her repulsive to him, cover her body with the silver scars of leprosy!"

"Maria! Maria! What are you doing?"

But it was plain, what she did. For as she spoke, her hands clutched at fiery globules rising from the slime. The corpse candles broke in her palms and she held her hands to her lips as though she drank! In her own mind she was drinking the souls in the will-o'-the-wisps!

I caught her, only intending to shake her out of whatever black spell held her. Her flesh was warm and human to my touch. She laughed softly, turned in my arms, put her own around me, pressed her body hard against mine. I kissed her! What possessed me to do that? What horrible thing had caused me to be guilty of this treachery to Lora?

I held her tightly. But I fought against the madness—and won. I set the girl back in the trail, forced her to precede me, outlined in the beam of the flash.

I locked her in, then hammered on the door of the main room. Lora her face livid, let me in. I staggered back in horror, unable to believe what I saw— *the silvery spots which covered her face and hands!*

CHAPTER FOUR

The Silver Pestilence

I STARTED toward Lora. Then I stopped. It wasn't fear for myself, for I knew that leprosy could not so quickly be caused by contact. Only long associa-tion with a leper caused it to appear in another; and yet, Lora seemed to have it! She had gotten it in a matter of minutes only though. Science said that the leprosy took seven years to incubate. And yet . . . .

"I've looked at myself in the mirror, Jim," said Lora hoarsely. "I know. I saw! You dare not touch me!"

"I'm not afraid," I said. "It's impossible! A nightmare!"

"A nightmare that you took Maria in your arms and kissed her—after she had swallowed a soul which gave her power to cover my body with *these?*"

"After . . . ?" I stopped. "Lora, what are you saying?"

"Only that I followed close behind you. I said that I wouldn't stay here alone, Jim. I didn't. I followed, and I saw. I heard every word she uttered. I was dreadfully frightened. I came back and looked at myself and saw—*this! these!*"

She held out her snow white arms to show the silvery spots. Again I started forward.

Behind me sounded the low laughter of Maria Tejeda. I whirled, almost mad at that sound. Maria stood on the threshold again, staring in at us, still wearing that gauzy nothing in which she had stood beside the slimy pool to drink—to drink *what?* It couldn't be, and yet there were the spots, and Maria was saying:

"Go to her, *Jaime!* Look at her! She will be a wrinkled hag in a few weeks, maybe even before the *padre* comes. Her limbs will drop off . . . . go to her, *Jaime,* and take her in your arms! Or turn and look at me, Maria Tejeda, and tell us both which of us is lovelier in your eyes!"

I started toward Maria. My hands were outstretched before me. My fingers were like the talons of a bird of prey. I swear that had I put my hands on

Maria then I should have torn her limb from limb. But she looked straight into my eyes—and laughed. It was the laughter of a fiend from Hell.

"I drank the soul which gave me power to do this to your white weakling," said Maria, holding her hands, palms to the fore, toward me, as though to force me back. "Destroy me, *Jaimecito,* and she will die of this dread disease! Touch me not, save at my whim, because you desire me, and I shall spare her. I shall even drink a soul that will help me to save her—!"

I was insane, I am sure, to have believed in such errant nonsense that not a man of reason would have believed in—unless he had been through what we three had gone through in El Gran Estero that night, and had seen what we had seen. I wouldn't have believed that I would have taken a native woman in my arms, yet the lips of Maria Tejeda still seemed warm against my own. I didn't believe that will-o'-the-wisps were the souls of women drowned for love; and yet . . . .

Again I looked in horror at the spots on the arms and neck of Lora Jaynes. I groaned in agony of spirit. Lora was looking strangely at Maria Tejeda.

"But *Jaime* must call either Belema Llansal or Divue Cerimarie, his guides, and start you out of the swamp," Maria said. "Sometime before you reach Sanchez you will be well again—and I shall stay here, with *Jaime!*"

"And if I come back?" Lora asked.

"I shall know, and the spots will return."

"Why must you have Jim? There must be many men you could have."

Maria spat on the floor of the cabin, advanced a step further into the room.

"I want no other man!" she said. "It is *Jaimecito* or it is no one."

LORA looked at me for a long time. Maybe there was a spell upon me, a ghastly spell of swamp sorcery, but I believed in all of it—and inside me was the wish that Lora would agree, and leave me here alone with Maria Tejeda!

And yet I knew that my brain, my reason, rebelled against the terror; and that what my brain wished was to destroy this hellcat as though she were a viper.

But something else inside me, something I did not know I could harbor in me, cried out for just one more touch of Maria's body against mine, one more caress of her lips. I wanted to feel her fingers through my hair again, the caress of her palms against my cheeks.

I wanted Maria!

And I stood there, a man of stone, staring from one to the other. Lora looked into my face—and knew! Maria looked into my eyes—and also knew, for she laughed.

"Maria," Lora's chin was suddenly high and proud, "it is only just that you should know the truth of what I feel. If you had not done to me what you have done, I would accept your challenge, fight you with your own weapons. For, with just our woman's weapons, Maria, I could hold him against you! I shall accept your conditions, Maria. I shall remain in Sanchez until you have discovered that even while he holds you in his arms, his heart sobs for me. I shall come back when you know for a certainty that he loves only me. What does it matter that you have him for a little while? I shall have him forever—if you keep your promise to me about *these!*" She held out her arms.

"If I lose him to you while you are absent, Lora," said the girl, using Lora's baptismal name with brazen effrontery, "then let him know now that if he leaves me and goes to you—he will find you as you now are! I hold the man I want against the world. I would barter my soul to Satan for the man I love: *Jaimecito!* When you go, Lora, you have lost. You might as well go on back to the United States. Maybe, who knows, he will tire of me. If he does, I shall not be the first who went into the quagmire to forget. But remember this, both of you; if his love wanes and he casts me forth, and starts back to you, I shall put the curse of the spots on you even as I die, and when he finds you again he will find you with the spots upon you!"

I could stand it no longer. Again I started for the girl. But Maria laughed.

"Kill me, *mi vida,*" she said. huskily, "and who will make this Lora whole again?"

A moan of anguish came from Lora's lips.

"I must think," I said. "I can't believe this."

I sat down on the edge of my bed. Water dripped from my still wet boots onto the floor with a sullen, murmuring sound. I raised my head to stare at Lora, and at Maria. My eyes held steadily on the window for a moment.

Outside, side by side, like two eyes, were twin will-o'-the-wisps. One rose above the other. They danced together, separated. I stared. They seemed to be trying to look in. I heard a hopeless sound behind me, knew that Lora had dropped down on her cot.

"Call one of the guides, Jim," said Lora. "What can this girl do to you? Even if she has you for a few days or weeks, she can never have you really, and when she has finished what has been between you shall be as less than nothing to me."

I groaned. I suffered agonies. "She would drive me mad!" I said. But even as I said it I thought of holding her in my arms, drinking deep of my madness, the madness of Maria Tejeda.

HOW much greater than either of us was Lora Jaynes. I knew that she, too, in that dreadful moment, thought of seeing Maria in my arms. I harked back to that, wishing for the passing of time to show me some solution to the ghastly dilemma. I heard Maria again at the pool, speaking to the rising will-o'-the-wisps. But now I knew that in the dark through which I had traveled, Lora had been, following. I shuddered in terror as I thought of the quagmire stretching all about her. I thought of the high courage which had sent her into the unknown to find me—and what it must have done to her to see me with my arms around the evil Maria Tejeda.

Tejeda! Tejeda! Where had I heard that name before? I remembered now. A Tejeda had slain her husband and, with her lover's help, in San Pedro de Macoris to the south, had buried him under the dirt floor of her house, into which she openly took her lover. A scratching dog had uncovered the horror, weeks later, and the woman and her lover had faced a firing squad.

There was horror in Maria's surname. I lifted my head to look at her.

"You have heard of Epifania Tejeda?" I asked.

She smiled. "Who has not? She had courage. She was not afraid to kill for the sake of her love. Neither am I. She was not afraid to die for her love. Neither am I, *Jaimecito.* She was my mother's sister."

So many women kept their original surnames, in Santo Domingo, because they did not marry their "husband"

"She was a bloodthirsty murderess, Maria," I said through set teeth, fighting for my reason as for my life. "I would rather die than have a woman like her. I don't know why I did what I did with you, save that there is a black cloud of madness on women of your name. You must be very like her. Men went mad for her."

"And for me," Maria shrugged. "But I have none of them, until now, when I desire—and will have—all!"

It was up to me. Maria, if thwarted, would blight Lora's life. I had brought that upon Lora. The least I could do was the best I could do. I loved her in spite of Maria's strange thralldom which gripped me, and against which I fought with all my heart and with all my soul— and all my reason!

Sweat beaded my cheeks like drops of blood in the flickering lamplight. The will-o'-the-wisps had vanished from the window. I heard the sucking sound of the quagmire through the light laughter of Maria which seemed still to hang in the cabin with us. I forced myself to make a decision, heard my own voice speak the fateful words.

"There is one thing you have forgotten, have overlooked, Maria," I said softly. "You can keep Lora as she is. You will if I refuse you. But you counted on my fear of the silver horror to make me avoid contact with it. Well, listen, you woman of the dark! I would rather take Lora as she is, knowing that in the end I should die of the spots of silver, than to do what you wish, to lie beside you, to be anything to you—but the master to the servant! Understand? I prefer a leper to a fiend!"

I didn't give Lora chance to protest. Sitting on the edge of her cot, she seemed to have been numbed by catastrophe. I jumped up, whirled around the end of my own cot, sat down beside Lora and put my arms around her.

My bare arms touched her bare arms. I rubbed my face against hers in spite of her scream of warning, and her struggle to keep me away from the spots of silver. I clung to her tightly, and looked into her eyes.

"Help me, Lora," I said quietly. "Help me to beat whatever it is that hangs over us. Help me with your love!"

A wail like that of a lost soul came from the lips of Maria Tejeda. Her face went white as she turned, jumped to the second door, and vanished into the night again.

CHAPTER FIVE

A Globule from the Ooze

WORDS came from my stiff lips almost against my will. "God Almighty!" I exclaimed, almost as though someone else had uttered them. I was staring in utter amazement at Lora's arm. Taunting Maria, I had dared to rub my hand back and forth across one of the silvery spots. Now I looked at the spot again—and saw only the smooth white skin of Lora, where the spot had been!

I jumped to my feet. I forced Lora to lie down on her couch, and I swiftly massaged her arm. One after the other the silver spots vanished under my palms. . . !

"Madre de Jesus! Virgen de Altagracia!" I didn't even think it odd that I spoke Spanish in my wild enlightenment. After all, I had spoken little else for months on end. "Lora, beloved! The spots aren't real. They . . . they're . . . ."

Then I remembered in a flash of understanding: those will-o'-the-wisps which had filled the room when I had wakened —they had broken about the head and face of Lora. Something in them . . . .

I jumped to my feet, while Lora held her breath and stared at the places on her arms where the spots had been as though unable to believe the truth of what she had seen. I went into the lean-to and cast the beam of the flash around the place—and found a small pan that was tucked under the boughs of Maria's pallet. It was still sticky with the slime of something she had been brewing. I tested the residue of whatever it had been with my fingers—

And knew at least some of the truth— Maria had done a very simple thing, for soap had been one of the ingredients of what she had mixed in that pannikin. Herbs of some kind, perhaps, from the jungle had been another. She had gone for them that first time she had left the cabin.

There had been nothing mysterious, nothing uncanny about it at all. I searched further, and found a hollow reed, like a cigarette holder, and knew how the "will-o'-the-wisps" had entered the room where Lora and I slept, with the blanket on a wire between us. Maria had simply taken the brew she had made, blown bubbles through the cracks in the wall until the room had been filled with them. She had waited for moonlight to show them to us. Then she had thrown away her brew and hidden the pannikin, entered the room where we were, and caressed me as I slept.

Lora had wakened and seen, because Maria had deliberately pulled the blanket that she should.

Lora had screamed—

The bubbles had touched her, some of them, and their breaking had covered her skin with a thin film, in spots, of the stuff of which the brew had been made —the herb from the jungle. "Bush medicine!" Many native women used it in their love potions. How simple when one knew!

Maria had used water from one of the same pools whose phosphorus content made the natural will-o'-the-wisps. Diabolical, yet easily comprehensible.

But what had made me take the woman in my arms as I slept?

What had made me kiss her, out there beside the sullen pool to the west?

All I could think of was the dark Tejedas, and that men went mad because of their beauty and the messages in their deep black eyes.

Now Lora was sitting up.

"Jim," she said softly, "we aren't yet finished with the horror. You know what she said? That if she did not get the man she wanted—you, Jim!—she would go into the swamp as the others had, and die for loss of him? Well, she has gone. Jim, we would never forgive ourselves if we did nothing to prevent her doing what she threatened. We've got to go back into the jungle again, and prevent her if we can. Maybe, Jim, she may yet be a good servant!"

"If we find her," I said hoarsely, still bathed in perspiration, "I shall send her back to Sanchez in the morning. I would rather delay my work for a year than keep her with us."

"Afraid of yourself, Jim?" asked Lora softly.

I didn't, couldn't answer that. . . .

WE hurried. I believed in my heart that we would be too late. I knew better now than to leave Lora behind. I was afraid for her to follow, not because I might again betray her, but that she might, now that we knew our happiness was safe again, slip into the quagmire and vanish, and I lose her after all. I would take no chances with that possible grim jest of fate.

So together we set out once more on the trail of Maria Tejeda.

"Poor woman!" Lora murmured once.

Even after what had happened Lora Jaynes could find room in her heart for pity for Maria Tejeda! How could I love any one but her, of whom I could never possibly be worthy, whose betrayal I would never cease to regret?

We hurried. The footprints of Maria were far apart, as though she ran. All about us the will-o'-the-wisps danced and flickered in the gloom, but they had lost the power to frighten either Lora or myself. We had gone beyond all thought of fear, save for the safety of Maria Tejeda.

Once I stopped and Lora bumped into me from behind. I thought I heard a woman sobbing. Maria Tejeda was taking desperate chances in her flight. There were many places where her feet barely escaped disaster in the bog.

I soon discovered whither she was going—straight to the sullen pool where she had eaten the souls of dead girls who had died for love, and where, for a mad moment, I had forgotten all loyalty to Lora Jaynes.

In spite of my knowledge that I had beaten the strange horror which had possessed the three of us, the sweat broke forth on me again. Maria *would* do this. If she were intending to die, she would die where, for a moment, she had been happy in the near-possession of her dark desire. Yet I hoped, with a feeling of sympathy which I instantly hated, that we would be in time.

But how would I feel toward Maria when I saw her again?

I had to know. There was just one way, if we found her alive. If her footprints ended on the lip of oblivion I would never know. I must look upon her again and know myself empty of desire for her. I think Lora must have felt this too, though she spoke never a word.

More will-o'-the-wisps.

I struck out at one of them. It broke with a popping sound, and a strange odor caressed my nostrils, the odor of decay, of pestilence, of the deep mysteries of El Gran Estero—almost the odor of some dank charnel house. For a moment I almost reverted to the overwhelming terror which had possessed both Lora and me when the will-o'-the-wisps had come

out of the jungle as we had sat beside our cabin to watch them advance into the clearing.

"There she is, Jim," said Lora. "Maria! Maria!"

The girl stood on the brink as I had last seen her, almost in the same spot. Now she wore nothing at all, and the beauty of her dusky body was an ache in the heart. Again she held her hands over the pool. She didn't seem to hear Lora at all.

"Maria!" I called to her. "Maria Tejeda!"

At the sound of my voice she turned, turned slowly, as though it were a vast effort. Her arms fell to her sides. Her face was very plain in the moonlight, touched with an ethereal expression that caused a tight hand to clutch at my heart.

The moon was high above El Gran Estero. Its light was brilliant. It struck eerie lancets from the globules of fire which came out of the pool. It touched tears that were like pearls of suffering on the drawn face of Maria Tejeda.

"I am not sorry," she said. "I would do it again, but I would take more time. I would fight you, Lora, with the weapons each of us possesses. But it is too late now."

We had slowed to a walk. She turned back to the pool. I held out my arms in protest; and she turned just once and saw them, and a little smile touched her lips. Once before I had come to her here, with my arms outstretched. She remembered, and that was why she smiled.

I wanted to rush forward. But Maria shook her head, and said: "You could never reach me in time, *mi vida*. You will remember those two words—*mi vida* —all the days of your lives, both of you, for I whispered them behind you when the corpse candles came out of the jungles tonight, whispered them through the cracks in the cabin. And I whispered yet others when the room was filled with my potions of love! Yes, always you will remember them!"

We were almost close enough for me to clutch her now. I heard a choked sob from her lips, the last sound that she uttered. And then there was the splash of sullen water as she stepped over the lip of the black pool and vanished.

SHE went in, a bronze statue, with her head back, her long black hair mantling her shoulders, her feet together, her hands clasped over her breasts. Just so would a Dominican girl have been postured in her coffin.

The water closed over her.

"Stand back, Lora," I said, my voice a hoarse croak.

Lora obeyed me. I rushed forward. I knew as I stood on the lip of the pool, that Maria had known I would keep Lora back, that I would advance to the pool alone. For her eyes, through the water, were wide open, staring into mine. There was a smile on her lips as she sank, already irretrievably lost in the quagmire which sucked at her brown feet.

It scarcely mattered. Even if I could have reached in and caught her black hair and pulled her out, it wouldn't have mattered. I had seen the hopeless determination in her eyes. She would have taken the first opportunity, before morning, to come back to the pool for this plunge.

She opened her mouth as though she said farewell through the water whose blackness was dimming the dark beauty of her face as she sank— and a bubble came to the surface and burst.

I turned back to Lora. Her face would never be whiter.

"Before God, Lora," I said, "I couldn't have prevented it."

Lora stared at the spot, then at me, her face a mask of determination. Then she moved quickly to the lip of the pool, and I followed, my heart in my mouth for fear that she had gone mad with our old madness and was going to follow Maria into the depths.

But it wasn't that.

A fiery globule suddenly came out of the ooze, rising, eddying, into the moonlit air above the pool. Lora leaned far forward to clutch it in her hands. It burst with a gentle popping sound.

Then I knew! I grabbed her hands, whirled her to face me.

"Why?" I asked.

"There was something about her, Jim," said Lora, as though she spoke the words of some uncanny ritual, "that made you put your arms around her and kiss her, not once, but twice, and I saw in your eyes, for one dreadful moment, that you *wanted* me to go out, to Sanchez. Maybe there was some truth, ever so little, in her belief that she could drink the souls of lost lovers, and partake of their gifts, however dark. Well, she told me, today—how long ago it seems!—that a woman must be all things to the man she loves. I wish to be whatever she may have been to you!"

She seemed to be in deadly earnest.

But I shook my head. "There is no need," I said.

I took out my handkerchief and rubbed her hands.

We went slowly back to the cabin, and both of us, I was sure, were thinking of Padre Castellanos and his power to forgive sins.

THE END

THE BLACK CHAPEL

O UT of the hoary past, from the musty crypts of time, still come vague voices which intone solemnly the words: "Fear begets courage!" The caveman, trembling at the flash of fiery lightning; the ancient bowing obeisance to a cruel god; the medieval man, oppressed by grim superstition, all were worshipping that greater, more powerful deity, *Fear!*

For Terror walks by night and crowds into our waking hours. Even men of to-day know him and have seen him face to face. Why, you ask? That is a just question, and it deserves a true answer —the answer sage men formulated in the dawn of civilization, when the first histories were scrawled on wet clay tablets: Fear begets courage!

Terror Tales offers the wise a proving-ground for their bravery. In this issue, for instance, have you not shuddered and trembled, testing the metal of your spirit? Have you not felt the cold fingers of dread crawling your spine? Have you not shivered at the grim menace of shapeless creatures which haunt the night, at the ghastly plans of twisted, mad brains? Have you not recoiled from the clutching grasp of fright?

Ah, yes! And by so doing, you disciples of dread, you have learned much. You have tempered your courage in a crucible of fear. You have strengthened the fibers of your bravery. You

have learned some of terror's many ramifications—have learned the lesson taught —to master your apprehensions.

And that is one of the greatest lessons in the world. It is the path to freedom and happiness. Only by breaking away from the pursuing fears of your life may you attain true peace of mind, happiness, and wisdom.

Nor have you yet finished your apprenticeship to fear, you learners! Much is to come. Fear's class-room will witness many another exercise before you have been graduated with honors from the spine-tingling school of fright.

The next issue—and all the issues to come—will contain new, courage-proving thrills for you. By means of them, you will overcome terror, escape from the toils of dread's binding slavery. Then, students of terror, you will know the mastery of despair. You will realize the cunning truth of the ancient maxim: "Fear begets courage!"

"I'll PROVE in Only 7 Days that I Can Make YOU a New Man!"

No other Physical Instructor in the World has ever DARED make such an Offer.

By CHARLES ATLAS

Holder of the Title:
"The World's Most Perfectly Developed Man"
Won in open competition in the only National and International contests held during the past 15 years.

Charles Atlas—
As He Is Today

Photo by Jael Feder.

I HAVE proved to thousands that my system of building powerful, big-muscled men begins to show real results *in only 7 days*—and I can prove it to *you.*

You don't have to take my word for it. You don't have to take the word of my hundreds of pupils who have added inches to their chests, biceps, neck, thighs and calves in only a few days. No sir! You can prove for *yourself*—in just one week—by the change you see and *feel* in *your own body*—that you can actually become a husky, healthy NEW MAN — a real "Atlas Champion."

All I want to know is: Where do *you* want big, powerful muscles? How many pounds of firm flesh do *you* want distributed over your body to fill you out? Where do *you* lack vitality, pep, and robust health? Where do *you* want to take off flabby, surplus fat?

Just tell me, give me a week, and I'll show you that I can make a *New Man* of you, give you bodily power and drive, and put you in that magnificent physical condition which wins you the envy and respect of any man and the admiration of every woman.

My own system of *Dynamic-Tension* does it. That's the way I built myself from a 97-pound weakling to "The World's Most Perfectly Developed Man." And now *you* can have a big, balanced muscular development like mine in the same easy way.

No "Apparatus" Needed!

You begin to FEEL and SEE the difference in your physical condition at once, without using any tricky weights or pulleys, any pills, "rays," or unnatural dieting. My *Dynamic-Tension* is a *natural* method of developing you *inside and out.* It not only makes you an "Atlas Champion," but goes after such conditions as constipation, pimples, skin blotches, and any other conditions that keep you from really enjoying life and its good times—and it starts getting rid of them at once.

Let Me Tell You How

Gamble a stamp today by mailing the coupon for a free copy of my new illustrated book, "Everlasting Health and Strength." It tells you all about my special *Dynamic-Tension* method. It shows you, from actual photos, how I have developed my pupils to the same perfectly balanced proportions of my own physique, by my own secret methods. What my system did for me, and these hundreds of others, it can do for you too. Don't keep on being only one-half of the man you can be! Find out what I can do for you.

FREE BOOK

Where shall I send your copy of "Everlasting Health and Strength"? Jot your name and address down on the coupon, and mail it today. Your own new "Atlas body" is waiting for you. This book tells you how easy it is to get my way. Send the coupon to me personally.

CHARLES ATLAS
Dept. 834
115 E. 23rd St.
New York, N. Y.

www.ingramcontent.com/pod-product-compliance
Lightning Source LLC
Chambersburg PA
CBHW080913020726
47502CB00008B/2445